# Ma Bo'le's Second Life

# Xiao Hong

# Ma Bo'le's Second Life

Translated from
the Chinese, Edited,
and Completed by
Howard Goldblatt

**OPEN LETTER**
LITERARY TRANSLATIONS FROM THE UNIVERSITY OF ROCHESTER

Library of Congress Cataloging-in-Publication Data: Available.

The translator has completed the original unfinished work and has placed it in a contemporary context. A full explanation is given in the translator's afterward.

*This project is supported in part by an award from the National Endowment for the Arts and the New York State Council on the Arts with the support of Governor Andrew M. Cuomo and the New York State Legislature*

Printed on acid-free paper in the United States of America.

Text set in Garamond, a group of old-style serif typefaces named after the punch-cutter Claude Garamont.

*Design by N. J. Furl*

Open Letter is the University of Rochester's nonprofit, literary translation press: Dewey Hall 1-219, Box 278968, Rochester, NY 14627

www.openletterbooks.org

# Ma Bo'le's Second Life

December 1984.

Margaret Thatcher's Conservative government has just signed a joint declaration to return the British Colony of Hong Kong to China in 1997, when the ninety-nine-year lease runs out. The news has captured the attention of the media and virtually all the colony's residents. But not David Ma, a graying, somewhat dour English-language storyteller for Hong Kong Radio. He has only one thing on his mind and he is livid.

**Ma Bo'le was a coward even before the war.**

"My father was no coward, not before, during, or after the war! I should know. Eccentric, sure, but a coward? Never!"

He cannot read beyond the first line on the sheet of paper he is holding before throwing it down on the table and looking unhappily at the woman sitting across from him.

She does not respond right away, just gazes at him, as if waiting for an ill-behaving child to get over a tantrum. She is local, of clear Cantonese stock—petite, with a small face ending in a pointed chin, hair cut short to exude efficiency. She wears an expectant smile. It does not win him over, but she will wait patiently, as she did moments before, when she explained what she was there for . . .

3

*. . . at the Hong Kong Historical Society we have come into possession of a handwritten manuscript from around the time of the Japanese invasion of Hong Kong, one that we think will interest you. It was discovered in an overlooked first-floor closet in a building on Lock Road in Tsim Sha Tsui that once served as the offices of a Chinese-language literary magazine. It shut down not long after the December 1941 attack. The manuscript was in poor shape, given all those years of heat and humidity, with mildew, mice, and insects making parts of it unreadable. Some pages were missing. Unfortunately, that included the first page, so we don't know its title or who wrote it. Interestingly, the writing and, to some degree, the tone, change after chapter fourteen, which implies that, for whatever reason, there were two authors, but I suspect we'll never know either of them. We are, however, confident that the manuscript dates from the early 1940s, and that it was likely being considered for publication in the magazine. The main character's name is given in the first line, as you can see . . .*

"Tell me, do you really expect me to dignify that insulting rubbish with a comment?"

While he is justifiably indignant over seeing Ma Bo'le reviled in print, hazy images of his father before, during, and after the war have already begun slipping into the crevasses of his mind, awakening memories that had long lain dormant. His guest notices what appear to be expressions of conflicting emotions on his face as he gazes into the middle distance.

"Please don't be angry," she says, "because this is where it gets interesting. Believe it or not, we think that the anonymous author was someone in possession of a wealth of information about your family, and wrote what appears to be a novel about you all, especially your father, beginning up north before the war, and ending here in Hong Kong a number of years later."

"My family, you say?" Ma's incredulity is palpable. "You must be joking. Who could possibly have written something like that? And did you say it's a novel, one that was written almost three decades ago?"

"That's right, and you, Mr. David Ma, are one of the characters in it, along with your mother, a younger brother named Joseph, and a sister called, interestingly, Jacob. Does that sound like your family? They are from Qingdao and came to Hong Kong via Shanghai, Hankou, Wuchang, and Chongqing. One of my colleagues recalled an interview you gave on local TV some time ago, and the story in this manuscript seemed familiar to her, familiar enough for me to come talk to you about it."

"My God, this is beyond belief. So that's what this is?" he says and points to the stack of paper she has placed in front of him.

"Yes. We asked one of our editors to work on it, and she has produced a readable version. That is what you see before you, Mr. Ma."

Though Ma's office is far from soundproof, and radio station activity produces an undercurrent of sound—noise, even—just beyond the door, he is oblivious to what is occurring around him as he tries to process the information he has just received and sort out his emotions.

"I see doubt in your eyes, but I would be surprised if you weren't curious about what is written in those pages. So, what do you say, may I leave it with you, in hopes that you will read it and, when you've finished, share your impressions with us? We would like to make it widely available in book form."

"Why in the world would you want to do that?"

"For several reasons. It was, after all, written and would have been published here in Hong Kong, which is of considerable interest to us at the Society. Many people in China saw the colony as a safe haven in the years before the war, and Hong Kong residents are justifiably proud of the city's role as a sanctuary of sorts from time to time. Your family's varied involvement with the city is part of that. But what's more, family sagas are wonderfully illustrative of how historical memory is created, and this one, partly because it is a novel, is a captivating read."

"I don't know what to say."

"Then say yes."

"All right, once I come to grips with the whole idea, I'll read it, and we'll talk again."

"On behalf of the Society, I thank you."

•  •  •

After shaking hands with the bemused Mr. Ma, the representative, Ms. Lam, leaves his office and takes the subway back to Society headquarters to report on her success.

David Ma still has trouble believing what he has just learned. After telling stories about ancient and modern life to a listening audience of Hong Kong residents, he has suddenly found himself a character in a novel and confronted with a story that is compellingly personal. Curiosity and trepidation pull him in opposite directions as he contemplates not only the awkwardness of reading about his own family, his father, in particular, but also the distinct possibility that his story could one day be made available to strangers, people who will be free to pass unflattering judgment. With a nervous look at the two-inch-thick pile of paper on the table, he gets up, goes into the bathroom to splash some water on his face, and, once he has regained his composure, sits down to read for the second time the line that started it all . . .

# Chapter One

Ma Bo'le was a coward even before the war.

Though not a brave man, he always had his wits about him. If he did not like how things were going, he fled, whether he had a destination in mind or not. He ran like a man one step ahead of a raging torrent. His catchphrase? Always look for the nearest exit.

It was escape that took him to Shanghai one year. He had told his father he wanted to enroll as a student at a Shanghai university, and since his request was met with silence, he made a second plea the following day. This time his father fumed, snatched his glasses off his face, and glared at his son.

That was a bad sign. Ma Bo'le could sense his wife's hand in it. But that was to be expected, since he was seeing another woman at the time, something that had already led to more than one argument. She had obviously gone bellyaching to his father, had probably told him he planned to go to Shanghai to be with that other woman. There was bound to be trouble if he stuck around. So he waited until his wife was off visiting her parents for a couple of days to ask once more for permission to study in Shanghai. This brought the issue to a head. "No, you cannot go!" his father thundered.

That night Ma Bo'le packed, convinced that the moment of escape was at hand. He crammed everything he could—more than a dozen toothbrushes, toothpowder, the works—into his wife's pigskin suitcase. Might as well take them all, he figured. He'd be a fool not to. If he passed them up now, he would not have another chance later. He also found and packed some hand towels and soap—Lux Soap, the best on the market. He'd have to wash his face wherever he went, and he couldn't do that without soap.

He then turned his attention to a stack of his wife's embroidered hankies, more than a dozen in all: muslin, cotton, satin, some of such high quality she could not bring herself to use them. The thought of taking these along could give him a lift. He laughed merrily, realizing the special use to which he could put them. Wouldn't it be rich if he gave them to . . . her? (The "her," of course, was his former paramour.)

Ma Bo'le was delighted. He closed up one suitcase and moved on to the next, stuffing his entire collection of neckties—twenty or more, old and new—into it. Then there were twenty-odd pairs of socks, some brand new, others so old and threadbare they were no longer wearable, and still others that had not been washed since their last wearing. This was no time to be fussy, so into the suitcase they all went.

But not everything found its way into the suitcases, and by the time he'd finished, the floor was so littered with rejects that the room looked like a junk heap. His wife's talcum powder covered the bed, white everywhere, and the floor was a repository for worn-out shoes, socks with gaping holes, plus a motley assortment of children's things. But what did he care—he wasn't coming back.

For reasons only he could fathom, Ma Bo'le hated pretty much everything about his opulent surroundings. His home life was lackluster, dreary, and irremediably dull. It was debilitating. Any young man experiencing it over a long period of time would waste away, vegetate, stagnate under a layer of moss. It was the sort of home that screws up a young man's head.

One glance at Ma Bo'le's father, Old Mr. Ma, and you know how bad things were: After rising each morning, the head of the household fell to his knees, eyeglasses in hand, and prayed to the Christian God for the better part of an hour. Sometimes he covered his face with his hands and remained immobile as a statue. Then, his prayers completed, he put on his glasses and retired to the parlor to sit at an old Chinese-style ironwood table and read the gilt-edged Bible given to him by a foreign missionary. Since this particular Bible was a prized work of art, he permitted no one to touch, let alone read, it, not even his wife. Just ask Ma Bo'le, who opened it for himself one afternoon, when he thought his father would not notice, and never forgot how that turned out. The old man revered his Bible more than he did the Ma family genealogy. In fact, ever since Mr. Ma's conversion to Christianity, the genealogy had been stored away, seeing the light of day only over the New Year's holiday, when it was casually displayed for anyone who cared to look at it. This in contrast to the family Bible, which, in all its forbidding sanctity, was in full view the year round.

In earlier days, Ma Bo'le's father was the quintessential Chinese Mandarin, with his long, bronze-colored and somberly patterned Mandarin gown, formal, high-soled footwear, and fingernails a half inch in length. But then, thanks to the ministrations of a Canadian missionary who was highly regarded by members of Chiang Kai-shek's Christian government, he'd converted to the foreign religion, a change that was marked as well by a fondness for the popular alien tongue. When his foreign friends from church dropped by, he called his servants "Boy" and had them serve his guests the fashionable drink: "Beer!"

When the beer was poured, leaving foamy heads in the glasses, he turned to his guests and said: "Bottoms-up!"

Mr. Ma's credo was: Western things are better than Chinese things. Western children are plumper, Western women are more accomplished, Western drinking glasses are more durable, and Western textiles are unmatched anywhere.

Owing to his exaggerated admiration for Westerners, he regularly lectured his sons on the glories of studying English and dressing in Western clothes. He must have been pleased with the results, for even his grandchildren got the message. Like children in the foreign community, they went around in short pants and suspenders, and greeted each other with: "Goo-da mah-ning."

Later in the day they switched to: "Goo-da day!"

"Hello, how do you do?" was how they greeted foreigners.

Dawei, the eldest grandson, was an anemic boy with small, almond-shaped eyes. His younger brother, Yuese, had a moon face like his mother's, the only difference being the stream of snot that often decorated his upper lip. Yage, the youngest, was nearly perfect, the apple of her parents' eye. A darling child with dark, fetching eyes and chubby arms, she hardly ever cried, and though she was only three years old, she looked nearly as old as Yuese, who was five. Their English names, chosen by their grandfather in honor of his favorite Biblical characters—David, Joseph, and Jacob—were how he insisted they be known.

But foreign ways were not all the old man taught his grandchildren. He also instructed them in Bible-reading. From time to time he would call them together, line them up at the table, and solemnly intone a passage from the Good Book. Given their juvenile understanding of things, these passages seemed to include little more than "Our Lord Jesus said," "Our Father tells us not to do this or that," "David rent his garments," "A shepherd in Bethlehem," "Pharisees as hypocrites," and so on.

These sleep-inducing sessions invariably led to confusion, with passages intermixed with Bible stories they'd heard in Sunday school. Standing there picking their noses or biting their nails as time dragged on, they stared blankly ahead and began to doze off. Long after their Grandfather had sent them outdoors, they were quietly rubbing their eyes and yawning instead of playing with other children.

Then there was Ma Bo'le's wife, whose mind, he believed, was never visited by a single thought. She had not picked up a book or written an entry in her diary since the birth of their first child. Day in and day out she made a show of burying her nose in the Bible, but without actually reading it. She may not have believed in Jesus, but with the family property hanging in the balance, it was a good idea to *appear* to believe. Father had made it clear that his estate would go only to devout followers of the Lord Jesus.

No one was allowed to buy anything on the Sabbath, not fruit and not vegetables. This restriction hit the children hardest in the hot summer months, when watermelon peddlers hawked their goods at the gate. It was necessary for their mother to plan ahead, buying and putting aside anything they hoped to eat on the Sabbath. Often the only way to keep them from misbehaving was to sneak out and buy them something to eat, and woe be it to her if the old fellow got wind of it. Naturally, he would say nothing at the time, since it was the Sabbath. But the next day he would call her out, stand her in front of the table, and read to the poor soul from his gilt-edged Bible.

Once, as Ma Bo'le's father was leaving church with his eight-year-old grandson Joseph in tow, the boy spotted a man in Western attire just beyond the church gate. Assuming he was a foreigner, he turned and greeted him: "Hello, how do you do?"

The man patted him on the head and said in Chinese: "For a little fellow you do well with English."

Upset by the discovery that the man was actually Chinese, he tugged on his grandfather's sleeve. "Grandpa," he said, "that Chinese man doesn't even know how to speak English!"

Ma Bo'le, who had gone to church with them, was disgusted. But, to be fair, he too held his fellow Chinese in contempt, often commenting on them with an expression he'd once heard a foreigner use when nearly run down by a rickshaw:

"Bloody Chinese!"

The way the Chinese crowded and jostled one another on public buses was a case in point. He pushed and shoved with the best of them, but only until someone knocked his hat off.

"Bloody Chinese," he'd complain, "must you push?"

If someone bumped into him while he was out walking and neglected to say, "Pardon me," he'd glare at the thoughtless pedestrian and curse:

"Bloody Chinese!"

When a servant once accidentally broke a drinking glass. Ma Bo'le glowered at him.

"Bloody Chinese!"

Did foreigners never break drinking glasses? He thought so.

While opening a piece of mail one day, in his haste he tore off a corner of the letter inside. His reaction to the discovery that some of the words had been torn off?

"Bloody Chinese!"

It was both an effective and a useless outburst. Those who understood the foreign words were likely to agree with the sentiment, and those who did not thought it sounded like a compliment, since the word "Chinese" would be a known and highly regarded entity.

Although Ma Bo'le held his hopeless, money-obsessed family in contempt, on the eve of his escape, he was, to his surprise, reluctant to leave. It was not an act to be taken lightly. Still, he gathered up everything and walked to the writing desk, where he emptied the contents of its drawers into his bag. The objects' usefulness did not concern him. By the time the clock struck 2 A.M., he had filled three suitcases and two bags.

At daybreak, the house began to stir. That spelled trouble, since his father would be waking up soon. He heard the sound of a door being opened.

The servants were getting up.

He broke into a cold sweat.

"What's more important in the long run," he pondered, "my freedom or these odds and ends? Once my wife is up and around, there go all my plans."

His musings were shattered by a throat-clearing sound from his father's room.

Displaying uncharacteristic courage, he snatched his hat from the hat rack and, without even stopping to knot his necktie, flew down the stairs and out the door, leaving behind everything he had spent a sleepless night packing. He was not a brave man, but he certainly had his wits about him.

Now he was on his way, walking down the street, his eyes darting left and right, as if he might be caught at any moment.

He entered a restaurant, pulled out a chair, and wiped his finger across the seat to see if it was clean. He always did that. If he was satisfied that the seat was clean, he sat down. If not, he sat down anyway. The important part of the ritual was the momentary hesitation, a signal that he was not an easy man to please. When the waiter brought the chopsticks, Ma Bo'le inspected them carefully. It was a curious examination, to say the least: Unlike diners who simply wiped theirs off with the paper they came wrapped in, he lifted them up to eye level to examine them closely. Then he drew out his handkerchief and wiped them from end to end, as if only his handkerchief were sufficiently hygienic to perform this operation. That, however, was not the case, for it was laundered in the same water he used for his weekly bath.

Western restaurants were another matter altogether: He trusted them implicitly. Without giving the chair a second thought, he pulled it out and sat down. (Admittedly, he would sometimes rub the tablecloth between his fingers, but only to marvel over the fine embroidery work.) When the cutlery was placed in front of him, a cloth napkin accompanied it. Then he picked up the utensils with confidence in their cleanliness and attacked his meat patty with gusto.

In the role of consumer, Ma Bo'le invariably tried to knock down the price of anything he planned to buy in a Chinese shop. He ignored the marked price. To his way of thinking, price was always negotiable. If a pair of men's nylon socks was marked forty fen, he offered thirty-five. If the shop owner refused to barter, he went ahead and bought them anyway. He would never consider going elsewhere to find a better deal, for he had already concluded that forty fen was not a bad price. If he went to one of the big department stores he'd have to pay at least fifty.

So why haggle if he thought it was reasonable? Elementary—if there was a chance he could get the socks for less, why not try? The cheaper, the better. And if he could get them for nothing, better still!

He disagreed, however, with his father's view that foreign products were superior. They held no attraction for him. He refused to sing the praises of foreigners. And yet he did not haggle in foreign shops. Never. Not even when he had the chance. It made no difference if the price was marked or not. If a foreigner said two yuan, then two yuan it was. Three yuan meant three yuan. Seeming to place no importance on money, he would reach into his wallet, take out the correct amount, and hand it over without a murmur. Admiration and intimidation are quite different animals.

•  •  •

Constantly on guard, Ma Bo'le appeared alert and happy. But in his eyes hid a trace of sorrow. Dark and lethargic, they often revealed a look of distrust. When talking with someone, he'd look the man up and down, from head to toe and back again before settling on the face, a process that could take a minute or more. Passersby might assume that he and the man he was talking to were complicit in something—good or bad. They might even detect a sense of intimacy that somehow defied expression. They would be wrong.

Our young squire was a genuinely sad soul. He enjoyed literature, especially sappy romances that gained popularity after the May Fourth movement in 1919, when translated novels from the West attracted young, impressionable boys and girls. He was given to sighing emotionally in the midst of reading a novel written by someone in a foreign country.

"What a great writer!" he'd say. "Bloody Chinese!"

He occasionally read a Chinese novel, but concluded that they were, in the main, inferior. Over time, his reading habits underwent a change, the focus shifting from love stories to hard-edged foreign works like the Russian classics. He actually discovered many stimulating passages in

these works, most notably Maxim Gorki's *My Youth*, in which he identi-
fied clear parallels between his and the Russian writer's experiences. In
fact, in some respects, his life had been richer and fuller: Had Gorki ever
spent time in a coal mine? Ma Bo'le had, often accompanying miners
down into his father's mineshaft to have a look around.

Chinese chronicles of prison life, in particular, were too loosely constructed for his taste; they lacked suspense and seemed thrown together.
Were he to write such a book, it would be an exposé of the darker side
of life behind bars. He would say what had to be said and criticize what
needed to be criticized. To him, that was the essential quality of anyone
worthy of the title "novelist." That was especially important in China,
where it was incumbent upon all writers to promote resistance against
the Japanese. He often sighed as he mused: "If I were a novelist, that's
what I would write. China won't be free until she stands up to her
aggressors!"

One thing led to another, and soon he began buying writing paper,
having made up his mind to become a writer in the service of a resistance
movement, in the event that one actually appeared someday.

Once the decision was made, he sat quietly at his desk for five or six
days, deep in thought. On the seventh day, he was so enraged over his
inability to write a single word that he ripped up every sheet of paper. Yet
even this deterred him only momentarily, for he went out and bought
more when he considered the notoriety he would gain with the publication of a timely patriotic novel. At first he used paper with a gilded
border, but he soon switched to regular foolscap, and, as days stretched
into unproductive weeks, finally settled on newsprint.

Nearly every conversation with friends during that period turned to
the issue of resistance against the Japanese, which gave Ma Bo'le the
incentive to buckle down and write.

He bought and checked out so many books they soon filled his
study—he even had to install bookcases in his wife's room to accommodate them all. One day, when she was in the kitchen frying fish,
one of the children went into the room, opened the glass doors of the

bookcases, and scattered Ma Bo'le's books all over the floor, tearing the pages out of some and trampling the rest.

"I borrowed some of those books!" he fumed. "What am I supposed to do if you ruin them?" Never before had he struck his children—he hadn't dared. His wife would have skinned him alive. But this time he was so enraged that he threw the screeching child down onto the bed and began spanking him.

Assuming that Daddy was playing, the child began to laugh and thumped the bed with his legs.

"You little monster," Ma Bo'le threatened, "just you wait!"

After the spanking, he locked the bookcase doors and then recommenced his daily trips to the People's Library to borrow huge quantities of books. His friendship with one of the librarians allowed him to take as many as he wanted without actually checking them out. Oh, he'd never read them, but his bookcases looked better full.

• • •

Then, one day, Ma Bo'le fell ill. While never the picture of health, there was nothing really wrong with him. A slight man, he shied away from medicine of all kinds, and on those rare occasions when he had a cold or indigestion, he simply smoked a few more cigarettes than usual. Now, cigarettes are not a known remedy for colds, but, as he saw it, neither were any of the available nostrums, so why waste the time and money? A cigarette was as good as anything. Besides, no one ever died from a cold.

But when one of his children came down with a cold he'd go out and buy some cookies.

"Eat up," he'd say. "Don't let them go to waste. Pretend the money was spent on medicine."

The last time one of the children was sick, Ma Bo'le sat attentively by the bed, sponging the feverish forehead with a cloth dipped in cold water, and the moment the sick child opened his eyes, Ma Bo'le reached for the cookie tin, opened it, and said, "Hungry? Daddy got these for you."

The child shut his eyes and panted. But eventually he woke up thirsty, and out came the tin, only to be ignored as the child took long, greedy drinks of water. Then he had an inspiration: If he steeped a cookie in water, it would go down with each swallow. So he poured a glass of hot water from the vacuum bottle, dumped in a cookie, and stirred the concoction until it cooled off a bit. After sipping it to check the temperature, he stood patiently beside the sickbed and waited, wanting to be ready when the patient awoke. But the child slept on until Ma Bo'le could wait no longer. He shook him awake.

"Thirsty?"

"No, I have to pee."

"Drink some water first, then you can pee. Come on . . ."

Quickly stirring the lumpy mixture, he poured it down the child's throat and, unfortunately, up his nose as well. Frantically clawing with both hands, the gagging child burst into tears and promptly wet the bed.

"Damn!" Ma Bo'le spat, and went to find the child's mother, leaving a string of curses in his wake. On his way out he picked up the glass and drained its gloppy contents. The mixture stuck in his throat momentarily, but by stretching his neck and massaging it vigorously, he managed to swallow the goo without further incident.

Ma Bo'le seldom bought anything for his children to eat when they were healthy, but when he did he put it well out of reach, like on top of the wardrobe. His little greedy-gut kids countered this strategy by moving a bench or table over to get to the goodies any way they could. At least that served to clear up the mystery of why all the teacups in the house were missing handles—they had come a cropper during the children's treasure hunts in and around the wardrobe.

One day, when her mother was out, Jacob climbed up to the wardrobe with her brothers in search of three large pears their father had hidden there.

They reached the summit of their ascent just as Ma Bo'le passed down the hallway and saw what was happening through a window.

"Aha!" he yelled. "So that's what you little brats are up to!"

Startled by her father's shout, Jacob toppled off the precarious perch and struck her head on a spittoon; from that day on her beauty was marred by a scar above her right eye.

With the knowledge that Ma Bo'le disdained the use of medicine, we should not be surprised that during this latest illness, he simply smoked a few more cigarettes than usual. Beyond that, he also took to wearing eyeglasses, like a true scholar, and even stopped making visits to his wife's bedroom.

Remarkably, he managed to write a short piece in his sickbed.

# Chapter Two

Ma Bo'le had no particular occupation; he lived a life of leisure and had done so since graduating from high school. He had made an earlier trip to Shanghai to take up studies at X University, but after flunking the entrance exam, he'd merely audited a few classes. His father had reacted by cutting off his allowance, so Ma Bo'le had forged some transcripts, written his letters on X University stationery, and told his father to write him in care of the university. It all came to nothing, and he returned home to live the life of a young squire once again. People like him normally want for nothing. But not Ma Bo'le, for his father had said:

"Don't try to get your hands on my money while I'm still alive."

Another of his favorite comments was:

"If you harbor the illusion that your father is getting too old to handle his own affairs, then gather up your things, your wife, and your kiddies, and set up house elsewhere."

Such drivel grated on Ma Bo'le's nerves, though he slept on a soft bed and dined on seasonable foods. He viewed his life as one of pure torture; he suffered the indignities of a house slave. As a result, whenever he saw that telltale look in his father's eyes, he fled from harm's way.

Going to the old man for a little pocket money was harder than digging gold nuggets out of the ground. And on those occasions when his request was grudgingly granted, he had to express his undying gratitude:

"Praise the Lord, thanks to God in Heaven!"

Having to beg for money made him seethe with anger, so when he returned to his room with his hard-earned alms, he'd throw it down on the desk and mutter:

"Bloody Chinese!"

But before many days had passed, the money would be gone, no matter how sparingly he used it, and something else would need buying.

Another source of money when he was broke was his wife. But when he asked her to part with some of her savings, she tossed it to him with a sneer and a snide comment:

"Some man you are! Instead of going out and earning your own keep, you're content to rely on a woman."

Once, after being turned down by his father, he took his case to his wife:

"The old guy's losing his marbles!"

To which she replied:

"Don't blame him. You're not a child any longer—you're pushing thirty! But it's always 'Father, I need some money.' If he didn't watch his money, he'd be in the same fix you're in. He'd have to sell his wife and pawn his children. All your hands are good for is taking money and stuffing your face. If you've got any talent for anything else, I'd like to know what it is. As far as I'm concerned, Father treats you better than you deserve. If you had a penniless father, you'd be out on the street begging."

Ma Bo'le's face turned white with rage.

"At least I'd go out and beg. You just tag along behind whoever's got money or power . . ."

There was more he wanted to say, but his wife collapsed onto the bed and burst into tears.

"You heartless animal, it's your fault. All my gold rings are gone. And what about that time you took off for Shanghai . . . my gold bracelet,

I want it back . . . and that woman, whose money did you use then? I never asked you to give it back, so why get mad at me? Neighbor women parade up and down the street with gold jewelry up to their elbows . . . we may not be as well off as they are, but we're certainly not poor.

"Being married to you would make any woman weep. You're always off to someplace new—Beijing, Shanghai . . . and when you run out of money, a letter isn't fast enough for you. No, always a telegram, demanding more. All I get from you in return is a hard time, and if you treat me like this now, what will happen when you don't need me anymore? You'll put a million miles between us, that's what!"

Not liking the way things were going, Ma Bo'le fled the scene.

Down the stairs and out the front door, he stopped briefly in the entryway to catch his breath. He shook one of the two fishbowls there, causing the fish inside to panic. The sight enthralled him.

"Wouldn't it be great to be a goldfish? All they need is water—they don't eat and they don't need spending money."

His ruminations were disturbed by the intermittent sounds of his wife's tearful grumbling upstairs, and plugging his ears did not help much. It was clearly the moment to move on, time to get away from the house and the sounds of crying. But as he turned to rush out the door, from the head of the stairs came a chilling cry:

"Give me back my gold bracelet! I want my gold bracelet!"

It sounded as if she'd come out of her room and was stalking the hallway. Every word rang out crisply. Instead of sticking around to find out, he fled as fast as his legs would carry him.

Meanwhile, his wife stayed upstairs, crying and carrying on. A blue hanky she'd embroidered with white flowers was soaked with tears. Her hair had fallen loose and was cascading down her face; even the bedspread was soaked. Her sorrow was like water spilling out of a bottomless glass—there was no stopping it.

She stood up and looked around—Bo'le was nowhere in sight—and she fell back onto the bed to recommence crying, even more pitifully than before. But this time it was short-lived; after a few wails for effect, she was back on her feet. With great force of will, she stopped the flow of tears, dipped her hanky in the washbasin, and wiped her tear-streaked face. Cool water on her feverishly hot skin refreshed her, although she was still a little light-headed and, of course, her eyes were red and puffy. She would have to wait a while before leaving the room, to avoid embarrassment.

So she sat down in an easy chair, picked up the daily newspaper, and began to read. But boredom set in, until an advertisement for new fashions from Shanghai caught her eye. Women were encouraged to shop early. Accompanying the advertisement was a photograph of a velvet dress, a lovely embroidered frock in a new style she'd not seen before.

That took her mind off her husband, but only briefly. Reminded of what she had to put up with, she heaved a sigh and forced herself to read more of the newspaper.

Her thoughts proceeded until she felt that life had begun to lose its meaning. Her mood was darkened further by her reflection in the mirror. Sensing that she had aged, she noticed that her complexion was poor, that she was heavier than ever, and that she had acquired something of a double chin. An additional effect of the added weight was that her eyes seemed smaller. She detected no trace of the graceful bearing of days past. Picking up a hand mirror, she smoothed back the hair that had fallen across her forehead, and looked to see if there were wrinkles below her hairline. On that score, she was pleased to note, she was holding up fairly well, and was reminded that several days had passed since she'd last plucked her eyebrows. It took so much time and effort to get the children to behave that her neglected eyebrows had grown together.

After searching through the vanity for her tweezers, and not finding them in any of the drawers, she recalled that the children had taken them to play with, and had a vague notion she'd seen them lying around somewhere, but for the life of her she could not remember where. "Those damned kids are going to drive me crazy!" she sputtered.

Still light-headed, she shuffled back to her chair and sat down, resting until she heard someone call to her from the hallway. She quickly stood up.

"Elder Mistress!"

It was a gentle, friendly summons from her mother-in-law, Lao Taitai. She answered with a sense of urgency:

"Just a moment, Mother, I'm fixing my hair—I'll be right out." The sound of her own voice, soft and ladylike, convinced her that life might not be so bad, after all.

Hurriedly, she brushed her hair and powdered her face. Even without rouge, she did not really seem much older. But as she was about to open the door, she noticed that her cheongsam was wrinkled from all that crying. She opened her wardrobe, which was filled with dresses of every style and color. No time to be choosy, she took out the first one she touched and put it on. It was a purple, rather plain dress that was far from new. But on her it looked nice, feminine, and quite elegant.

Her hair was styled in a tight permanent wave, but since she had been forced to touch it up, it wasn't as neat as it might be. She was wearing fawn-colored nylons and blue satin house slippers embroidered with yellow flowers.

Gliding across the room noiselessly, she stole a final look in the mirror before shutting the door, convinced that no one could tell she had been crying. With renewed self-assurance, she walked down the hall, accompanied by her fragmented reflection in the hall windows.

When she arrived at her mother-in-law's room she learned that the older woman merely wanted to tell her that the daughter of Pastor Ma had just returned from Shanghai, bringing back some black gauzy dress material. Afraid that people would laugh at an old woman in a dress made of such material, she wanted her daughter-in-law to have it.

"Praise Jesus," the younger woman exclaimed.

Respectfully, she accepted the boxed material in both hands and, as she was leaving with the gift, her mother-in-law whispered:

"Make a nice dress, but for goodness sake don't tell . . . don't say a word to Younger Mistress, or she'll take offense."

Ma Bo'le's wife returned to her room, took the material out of the box, and draped it around herself. One look in the mirror was all she needed to regain her self-confidence. It was proof that she had gained her mother-in-law's favor. Thanks to her diligence in reading the Bible the first thing every morning, she surmised. As her father-in-law, Lao Taiye, had said succinctly:

"The most devout believer in the Lord Jesus will fall heir to the lion's share of my wealth."

Now she began to worry that her recitations from the Bible might not be quite loud enough. Lao Taitai could hear her, but she wasn't so sure about Lao Taiye, who was a little hard of hearing. She resolved to increase the volume beginning the next morning.

After folding the material and putting it away, she went down to the kitchen to have the servants start dinner.

How had she let a gold bracelet and a few paltry gold rings upset her so? The future held so much more than those baubles. All she had to do was show a bit more devotion to the Lord Jesus.

The recent argument with Ma Bo'le was forgotten.

# Chapter Three

Ma Bo'le's father was a member of the gentry class in Qingdao, a medium-sized city in Northern China. Rich, yes, but not a member of the upper crust. Having been born into a poor family, he was terrified that someday he'd be poor again, and this made him a cautious man. His savings amounted to tens of thousands of yuan, but most likely less than a hundred thousand. No wonder he kept such a close rein on his sons. This much could be said for him: he practiced what he preached. He rose early and went to bed late, and for many years had been a devout follower of the Lord Jesus.

Ma Bo'le did not give a damn about any of this. As far as he was concerned, his father's impoverished background belonged to the past, and to his father alone. What got to him was the way the old tyrant smugly grilled him every time the subject of money arose, wanting to know exactly what he needed it for. He was fed up with this routine. He had started out as the heir apparent in the family, but soon despaired of ever going beyond the "apparent" stage. His brother, who knew how to bow and scrape, might well walk away with the bulk of the estate, even though he was younger. They did not get along. Nor did their wives—for obvious reasons.

Despite the life of ease he led, Ma Bo'le detested rich people; he was disgusted by wealthy merchants, hated compradors, and held bankers in contempt. He took pleasure in deriding members of the local gentry. His dislike for his father extended naturally to all people like him. He considered the rickshaws owned by wealthy families the epitome of ostentatious wealth. The Ma family had one, and he refused to ride in it.

"It's unnatural for one man to pull another," he would say. "Ahead a poor man struggling, behind a sick squire snuggling." To him this anonymous limerick said it all. For the man pulling the rickshaw it was a life-and-death struggle, while the customer leaning back comfortably in his rickshaw looked every bit the sick squire.

He recalled the time he unadvisedly jumped onto the seat of his father's rickshaw and ordered the puller to give him a ride. The man threw down his towel, turned to him, and said:

"I work for Lao Taiye. I'm not going to serve you too."

Bo'le climbed sheepishly down off the rickshaw. Even the polished brass headlamps seemed to mock him. He was so angry he felt like kicking them in, and as he walked out the gate, he turned and glared at the offending lights.

"Bloody Chinese!"

Ma Bo'le found it especially distasteful to make friends with wealthy scions of his generation. "Rich people are no damned good," he often said, mostly when he was alone. "Their entire household is mean, from their servants to children."

The trouble with associating with rich friends was that money had to be spent, even if you needed to beg your father or pawn your wife's jewelry to get it. If you were invited to a movie, you had to reciprocate. If you were asked to dinner, it was your turn next. If someone bought you tickets at a dance hall, you'd have to buy some for him and stuff them into his pocket. And to do things right, you would have to buy more for him than he had bought for you. But all this could be avoided by making friends with the poor. They are easier to deal with: when you have money in your pocket, they are content with a simple meal of dumplings or won-ton soup.

True to his ideals, in high school Ma Bo'le made friends almost exclusively with his needy classmates, and the few friends he had as an adult dated from that time. None enjoyed anywhere near his personal wealth. There was, of course, a drawback in befriending the needy, and that was they were usually in a borrowing mood. If they found out he had money in his pocket, sooner or later he would have to lend them some or treat them to a meal. Which was why he kept his wallet well out of sight when he was with his hard-up friends.

There was method to Ma Bo'le's madness in wanting to become a writer: he was tired of always being short of cash and having to beg his father or his wife for spending money. He had high hopes of selling his work. But sitting at a desk and producing nothing was a waste of time. So he changed his mind, figuring that the quickest road to riches was in commerce, and this led to yet another trip to Shanghai, where he planned to open a small publishing house.

This time he would go with his father's blessing—escape would have nothing to do with it. His father assumed that his son's plan to go into business was evidence that he finally realized the value of money, and was moved to the point of coming up with the capital.

Even his wife was secretly hopeful that he would find success in his new venture, and she began to show him a bit of respect. On the eve of his departure, she went into the kitchen and personally prepared a fish for his dinner, just as she had done for the foreign missionary when he'd visited their home. The difference was that for the foreigner she'd cooked it Western style, fried in batter.

She walked into the dining room followed by a servant carrying the platter, saying as she reached the dining table:

"Bo'le, I want you to enjoy a good meal tonight. As you know, fish stands for 'plenty,' so this can symbolize the success of your forthcoming business venture. Who knows, you might make your fortune . . ."

Bo'le's mother, who was equally pleased, felt obliged to make a minor correction:

"Our young master is going to open a publishing house, not start a business."

Father's contribution to the general discussion was lengthy. He did not wear glasses hooked over his ears like other people; rather, he fastened the frames over his temples, grasshopper style. The lenses were made of transparent stones, supposedly dating from the Qianlong period in the mid-eighteenth century. They made his eyes look cold and steely, and since he needed them for nearsightedness, he was never without them. The only thing that occasionally bothered him about this particular pair of glasses was the annoying and inescapable fact that they had not been made in the West. More than once, a foreign parishioner from his church had brought pairs of the smaller, lighter foreign eyeglasses from Shanghai or Hong Kong for him, and he was eager to wear them, if only for a short time, such as when he went to church.

But it never worked, no matter how hard he tried. Western-manu-factured glasses were made to fit over the bridge of the nose, and with his typically small Chinese nose, they kept slipping off. Since nothing worked, he always went back to his Qing dynasty relics, the ones with lenses as big as saucers. On this occasion, he adjusted his glasses and said:

"You're getting on in years, you know, and you must not be afraid of making mistakes. Jesus said, 'To do wrong and make amends is not a sin.' Like you . . . in the past . . ."

He sighed before continuing:

"We do not need to be reminded how you once ran off to Shanghai . . . Ah! But that is water under the bridge. There probably isn't a man alive who hasn't run off to sow his wild oats in his youth. But when a man approaches the age of thirty, it is time to take hold and get something done, if not for himself, then for his children and his children's children . . . why did Jesus allow himself to be nailed to the cross, if not for his people? A man must take into account the well being of his descendants. If thoughts of you had not figured into my actions, I might have squandered every cent I had on myself. Look at me: all day long, if I'm not in church, I'm over at Pastor Ma's house. Don't think I don't know that you all believe I'm wasting my time and that I think too highly of the foreigners. If you want to know the truth, I would prefer to lie around the house like a proper patriarch. But that is not how it can be. They are better off than we are. Their food, their clothes, everything they do exudes taste and refinement.

"Could we Chinese get along without those foreigners? Oh, sure, they sacked Beijing during the Boxer Rebellion, but that was for our own good. If they hadn't attacked, do you suppose we'd have as many churches as we have now? Why do you think they worked so hard to build all those churches? They did it for us, the Chinese people. There isn't a single Chinese moral code that compares with theirs. We are an unsanitary race. Everywhere you go you find eight to ten people living in a single room. Now take a look at the foreigners, go to their neighborhoods if you want to see urbanity. You would think their homes were deserted, they're so quiet. Why, they don't even allow their children to sleep with their mothers. Instead, they outfit special rooms for them called nurseries. The foreigners are different, and we need to model ourselves after them."

Mother sat quietly at the table. But when dinner was finished, she went to the altar and knelt before the Virgin Mother's statue, where she prayed for a full half hour.

"Lord Jesus," she intoned emotionally, "take pity on our son. He has always been a good and honest boy, just a little timid. I beseech you, Lord, to bestow upon him the gift of courage. He has always obeyed the Lord's commandments. Dear Lord, Father in Heaven, having given him this opportunity to go to Shanghai, you must also instill in him the common sense to make it a success. Let him recoup his investment by the end of the first year, let his investment yield interest by the second, and let him be rolling in gold and jade within three to five years . . . Dear Lord, Father in Heaven."

Bo'le was more moved by this heartfelt plea than at any other time in his life. He had now gained the respect of his family. Back in his room, he paced the floor, hands clasped behind his back, lips clamped tightly shut. He stared straight ahead with fiery determination, for now he was imbued with the notion that he was but a step away from becoming his own man.

He had never believed in Jesus, but today he wasn't so sure. Maybe he believed, after all, for when his mother rose from in front of the statue of Mary, he fell to his knees. This was unheard of. His mother immediately parted the door curtains to let his father see what was happening from the living room.

In the past, Father had often commented that Ma Bo'le was not a true believer.

"He doesn't even say evening prayers," he complained.

At such times, Mother would speak up for her son:

"Be patient. Someday he'll learn to believe."

Now, here he was, kneeling of his own free will, and it wasn't even evening prayer time.

The moment Father witnessed the scene before him, he fell to his knees in front of the cross and offered up a prayer of thanks that Jesus had finally won over his son's heart and earned his devotion. He thanked the Lord for blessings bestowed. His prayers lasted half an hour.

Seeing her husband join her son on his knees in prayer, Mother quickly went to her elder daughter-in-law's room, but it was empty. She hurried back to the living room, her jowls shaking like jelly. In the hallway, she met her daughter-in-law, who was scolding the child in her arms.

"Mother," she complained loudly, "this child is just asking for a spanking. Every time she sees a peddler, she wants to buy something. She won't listen when I tell her that she's not allowed to buy things on the Sabbath . . ."

Mother quieted her with a wave of her hand and the blank look that always accompanied an important event.

"Hush now. Come see who's on his knees praying!" she caught her breath, in obvious excitement, then continued: "Hurry up, join your husband and ask merciful God in Heaven to watch over Paul and convert him into a true believer."

(His father had given him the name Bao-luo, the Chinese equivalent of Paul. But he did not like having a foreign name, so he had changed it to Bo'le, though his parents continued to call him Paul.)

She pushed her daughter-in-law into the other room. "Even your father-in-law is praying . . . hurry now . . ."

Although the Ma house was not a church, a religious image decorated every room, as well as the hallways and the servants' quarters. To be sure, the latter were less well appointed: In place of the inlaid frames that enclosed images in other parts of the house, here they were simply tacked to the walls to be replaced by new ones each year, like New Year's scrolls. As time passed, the images turned black with dust and dirt and became tattered.

Lao Taitai had not run through the house in vain, for now there was a kneeling figure in front of nearly every religious image.

The elderly housekeeper Mama Geng was kneeling in the kitchen. Born in a Shandong village, she had answered the call of Jesus soon after coming to the city. Back in her village she had been a Buddhist, but those beliefs had been supplanted by the persuasive powers of a European missionary.

Mama Geng went to church every Sunday. As one of the foreign God's most devoted followers, her prayers were accompanied by loud sobs, for she had lived a tragic life, a fact of which she never failed to remind Him:

"Dear God, take pity on me. I lost my mother when I was ten, was married at fifteen, bore three children over the next three years . . . their father ran off before the third child entered this world. He said he was going north to Shanhai Pass and would be back the next year. That's the last I saw of him . . . dear God, take pity on me . . . my children are grown now, so don't allow them to go to Shanhai Pass. Dear God, drive the Devil out of their hearts, and if they have to die in poverty, let it be in our village."

Mama Geng was as clumsy and slow-witted as a woman could be. She never got things right. But she had a good heart, which was why Lao Taitai put up with her.

Lao Taitai next ran into the slave girl as she was walking upstairs with a basin of water. She called her to a halt. The little girl was a motherless child, not because her mother had died (or, for that matter, her father), but because they had been too poor to care for her. One day her mother had simply bundled her up and sold her in the town square like a lamb. Only two years old at the time, she had been bought by a servant in the employ of one of Lao Taitai's neighbors. When the girl was seven years old, Mrs. Ma had purchased her from the servant. The price had been thirty yuan, a sum Lao Taitai never forgot. Nor did she let the girl forget; whenever she was displeased for any reason at all, she launched into a familiar tirade:

"You cost me thirty yuan, money that would have been better spent on goldfish. Goldfish may not make much of a meal, but at least they're nice to look at. You're neither."

The girl was a good worker. Her only fault was a penchant for pilfering food. Since she was free to come and go in the daughters-in-law's rooms, she searched for sweets when they were out.

Lao Taitai had beaten her more than once over this habit, and each time the girl had sworn she'd never do it again. Lao Taitai, taking pity on her, would lower her hand and say:

"The Lord does not cotton to oaths." She never beat the girl without regretting it afterwards.

Now, having been stopped by Lao Taitai's shout, she laid down the basin and fell to her knees in the hallway, instinctively assuming that she was about to pay for some unknown transgression. She knelt obediently, covering her face with her filthy hands.

Lao Taitai went back downstairs, where she spotted the rickshaw puller polishing headlamps. She shouted to him:

"Hurry up and pray for Young Master . . ."

Assuming that something bad had happened to young Ma, he dropped everything, ran to his hut, and knelt before the image tacked up on the wall.

The man had once hawked clay utensils and earthenware bowls door to door. Things had been going well for his family until misfortune visited him in the form of typhoid fever. Since he had no savings, he refused to go to the hospital, relying instead on traditional Chinese herbal medicine. He was sick for over a year before his wife and daughter contracted the disease and died in front of him.

To his illness was now added the grief of mourning, and by the time he was back on his feet physically, he was dangerously close to insanity.

He was a pale, sickly man whose past illness was written on his face. He rented a rickshaw and went out looking for customers, but he never earned more than a few fen, even when he was out from dawn to dusk. He spent most of his time resting, complaining that he did not have the strength to pull a fare. If a prospective customer jumped into his rickshaw, he might say:

"I haven't got the strength." Or:

"I'm too sick."

Somewhere along the line, Ma Bo'le's father met this man.

"Since your health is poor, why not come to God," he counseled him. You can ask him to heal your body."

The following Sunday, the pale man appeared in church, where he learned how to pray, and when Ma Bo'le's father saw the extent of the man's devotion, he brought him into the household to run errands, sweep the compound, and perform odd jobs. For this he gave him three meals a day—rice porridge for breakfast, and flatbreads for lunch and dinner.

At the time the family had a rickshaw puller, a fast runner with no shortcomings. But he demanded a monthly wage; by having the new man pull the rickshaw in addition to his other duties, the family could save ten yuan every month. So the original puller was let go and replaced by the pale-faced man, who pulled the rickshaw at an agonizingly slow pace. Each time he tried to make it up an incline, he frothed at the mouth like a sickly old nag. Gasping for breath, his energy spent, he looked as if he might collapse.

Lao Taiye would continue sitting on his perch, content that the savings were worth a bit of anxiety. "If he were a fast runner, he'd want a wage, and Lord Jesus said that a man should not be greedy."

Upon reaching his destination, Mr. Ma would alight from the rickshaw and take a long, sympathetic look at the gasping, hacking figure before him. Reaching into his coin purse, he'd fish out five fen and tell the rickshaw puller to buy a cup of hot tea to make him feel better.

The man was treated well by every member of the Ma family, young and old, and he knew it. Any time Lao Taitai saw that he was a little under the weather, she treated him to a cup of local spirits. In fact, only the eldest son of the family came up a little short in compassion, though even he never abused the fellow.

But then one day, after bringing Lao Taiye home, the rickshaw puller's strength gave out. Bo'le suggested taking him to a nearby hospital, but his father objected:

"That hospital is run by foreigners and is very expensive."

"I don't mean to get medical attention," replied Bo'le. "They have a morgue."

"Do you think he's going to die?" Father asked.

"Of course he is, and it's not a good idea for him to do it here in front of the children."

The rickshaw puller lay on the ground just beyond the gate, foaming at the mouth. Lao Taiye stepped forward and began to pray for the unfortunate man.

Lao Taitai stood in the doorway, wiping her eyes, which were filled with tears of pity for the helpless man.

People watching the excitement looked on quietly—no one said a word. Mama Geng broke the silence by urging Lao Taiye:

"Carry him inside—he's not going to die."

But Lao Taiye shook his head:

"Lord Jesus does not like to work in cramped spaces . . ."

So Mama Geng turned to Lao Taitai:

"Please have him taken inside."

Lao Taitai continued to rub her eyes.

"Shut up!" she said.

Meanwhile, the object of all this concern lay on the ground just beyond the gate, soaking up sunshine amid a circle of witnesses.

Lao Taitai went back upstairs.

The man did not die, after all.

A din arose from the sound of prayers on Ma Bo'le's behalf that day as the postman walked up and rapped on the window of the hut. "Mail!" he shouted. There was no response, which he found peculiar. Then he heard the hum coming from the house.

Christianity had gained a foothold in town. In fact, many of the city's postmen were Christians, so he knew the sounds of prayer when he heard them. A glance at his watch assured him that it was too early for evening prayers. It was a rare sight indeed to see a family praying together in the middle of the day; the only possible explanation was that something had happened—maybe the birth of a child, for they were gifts from Heaven. Then when people died, their kinfolk hoped that they would return to Jesus's bosom. And so they prayed.

He strolled into the compound and up to the house, where he spotted the slave girl kneeling in the hallway. He left, feeling perplexed. Continuing on his route, he proceeded to the house next door, where he related what he had just seen to the gatekeeper, who ran over to the Ma house, stopping at the gate to look around. He returned and passed the news on to a servant, who then relayed it to the eldest daughter of the family she served.

It did not take long for a crowd to gather outside the gate of the Ma house. Since they had no business inside, the people had to be content with craning their necks to get a look inside. Some guessed that Lao

Taiye had died. Others, recalling that one of the grandsons had run a fever a couple of days earlier, assumed that his illness had gotten worse. Then there were passersby who stopped only because they saw a crowd; they had no idea what was going on and just stood with the others looking around.

The Ma family's elderly cook, a blue apron tied around his waist, strolled nonchalantly up to the gate carrying a wine jug. The crowd stopped him before he could enter the compound.

"What's going on at your place?" they asked. "What's happened?"

"Nothing," he said.

The people surged up to him.

"Don't push," he complained.

As he entered the courtyard, he was greeted by prayerful sounds coming from the house. He opened the kitchen door, where he saw Mama Geng kneeling on the floor. He unhesitatingly set down his wine jug and joined her.

Only twice in his life had Ma Bo'le been the beneficiary of such solemn prayers: once when he was born, but of course he had no recollection of that occasion, and today. The sense of solemnity was overwhelming.

# Chapter Four

Not long after the prayer-fest, Ma Bo'le was in Shanghai to open a publishing house with his father's capital. How much money his father had given him, whether it was a few hundred or three thousand, remained a secret to outsiders.

The venture was located in a three-story building on a quiet street in the French Concession. All things considered, it was lavishly appointed. Business was conducted on the ground floor; the office—his private domain—was on the second floor; and the upper floor had been turned into living quarters for his employees, some friends he'd made on his previous trip to the city who were down on their luck. That included a man named Chen who had audited classes with him and was good with figures. Ma Bo'le hired him to be his bookkeeper.

Altogether there were six or seven rooms, furnished with half a dozen desks, each covered with a sheet of glass. Ma Bo'le had bought all the necessary inkpots, scissors, glue pots, thumbtacks, and odds and ends for slightly over fifty yuan.

He hired a servant to run his kitchen. She lit the fire, warmed the stove, and prepared for the arrival of Ma Bo'le's visitors, at which time the kitchen would be filled with cooking smells of chicken, duck, fish, and more, as the dinner parties began.

For whom did Ma Bo'le throw out the welcome mat? His honored guests were budding poets, prospective poets, would-be poets, and a few aspiring novelists who were gathering material for their first works. His new circle of friends had been rounded up in a matter of days. There was no lack of intimacy in these friendships—it was all for one and one for all. When there was food, everyone ate; when there was liquor, everyone drank. No disputes ever disrupted the camaraderie.

Ma Bo'le told them about his own novel in progress, discreetly omitting any mention of what had motivated him—the prospect of making money with his pen. He limited himself to a discussion of his central theme and how he hoped to lend his pen to the cause of national salvation. "If the Chinese are to be roused out of their lethargy," he told them, "it's up to us writers. The responsibility is ours—every one of us . . ."

When he was in an expansive mood, his guests were assured of being treated to this patriotic outburst. The consensus among his acquaintances was that Ma Bo'le showed more promise than any of them.

The good times held on for a few weeks, but before long, the luster began to wear off Ma Bo'le's publishing house, which had yet to begin the arduous task of publishing books. One day, he told bookkeeper Chen to perform an audit, since he was concerned about expenses. With the results in hand, he asked:

"Is this figure accurate? Is it that much, really?"

He spent the morning at his desk, pencil in hand, checking and rechecking the figures. This constituted the first time since the opening that he'd actually done any "work," and it was exhausting. So he lay down to rest for a while, and then went back to give it another try. The figure that had so alarmed him stubbornly resisted every one of his mathematical assaults, remaining the same as it was when first arrived at by bookkeeper Chen. "That's hard to believe," was all he could say. "Where could I have spent nearly two thousand yuan? I only bought what I needed. I didn't throw it away on non-essentials. Where did the money go?"

He had only to look at the figures in his hand to get the answers he sought, for not only were the expenditures itemized, they were dated as well. Every fen had been spent with his approval. There were no surprises: desks, chairs, wardrobes, spittoons . . . even the tins of cigarettes he'd bought for his guests, he'd recorded it all. There was no getting around it; the figure was accurate. But even after accepting what was in front of him in black and white, doubt was still written on his face. And by the following day he'd formulated a plan to cut his losses—he'd sublet the downstairs. Putting his plan into action, he hung a red-bordered sign on the front door:

ROOM FOR RENT

SANITATION FACILITIES INCLUDED

LOW MONTHLY RATE—ONLY FORTY YUAN

Bo'le and his bookkeeper nearly came to blow over the words "Low Monthly Rate."

"Why do you need to write that? If someone's interested in the room, they'll take it; if not, they won't. If any of your friends saw it, they'd figure we could not make a go of the business."

But Bo'le's mind was made up—the disputed words stayed.

Once the sign was finished, he pasted it up, and this too nearly led to a fight. Bo'le wanted to put it up high, the bookkeeper wanted it lower so passersby could see it more easily. But Ma Bo'le countered with:

"If I keep it low, some damned kids will tear it down."

Bo'le personally slopped on the paste, took the sign outside and stuck it up. He had to stand on his tiptoes to get it at the desired height. Inadvertently, he used more paste than he needed, so once the room was rented, no matter how hard he tried, he could not tear down the sign completely. After the tenant moved in, he quit trying and let the rains finish the job for him, which they eventually did.

When Bo'le's friends dropped by, they opened the downstairs door, walked in unannounced, and called out:

"Bo'le, are you home?"

The tenant never quite got used to that.

"The place was too big for us," he'd tell them upstairs, "so we moved everything up here."

He'd wanted to say they'd moved the business section, but since they hadn't done any "business" so far, it did not seem appropriate.

The net result was a decline in the number of friends and a notable lack of enthusiasm among those who continued to drop by. He stopped putting on the feedbag, limiting his hosting responsibilities to engaging them in long chats. Few were particularly enthused about sitting around and talking, and the general atmosphere cooled; there was less and less to talk about. Conversations that managed to get off the ground were more orderly and less spontaneous—there was no longer any life to these gatherings.

The second-floor furnishings now consisted of three desks, a wardrobe, two bookcases, and some chairs. Plus Ma Bo'le's bed. There was barely room to walk, in part because of the haphazard way it was arranged.

All this chaos affected Ma Bo'le, who no longer wore a tie and gave up wearing socks inside his sandals. Before long, he even stopped getting dressed in the morning, lolling around all day long in his pajamas. And on the days he washed those, he went around in an undershirt and shorts. He gave up washing his face and brushing his teeth in the morning, limiting his activities to reclining in a chair or sprawling listlessly on the bed in a sort of half sleep. "What am I going to do when the day comes?"

He always had a particular "day" in mind, but it was a secret known to him alone. For all anyone knew, it referred to the day when he would shut the publishing house door for the last time.

And so it went: Before long, the third-floor rooms were sublet, then the garret.

The enterprise now occupied the second floor alone. It was all there in one room—bookkeeping, general affairs, everything.

Bo'le and a couple of his friends ate and slept in the same room. The friends were his employees. This unseemly arrangement was resolved when he bought a screen and separated his quarters from theirs. The retrenchment made life easier. What it failed to do was breathe life into a venture that was on its last gasp. Things might have been different if he had found a way to actually publish something. He was collecting forty yuan for the downstairs room, twenty for the third floor, and a total of fourteen for the two garret rooms. Since he paid seventy a month for the whole building, by subletting most of it, he netted four yuan a month. That, at least, was reassuring. By saving the earnings for a couple of months, he'd have enough to buy a ticket home. Nothing reassuring about that, unfortunately.

Ma Bo'le's publishing venture lasted three months, during which he had spent in excess of two thousand yuan. He had not printed or sold a single book.

• • •

Ma Bo'le's return home took his wife by surprise, but she reacted indifferently to the reality that his business had failed. No arguments, no questions; it was as if the news did not register. She employed the silent treatment, avoiding direct contact by a series of sidelong glances. Sometimes she looked at him as if he were a total stranger.

When the maidservant came to call them to dinner, his wife picked up Jacob and walked out without her usual comments of:

"Dinnertime," or "Let's eat."

Her silence did not affect their little daughter, who looked back over her mother's shoulder, clapped her hands, and called out, "Daddy!"

All this brought tears to Ma Bo'le's eyes.

He was partial to the children, who were not aware that their daddy had returned home in disgrace. During dinner, no one at the table spoke to him, and he was not invited to join their conversations.

Father had not said a word at mealtime for a couple of days. His silver chopsticks clanged against his rice bowl as he ate. After he finished his first bowl of rice, Mama Geng came up to give him a refill. He waved her off, put down his rice bowl, rose from the table, and walked away, followed by his younger son, Ma Bo'le's brother and rival for their father's affections, such as they were, and inheritance.

The big family cat jumped from its perch on the windowsill onto the cushioned chair Father had just vacated, where it crouched and purred. It was black, and very well fed. It returned Bo'le's stare.

The prodigal son had no choice but to get up from the table before a second bowl of rice, thus leaving the dining room neither full nor hungry. Later on, his father even refused to eat at the same table with his older son, taking his meals alone in the living room. When he finished, he rinsed his mouth so loudly that Bo'le felt personally threatened.

Mother's mood was dampened by her husband's obvious displeasure. The maidservant stood off to the side, not daring to say a word.

When Jacob clamored that she wanted some egg-drop soup, her father spooned some into her rice bowl. But before she could get the first spoonful to her mouth, her mother snatched the bowl away from her.

"With your bad stomach the past couple of days," she complained, "I'm not going to let you fill up with soup."

Jacob started to bawl.

"What harm can a little soup do?" Bo'le asked.

His wife responded by picking the child up and walking off without giving him a passing glance.

Bo'le's family had begun treating him the way Satan was treated in the Bible. Now even little Jacob would no longer let him near her. So he decided it was time to move out of his wife's room and into his study. And that is what he did. He took all his trunks, in which were stored his clothes, his shoes, and his socks. Even things that had accompanied him on two sojourns to Shanghai went along. It was as if he and his wife had negotiated a formal separation.

She took the move with equanimity—not a word or a second glance. No sign, verbal or visual, that she approved of his action, or, for that matter, opposed it. He got the message that he was free to do as he pleased, that it was no concern of hers.

On the final trip, when he came to pick up his soap dish, he gave his wife an ugly look after opening the door with a ferocious kick. He then made a show of searching the room, pretending not to notice that the soap dish was on the dressing table, keeping a furtive eye on his wife the whole time. As he rummaged through drawer after drawer, he glanced at her out of the corner of his eye to see how she was taking it. All the while she was lying on the bed playing with her daughter.

"Bloody Chinese!" It was a muted protest

They were sad days for Ma Bo'le. At night he opened his window and looked outside—the moon was out, and he intoned thoughts that came to him.

"When the moon comes out, the sun disappears."

"When it rains, the streets get wet."

In the autumn, fallen leaves covered the courtyard and lined its corridors. Night winds whipped them against windows as Ma Bo'le tossed and turned in bed, his mind flooded with chaotic thoughts. In fact, he thought so hard that his head began to ache. He felt a little better after getting up and drinking a cup of tea. Looking out the window into the dark night, he embarked upon a soliloquy:

"Without the moon there's total darkness.

"Leaves fall to the ground when autumn arrives."

This led him to a series of related musings:

"The rich look down on the poor.

"Officials look down on the common people.

"My wife looks down on me.

"When the wind dies down, the leaves stop falling.

"If I were rich, my wife would look up to me.

"If I were rich, Father would still be Father, the kids would still be my kids.

"That's what life is all about.

"Life is being alive.

"Death is not being alive.

"Suicide leads to death.

"When it's time to flee, you have to flee."

The thought of escape was tempting, but he knew that this was not the right moment. Bo'le stayed home for a long spell this time, some seven or eight months.

• • •

That summer, a fleet of eighty Japanese warships visited the city. They anchored off the coast in a line that stretched nearly out of sight. The city buzzed with news of their arrival. Everyone knew that the ships had no intention of attacking Qingdao and were only in port for shore leave or as part of war games. But it still terrified the populace, especially the lower classes, whose illiteracy prevented them from reading the daily papers. They got their news from rumors and misunderstood the term "war games" to mean that the Japanese were going to be playing their games on them.

In the streets and byways of Qingdao, the people talked about nothing else. Everywhere you looked you saw rickshaw pullers, bean curd peddlers, teahouse proprietors—people from all walks of life—pointing anxiously at the great amphibian creatures lying off the coast of their city. "Why don't they play their games in their own country?" people asked. "Why come all the way to China?"

A drastic change occurred following the arrival of the warships. Prostitutes—Annamese, French, Korean, and others—gaily and seductively greeted the squat Japanese sailors in a variety of languages, all the women attired in clothing appropriate to their national origin. They strolled up and down the beachfront, where waves lapped against the shore as if summoned by the sounds of their gaiety. At high tide, the mobile breakwater washed up closer to the shore, where it disgorged its complement of men to the raucous delight of the prostitutes wading in the rising water. The girls of this multi-lingual sisterhood joyously welcomed the runty visitors. With every look, with every touch from these newcomers, the girls exploded in gales of laughter. Normalcy returned only when the beached sailors began walking off with their chosen escorts, although as they departed, the girls continued to laugh and joke until the streets swayed with sounds of merriment.

In other quarters, many of the city's Japanese occupants posted signs of welcome on the walls of their houses, inviting sailors of the Imperial Navy to be guests in their homes. Virtually every Japanese household displayed such a sign; to them, what was happening in the city counted among the most magnificent, most spectacular, most extraordinary events in the history of man.

Within a few days, every Japanese household in Qingdao had taken in one or more of the naval heroes, who were distinguished by flat caps with two small black streamers attached to the rear. The men came in twos and threes, and some homes took in as many as four or five. In each case, although visitor and host were meeting for the first time, they took to each other like long lost cousins. Housewives, no matter how young, drank toasts to their guests; naturally, from the sailors' perspective, the younger the better. Lodging with compatriots was as much fun—and not nearly as fraught with risks to their health—as being with the women who spoke all those different languages and who had formed a beachfront welcoming party. The younger the women, the livelier the atmosphere. The sailors sat cross-legged at low Japanese tables, the women knelt beside them respectfully. The sailors behaved like true guests, eating some, drinking a little, and chatting with their hosts. At least most of them did.

Ma Bo'le had read in the newspaper that local Japanese were entertaining sailors of the Imperial Navy on orders from Tokyo in the name of the Emperor. Having received directives on where they were to be quartered, the sailors had no say in the matter. Nor did their hosts, who did not know the names of their guests or what they would be like until they showed up on their doorsteps.

One of Ma Bo'le's neighboring families was Japanese, as it turned out. He watched their antics through a window, and he watched, and he watched, until finally he was treated to a show. A drunken sailor pulled the lady of the house to him, and started ripping off her clothes.

The sight incensed and repelled Ma Bo'le.

"Bloody Chinese!" he muttered, blissfully unaware of how inappropriate, though heartfelt, the outburst was on this occasion.

It was an extraordinary occurrence, one that would be repeated the following day, when Bo'le went outside to get a closer look at the show in the Japanese home. Before long, the sailor appeared on the scene. The lady of the house was wearing a different kimono than on the day before. Bo'le had observed the activities at this house for some time, since the couple who lived there appeared to be newlyweds and were always carrying on. He had personally witnessed quite a bit of activity, though he would not allow himself to get too caught up in the unfolding drama. That would have been mortifying.

Not much happened at first: hostess and guest had eaten a little, drunk a little sake—nothing out of the ordinary. Everything normal. But then it got interesting when the sailor pulled the women to him. To Bo'le's dismay, the man stood up and pulled down the window shade, so he missed the main event. But the presence of the warships left him with a clear picture of what the future held.

He was convinced that a Japanese attack was imminent. He did not know when or where, but he had no doubts about its inevitability. This conviction was only partly rooted in the arrival of the warships, for he had also observed an example of Japanese military-civilian cooperation right next door, which was how he termed the entertaining of the Japanese sailors by their civilian countrymen (and women). What was the goal of this cooperation? Ma Bo'le had the answer: It was to attack China.

# Chapter Five

On the heels of the July 1937 Marco Polo Bridge Incident, when Japanese and Chinese forces exchanged fire on the bridge between Beijing and Tianjin, Ma Bo'le boarded a foreign-registry steamship and sailed once again from Qingdao to Shanghai—he had gotten away, knowing that his days in his father's house had come to an end. The future—for him and for China—looked bleak. Prior to his departure, he had calculated that the city would fall within a few days, anticipating his wife's joining him in Shanghai shortly after that. She would be sure to bring plenty of money, and he would be set. He knew he could not go home, and that was a crippling thought, for this time, return would be more humiliating than ever. He dreaded the thought of the treatment he would receive at the hands of his father, his wife, even little Jacob. If that happened, he would never again be able to hold up his head. As the ship steamed into port and nestled up to the pier, Ma Bo'le was perched high above the waterline at the railing. From this vantage point he could see the throngs of people who had come to meet the ship. He knew that no one was there to meet him, since he had told no one at home that he was leaving—he would send a telegram after giving his family time to come to grips with his absence.

No one in Shanghai knew that he was coming either. But that did not stop him from searching the sea of faces until all the passengers had debarked and the crowd on the pier had dispersed. Then he returned to his third-class cabin, rolled up his bedding—the only thing he'd brought with him—and left the ship, which displayed none of the characteristics of a refugee vessel. For that matter, Shanghai displayed none of the characteristics of a refugee city. No one was fleeing *to* the city, and no one was fleeing *from* the city. Peace reigned. Everything was normal in the International Settlement, and the tall, buildings along the Bund were stately as ever; double-decker buses continued to ply their routes in peace; the sound of trolley bells filled the air; women strolled the streets and avenues, carrying parasols or shiny leather handbags, decked out in fashionable dress and elegant footwear. Most wore peep-toe shoes, and since they preferred not to wear stockings, they looked fresh and comfortable, especially those in the double-decker buses who favored gauzy, floral dresses in crisp yellows, light blues, and creams. In their filmy, airy outfits, they looked as cool as a spring breeze, so cool that one might worry about their catching cold, even though it was July. Storefront windows, too, were dressed in their finest. Some small shopkeepers had even set up gramophones in their doorways.

He boarded a trolley and rode it past Sincere Company, Koon Sang Yuen Restaurant, and the Sun Company, all packed with customers—no hint of panic there.

The neon signs of the Great World Theater, the Wing On Company, and Sun Company proclaimed their existence, lighting up the night sky. Nanjing Road, King Edward Road, Foochow Road, and Avenue Joffre were flooded with light as bright as the sun. Throngs of people crowded the movie houses; vehicles of every imaginable type—automobiles, buses, trolleys, rickshaws, and bicycles—filled the streets, their horns and bells shattering the calm. All this vehicular activity threw the scurrying pedestrians into confusion. The worst was Nanjing Road, where seemingly endless lines of pedestrians wove in and out among passing trolleys and automobiles.

At the Sincere Company intersection, a traffic cop reigned over this chaos from his perch atop a platform. A dark-skinned Sikh with a massive beard and turban, he directed the flow of traffic majestically. His commands reached the ears of every driver and pedestrian in the area. To let one line of traffic pass, he showed the green light, and across the intersection they went; to stop a line of traffic, he showed the red light and brought it to a halt. He exercised his power with authority.

Everyone was acting too normal for Bo'le's taste. The presence of this refugee from Qingdao in their midst went unnoticed. Wearing heavy clothes, including a filthy shirt and scuffed shoes, he walked along the Bund and down Nanjing Road, sporting a five-o'clock shadow and looking dark and dirty. Everything was as peaceful, as safe and secure, as could be. But there were dark days ahead.

"Bloody Chinese! The Japs will be here any day. You should be home preparing for war!"

Soon after his arrival, he rented a room on Rue Frelupt in the French Concession.

The garlic-infused room, located by the main floor stairwell, was as dark as a morgue. The layout was unusual, to say the least. None of the rooms on the ground floor, including his, had a window. This defect was the first thing he noticed when he was shown the room, and it was what sold him on the place. Sure, he knew that poor lighting was bad for the eyes and that there could be no ventilation in a windowless room. Intolerable? you might ask. Not when you take into consideration the low rent. Ma Bo'le was of the opinion that a refugee should live like one. Economy took precedence over everything else.

He kept his electric light on day and night, and was oblivious to the alternation of day to night, the howling of the wind, the falling of rain, and the crashing of thunder, none of which affected him. He paid nothing for electricity, so what did it matter? Besides, he had grown afraid of the dark. The electric light was his private sun, always shining down on him. Cut off from blaring horns and other street noises, it was as if sound had ceased to exist, that Mother Earth had grown mute. Once in a while, neighborhood kids bounced rubber balls against the wall, producing a dull thud that sounded as if it were coming from miles away. Sometimes they scraped sticks against the wall—*shua-shua* . . . Where's that sound coming from? What is it? He tried and he tried, but could not make it out, sensing only that it came from a great distance away.

In the interest of economy, he stopped going out for meals. For no matter how inexpensive restaurants were, it was still cheaper to cook for himself.

He bought a charcoal brazier, a small iron wok, and a spatula, and then cooked his own food. At first he confined his culinary labors to the kitchen, but it only took a few days to realize the disadvantage in that: he noticed that someone was using his cooking oil, that his soy sauce bottle was being emptied at an alarming rate, and that his supply of charcoal was shrinking faster than it should have. Shanghai rooming houses were equipped with a single kitchen, which everyone shared, and this worked to Ma Bo'le's distinct disadvantage. His suspicions were confirmed when he saw the landlord's servant use some of his oil to fry eggs, so he moved the brazier and his supplies into his room, where he began cooking meals at the head of his bed. He stored the oil, salt, vinegar, soy sauce, and all the rest under his table and bed. The small space was made even smaller by the accumulation of these bottles and cans.

One day he discovered a glass full of chili paste he had prepared four or five days before and promptly forgotten. By now it was covered with a layer of green fuzz that gave off a strange, rank odor. What a shame. It was, of course, inedible, but it hurt to think of the waste involved in getting rid of it. After long deliberation, he scraped it out of the glass with his chopsticks into an old newspaper and threw it out. No need to wash out the glass, which now became a container for hot-pepper oil. In the artificial light, it was impossible to tell that the glass was dirty. All it really needed was a good wipe. Things would get a lot worse on the refugee trail.

This thought provided him with the excuse he needed to stop washing his wok after each use. Every day after finishing lunch, he simply covered the wok with its lid; then, come dinnertime, he uncovered it, scraped it noisily with his spatula, dumped in some new rice, and cooked his meal. He repeated the procedure daily, allowing the accumulations to follow their own nature. As the residue gathered and dried on the outside, the wok slowly expanded in size.

Meanwhile, Ma Bo'le's chopsticks grew thinner with each use, as did his chopping board, for he never washed them. He relied on scraping to remove foreign objects. The effect on his wok was a gradual scraping away of the inside, although the buildup on the outside compensated for this erosion, leading to a consistency in its overall thickness. The only utensil that neither shrank nor expanded was Ma Bo'le's rice bowl. He cleaned it with the same scraping technique as everything else, yet it somehow maintained its original dimensions.

Owing to his preference for scraping, everything he owned—pillow, comforter, shoes and socks—were transformed in one way or another. Sooner or later, they all got dirty, at which time he set to scraping them clean. The wok, his rice bowl, and his chopsticks he scraped with a knife; for his hat, clothes, and socks he relied on his fingernails. He also had a sliver of wood, which he used on his shoes. After coming in out of the rain, he used it to scrape the sides of his mud-caked shoes. Then, once the weather cleared, he gave his shoes another good scraping before stepping outside. Not surprisingly, the prolonged application of this procedure, coupled with his refusal to apply shoe polish, produced a spotty erosion of the leather, giving his shoes a mottled appearance. But if he noticed this state of affairs, he gave no indication of it. He continued to walk in a stately manner, never losing his poise or manifesting self-consciousness or timidity. In fact, he viewed with contempt the glossy shoes and slicked-down hair of those around him.

Ma Bo'le was alone and lonely. His little room was dark and stuffy. There was nothing to see and nothing to hear. But when he went for a stroll, he was furious over the scenes of peace and prosperity that greeted his eyes; there was no sign of preparedness for the approaching Japanese attack. His anger was rekindled each time he saw the opulence around him and the serenity, as if nothing could disturb the city's equilibrium.

Ma Bo'le walked down Nanjing Road, cursing to himself. Everything was too normal; the prospect of change seemed remote, and he was livid. Noticing that shirts were on sale at Sincere Company for eighty or ninety fen, he considered buying one. Though they were of poor quality, they might serve his needs when he left the city. But in his state of anger, he could not bring himself to make the purchase. He could not be bothered about clothes when he was fleeing for his life!

Then a flash of light caught his attention. A youthful peddler walked up with strings of water chestnuts. Ma Bo'le looked thirstily at the water chestnuts, which sold for three fen a string, and considered buying one. But he reminded himself that he was a refugee, and that in times like these, economy took precedence over everything, so he decided to pass them up. But the boy pestered him until he cursed angrily:

"Bloody Chinese!" He gave the boy a swift kick.

Just then, a foreigner walked up behind Bo'le and stepped on his heel.

"Bloody Chinese!" But then he discovered that it was a foreigner.

"Sorry, sorry!"

The man walked on scornfully, without acknowledging Ma Bo'le's existence. He was a big man, so the best response was no response at all, and he let him pass unmolested. Not that he held foreigners in esteem, but what could he do?

His stroll one day took him by a lottery stand. It looked like a New Year's celebration, replete with red bunting. The signs, the curtains, were all red. The stand was chaotic with activity, and that evoked a familiar response:

"Bloody Chinese!"

He put more feeling into this outburst than usual. Sparks nearly flew from his eyes and his hands trembled. The scene, which he would witness time and again, appalled him:

Gramophones blare their so-called music—shrill, cacophonous noises that are a cross between weeping and laughing. People pace in front of the stands, tempted to buy a ticket, yet afraid of throwing one yuan away on a loser. But if they hold onto their money, they will be passing up the opportunity to pick a winner. In addition to the top three prizes, many lesser amounts are at stake: by simply matching the last two numbers, you can win thirty or as much as fifty yuan, down to smaller prizes of two and three yuan. There are even one-yuan prizes—everyone's best chance. Even if you don't win the sweepstakes and have to settle for the one-yuan prize, at least you get your money back. And if, by some stroke of luck, you are the second- or third-prize winner, well, what a day that will be! An instant millionaire, with an automobile and servants to do your bidding.

People crowd the entrance—maidservants, rickshaw pullers, shopkeepers, fortunetellers, vagrants and idlers, people of all classes and from all walks of life—calculating their chances as they stare at row upon row of pink lottery tickets, trying to spot the one that will make their fortune. Suddenly they stop, point and say: "I want that one!" The ticket seller takes down a series, which includes as many as ten or twenty or as few as two or three connected tickets, like postage stamps. But you won't see people in a post office pointing out which particular stamp he wants. If you put down five fen, the clerk gives you a five-fen stamp; if you put down one fen, you get a one-fen stamp. Just try to ask for a particular stamp—you'll get an earful.

Lottery tickets are different. If the buyer does not like the looks of any of the tickets in the row he's selected, all he has to say is, "Not this row, that one," and the seller puts the one back and takes down the other, even though the two are identical. All this indecision sooner or later confuses the buyer, until he senses that the critical moment has arrived, and he zeroes in on one ticket out of all those in front of him. The onlookers believe that something has caught his eye. But no, it's just a shot in the dark, and the outcome is very much in doubt. With confusion clouding his vision and dulling his mind, he tears off the ticket nearest him. For some even that does not end the process: experiencing a sudden change of heart, they see another ticket that looks more promising than the one they have selected. Still unruffled, the seller makes the switch for him, even if he has to repeat the process two or three times, or more.

Among the packed crowd of hopefuls are some who study the choices carefully, fingering the tickets in front of them for the longest time. But they never buy, choosing instead to back off and watch other people. Sometimes the strangest thing happens: One daring fellow steps forward and buys a ticket, encouraging others to take his lead and step up to buy their own. Our timid observer unexpectedly falls in behind the others, sensing a change in the atmosphere, as if the carefree manner of the first customer proves that he, too, is destined to be a winner. Maybe by sweeping in on the other man's coattails, everyone's chance of winning is enhanced. But carefree customers are a rarity here. While most people study the situation carefully, many never go beyond the study phase. They neither buy nor move back to watch others, but simply return home empty-handed. After thinking it over, they promise themselves to go back the next day.

Rich folks also buy lottery tickets, but they seldom bother to pick and choose, nor are they overly concerned about the expense. They shell out ten, twenty, even a hundred yuan at a time, like buying a pack of cigarettes or some daily necessity. Their nonchalance is just as apparent when they get home with the tickets: Jotting down the numbers in their diary or a private journal, they put them out of their minds until the day of the drawing, recalling only the pleasure involved in the purchase.

Despite his strong disapproval, Ma Bo'le was sorely tempted to try his luck, if only for one yuan. The thought of never having to beg for money from either his father or his wife had him reaching into his pocket to fish out the piece of paper that would make him rich, but someone shattered his illusion by snatching the hat off his head before he could step up. He spun around to catch the thief and discovered to his surprise that it was Chen, the bookkeeper from his publishing venture.

The man looked like an opium addict, with one eye bigger than the other and a pale, sickly complexion; he was thin and sort of dried out.

"What's the matter with you, snatching my hat like that?" Ma nearly said. But he thought better of it, since it would not look good to engage in horseplay on a Shanghai sidewalk. So, after shaking hands with Chen, all he said was:

"Where are you staying? What have you been doing lately? Your stomach still acting up?"

They chatted for a while, and when they were about to part, Chen handed him back his hat. Ma Bo'le examined it closely.

"Hey!" he exclaimed. There was a hole in it. "All right, who did this? Where did this come from?"

While Bo'le concentrated on his hat, Chen gave him some advice:

"Old Ma, it's about time you got yourself a new one. I never saw you wear a hat before, and now, a year later, you're wearing one. I thought it was you by the way you walked, but I had to check under your hat to be sure."

With that he turned and left.

On the way home, Bo'le racked his brains trying to figure out how his hat had gotten a hole in it. The answer did not come until he was back in his room preparing a meal. As he fanned the brazier to get the fire going, one of the many sparks landed on his hand. He felt the pain at once and knocked the ash off before it did much damage—the burn was the size of a grain of rice. Then it dawned on him that a hot ash must have landed on his hat. He hurried over to his bed to see if there were holes in his pillow or bedding. It didn't look like there were, but he couldn't be sure. There might be, so he turned the brazier to face the wall. That way the sparks set in motion by his fanning would hit the wall and bounce harmlessly to the floor. What happened to them then was no concern of his, so he fanned the fire more energetically than ever. This made sparks fly, some of which bounced off the wall and landed in his hair and on his face. But that did not faze him, since they were ricochets, not direct hits. He found that by moving left or right as he fanned, he could aim his fiery projectiles in one direction or another, a discovery he turned into a sort of game, lining up bottles and other items as targets.

Meals were the only interruption in Ma Bo'le's otherwise idle days. So he put his heart into his cooking: Stripping down nearly naked, he threw himself into his labors. He would be bathed in sweat, from head to toe, clad only in shorts, an undershirt, and a pair of wooden clogs.

But this only happened twice a day; he passed the rest of the time in idleness. Since he had to keep busy at something, he spent the long hours grooming or making repairs to his socks, his shoes, and his suit. When the soles of his socks had hardened from long wear, he first scraped them with his fingernails, and then kneaded them between his fingers until they softened up. If his trousers were splotched with food stains, he likewise put his fingernails to work. His shoes were the only exception—the sliver of wood replaced his fingernails. For everything else, fingernails worked just fine. If he had food stuck between his teeth, what better tool than a fingernail to fish it out? It was also the ideal tool for removing a stray eyelash or for clearing out a stuffed nostril. When his scalp itched, drastic action was called for: He would dig all ten nails in and scratch for all he was worth. The inside of his ear presented a problem, for it did no good to scratch the outside, and his nail was too short to reach an itch inside. Anxiety usually set in then, manifesting itself in a furious scratching of his ear.

A long time had passed since Ma Bo'le's last bath. The major drawback with public baths was that they were unsanitary, and his rooming house was not equipped for bathing. Since economy was paramount, he settled for rubbing himself down with a towel. He had always perspired freely, and these days, at each of his two daily meals, he worked up quite a sweat. "Sweat is just water," he reminded himself. "If I rub myself down with a towel when I'm sweating, isn't that the same as taking a bath?"

If he had nothing else to do, he simply lay on his bed. The floor was littered with leek skins, which gave off an odor so strong it nearly floored anyone who entered the room. But onions and leeks were among his favorite foods, especially raw, and after eating them, instead of airing out the room, he turned off the light and went out for a walk, closing the door tightly behind him. The reek of onions and leeks thus imprisoned in his room soon became his constant companion. He seldom noticed the smell, and when he did, he wasn't bothered. Economy took precedence over other considerations, after all, so he was perfectly content with his surroundings. And even on those rare occasions when something vexed him, a single thought brought him contentment:

"These are refugee times . . ."

Unavoidably, each time he returned from an outing and opened the door to his room, he kicked over some of the bottles of oil or cans of salt that were scattered across the floor and constituted hidden obstacles in the pervading darkness. But even this did not faze him, no matter how often it happened. In fact, it happened very often, and each time, he calmly bent over and righted the toppled containers. The idea of stacking them away never occurred to him; he just left them all over the place, so that the next time he entered the room, he'd kick them over again, and right them again, over and over.

This, too, he reasoned away with ease:

"These are refugee times."

He made daily trips to the neighborhood market, shopping basket in hand, like an ordinary housewife, where he haggled over everything. He'd buy three fen worth of bean sprouts, then reach into the peddler's basket and scoop up an extra handful—not much, no more than ten or fifteen stalks—for it was his philosophy that more is better than less.

If he was buying a fish, he'd wait until the fish had been weighed and the price settled, then demand that it be exchanged for a larger one. Generally speaking, there would be little if any difference in size between the two, but he would argue over the exchange until his face turned red. As with bean sprouts, Ma Bo'le would invariably snatch a few extra stalks of spinach or leeks after the sale was made. This routine was broken only with the purchase of bean curd, for he could neither reach in and take a little extra nor ask for a larger piece, since every piece was the same as every other piece. Like a sheet of lottery tickets, each square was identical. With this commodity he had no choice but to stand helplessly by and allow the tradesman to hand him any piece he pleased.

Though Ma Bo'le was now safely settled in Shanghai, he had made plans for further flight if it became necessary. The only hitch was that the Marco Polo Bridge Incident had occurred way up north, and the Japanese had not followed it up with an attack on Qingdao, let alone Shanghai. Every time he tried to win converts to the cause, the response went something like this:

"Old Ma, you're going overboard on this. Why don't you pack up and head back to Qingdao? Look at how you're living here. Why punish yourself by staying cooped up in that dark room? You're always talking about the danger Qingdao is facing. Do you think you're the only Qingdao citizen concerned for his safety? Buy a steamship ticket and go home."

He responded with a cold, hateful stare, bemoaning the appalling lack of patriotism and nationalistic sentiments.

"Things are worse than I thought. If all Chinese feel the way you do, China will surely . . . surely . . . Bloody . . ."

He could not bring himself to say it, but he was despairing over the nation's future.

# Chapter Six

At night, the crowds on Nanjing Road were so dense there was barely room to walk. From time to time, Ma Bo'le took an after-dinner stroll into the area, aimless walks to simply blend with the crowds and relieve the lonely boredom of his solitary existence.

Loneliness should not have been one of his concerns, owing to his refugee lifestyle, but somehow it crept up on him. If becoming a refugee had been the only problem facing him, nothing could have drawn a cry of protest out of him or broken his resolve to withstand the worst that life had to offer. The one hardship he had not anticipated, however, was an inability to spread his message—no one believed him. When would the people come to their senses? Each time his alarm over the inevitable Japanese attack fell on deaf ears, he felt like a spurned savior. His innate sadness had the added dimension of frustration and anger.

As he walked along, cursing to himself, everything was too normal; the prospect of change seemed remote, and he was furious. Short on money and in a debilitating funk, he turned on his heel and left Nanjing Road to return home, where he knocked over the usual bottles and jars and was met by the overwhelming odor of leeks. He lay down and slept through the night.

The following morning, he awoke at six or seven o'clock with a nagging feeling that things were not going as they should; he had a premonition of disaster.

He paced the floor, despairing over his future.

His original scenario had been that within a week of the Marco Polo Bridge Incident, the Japanese would attack Qingdao, and Shanghai two or three weeks after that. The incident had given him a measure of confidence, but it had been nearly a month, and neither Qingdao nor Shanghai had experienced a single shock wave. Maybe he'd guessed wrong. What if the Japanese had decided to move north from the Marco Polo Bridge? Or west? Or into the central plains? What if they had decided not to attack Qingdao or Shanghai at all? That was certainly possible.

Self-pity held him in its grip.

After giving free rein to his sadness, Ma Bo'le lay down on his bed, too lazy to cook and too spent to find anything else to do. His hair had grown long, and his face was pale and drawn. His clothes were filthy: his trousers were splattered with cooking oil and his socks had developed holes. He no longer wore a tie and kept his shirt cuffs rolled high, exposing skinny arms that had never done an honest day's work. His shirt had not been washed in so long that a sweat stain had formed down the spine. Every time the shirt was soaked with sweat, he took it off and laid it across his bed to dry out, though he usually put it back on before it was completely dry.

His self-pity increased. When the sky was overcast he said:

"It's a gray world we live in."

When the sun came out, he said:

"When the sun's out, the sky clears up.

"When the sky clears up, the streets are soon dry.

"When the streets are dry, it looks as if it had never rained."

With these commonplaces out in the open, he went on:

"Life isn't worth living if you're broke.

"If you're going to flee, it's best to be the first out.

"When the Japs attack Qingdao, my wife will have to come to Shanghai. She'll bring money and my problems will be solved.

"If the Japs don't attack Qingdao, then my wife won't have any reason to come, and I'll have to go home."

Ultimately, the happy day arrived. All his sorrows were swept away, thanks to the sight of packed vehicles streaming along North Sichuan Road. It was a scene of desolation, but the crowds thinned out when he reached the northern side of the Suzhou River Bridge, and continued thinning as he went north, up to the main post office, where the trolleys were empty. Japanese policemen were out in the streets, most of the storefronts were boarded up, and scraps of paper were swept up into the air by the wind. A string of vehicles—trucks, pushcarts, rickshaws, and the like—proceeded down the street toward the Suzhou River Bridge, filled to overflowing with pots and pans, cats and dogs, and other objects too numerous to count. The vehicles climbed to the top of the bridge. But instead of heading north, they followed the southward flow of the river.

Ma Bo'le looked on excitedly. "Aha! They're on the move!"

He walked up to a woman with a baby in her arms and asked what was going on.

"Oh, it was terrible! The Japanese attacked the Chabei District. Everyone's fleeing for their lives, everyone!"

She pointed north, and then ran off.

It had finally happened, and he was elated.

So he strolled along North Sichuan Road, observing how the new refugees were conducting themselves. With renewed courage, he kept to the side of the road as vehicle after vehicle passed him from the opposite direction.

Before long, he spotted a company of Japanese policemen coming his way. Luck was with him. They did not stop. He hopped onto a passing bus and rode it home.

All day long, Ma Bo'le was so excited he could barely contain himself. He went to see every friend to whom he'd previously tried to spread the word:

"Have you seen the refugees pouring into North Sichuan Road?"

A few had heard spotty reports, but most had not. Ma Bo'le was quick to fill them in on the details, adding whatever was necessary to spice up his story, until the situation sounded far more serious than it actually was.

"Shops on North Sichuan Road are boarded up. There's hardly a person left in the area. Japanese policemen are moving the remaining people along with bayonets . . . refugees are scurrying like rats leaving a sinking ship. Carts are piled high with beds, pots and pans, men, women, and children. Such a tragic scene, truly tragic . . ."

This last line was invariably accompanied by a mournful expression and a surreptitious look to see if he was being convincing enough. If he had doubts, he was prepared to give a repeat performance. But if he was happy with the effect, he stood up and was off to see the next person on his list. There simply weren't enough hours in the day. By the time he had visited the seventh home, it was eleven o'clock at night. Back in his own room, he was tired, hungry, and exhausted. His legs ached so much he could barely stand. A muted sound like the *clickety-clack* of a train raced through his head. He somehow managed to get his shirt unbuttoned before flopping down on the bed and sleeping straight through the night.

It was the best sleep he'd enjoyed in a very long time. It was almost as if he'd taken leave of the suffering of this world and been transported to another level of existence. He had no feelings, no memory of the entire night. He neither dreamed, thought about what the future held, nor relived the past. He wasn't conscious of the fact that flies landed on his face or that representatives of Shanghai's legion of cockroaches cavorted on his exposed chest. He was dead to the world. The next morning, he awoke in precisely the same position as when he'd fallen asleep. His legs stuck straight out, still sporting shoes and socks, and he looked more like a man about to go for a stroll than one who had just awakened from a sound sleep.

A night's sleep of such comfort comes to a man but a few times in his life. This was especially true in the case of someone like Ma Bo'le, who calculated every aspect of his life well into the future. He spent his nights trying to determine what fate had in store for him. Though not an insomniac in the strictest sense, he nonetheless slept poorly more often than not.

Now that he was awake, he reacted as if he were seeing the world for the first time—his mind was a blank. His eyes were open, but he had no idea where he was. Even after staring straight ahead for what seemed like ages, he was still conscious only of the pale glow of the overhead light that enveloped him. He shut his eyes like a man trying to comprehend a deep secret. But it was no use; his mind would not function, and everything was shrouded in mystery. He remained in the grip of confusion for some time before getting up to look for his shoes. He found them right where he'd left them—on his feet—and he recalled that he'd gone to bed fully dressed. This recollection jogged his memory of the plight of the refugees on North Sichuan Road.

After splashing some of last night's dirty water onto his face, he ran outside, without brushing his teeth, to see what was happening in the neighborhood. Just as he'd thought, the evacuation was no figment of his imagination. But he was shocked to see that the refugees had even begun pouring into this quiet, out-of-the-way spot.

Everything about the people passing in front of him with their beds and their toilets, creating mass confusion, was as he'd predicted. He whistled in amazement, then turned and went back inside, feeling very cocky. As he entered the room, he kicked over the usual bottles and jars.

After bending over and righting them, he hurriedly made some fried rice, rushing so he could go back out, take a look around, and see how today's evacuation compared with yesterday's. He was in such a good mood that he dumped in five eggs, five times his normal consumption.

"I might as well eat them now, because the Japs are about to attack!"

Despite the five eggs and all the rice, Ma Bo'le was still hungry, since, as he realized, he'd gone to bed the night before without dinner.

As soon as he finished his breakfast, he left his room, closing the door behind him and sealing the odoriferous mixture of onions and grease inside. His bony frame hurried down the street, head held high as he strode proudly along, an occasional whistle a display of self-assurance. He gazed appreciatively at the refugees moving down North Sichuan Road.

By nightfall, confusion reigned in the French Concession. Refugees were streaming into the area from Rue Lafayette and Rue Chapsal. Retail establishments—oil shops, salt shops, and rice shops—were packed with customers fighting over dwindling stocks of merchandise. If war really came, there would be shortages of everything, including food and drink.

A depression settled over Ma Bo'le from that night on. He experienced a loss of drive, passing listless day after listless day right up until the outbreak of hostilities at Hongkou Park.

By the third day of the exodus, virtually all Shanghai residents had heard and believed the rumor that "war would come to the city tonight."

The last vehicle passed down North Sichuan Road that night, escorted by British soldiers. The presence of this solitary truck lumbering down the road made for a desolate sight. An international evacuation truck, it carried Belarusians, British citizens, Jews, even a Japanese or two. It had been sent by British security authorities to help their citizens make their escape, while the others had begged their way on board.

The bombardment was imminent. North Sichuan Road was so quiet that even birds were stilled. Every house and shop was empty; there wasn't a soul in sight. The street, usually thronged with vehicles, was deserted; the area was heavy with the anticipation of war. Bits of paper, litter left behind in the evacuation, swirled into the air.

During the night, every Japanese family on North Sichuan Road had moved into an elementary school run by and for Japanese citizens. For that matter, virtually all the Japanese citizens in the city had taken refuge in the school. They were there for two reasons: first, they were afraid of possible confrontations with the Chinese; second, the Japanese authorities were concerned that some of them might oppose the war and throw in their lot with the Chinese. Therefore, strict control measures had been put into effect: all Japanese citizens were to congregate at designated locations. That way, when war broke out, the authorities had only to round them up and put them aboard warships for the trip back to Japan.

There wasn't a living, breathing soul left anywhere on North Sichuan Road, except for the occasional troop of Japanese soldiers and, from time to time, a stray dog that had been left behind by its master.

Meanwhile, tension reigned in the International Settlement, where gossip ran rampant. Newly arrived refugees, not yet acclimated to their new surroundings, got into interminable squabbles and shouting matches—peace and quiet was on the decline. The oppressive summer heat and the ominous rumors provided the stimulus people needed to keep arguments going all night long.

When dawn broke, the people listened in vain for the sound of artillery fire. Maybe they would begin shelling that night.

The day's activities proceeded on a regular basis—meals, laundering, shopping. Nothing changed. Confusion and panic was on nearly everyone's face, but to Ma Bo'le the people looked about the same as usual, oblivious to the impending danger as they blithely went about their daily business. He was not interested in the actual outbreak of hostilities. To him, that would be a commonplace event. Since there was no longer anything he wanted to see or hear, his excursions in the neighborhood ceased. As far as he was concerned, it now belonged to history.

As a result, rumors that the attack on the city would begin that evening made him yawn. He was blasé, though he wore a frown, and his normally sad eyes were sadder than usual. Putting aside thoughts of the looming Japanese attack—word of which he had spread among his friends only days before—what occupied him now was where he should go when the attack actually came.

"In every situation a man must look for the nearest exit," he reminded himself. "I must be prepared when the Japs come."

In his lexicon, being prepared meant escape, but "be prepared" sounded better.

Actually, the time for making preparations was long past; now he had to put a plan into action. If he waited till everyone else had gotten out, there would not be a truck or a ship left to take him away. Once war broke out, they would be used for transporting troops or supplies. Who would care about a bunch of refugees then? He had to get out soon, for there might not be a second chance.

Everyone in Shanghai was in an uproar—everyone, that is, except Ma Bo'le, who accepted it all in silence. He calmly smoked a cigarette as he lay in bed, his feet propped up on the footboard, eyes half closed as he dreamily stared at the dim light of the overhead bulb. The artillery fire had commenced some time before, as early as dusk.

On August 14th, the day after the outbreak of hostilities, Japanese and Chinese aircraft clashed in a series of dogfights over the Huangpu River. A mixture of airplane exhaust and smoke covered half the sky; spent bullet casings peppered the ground below. People stood outside, faces lifted skyward as they watched the airplanes draw ever nearer— each approaching sortie increasingly paling their expressions. In these early stages of the war, no one quite knew where it was all going.

It rained the next day, and gusty winds swept the city, leaving in their wake a layer of fallen leaves. The French Hospital was filled to overflowing with wounded soldiers. They had been brought there in vans, whose camouflage made it clear that they had come from the front. Nurses wore Red Cross armbands, while the soldiers wore red marks of a different kind on their uniforms. Each van loaded with wounded men was greeted by respectful and somber stares all along the route of approach.

Ma Bo'le walked the streets in glum, silent concentration over his own predicament, his head lowered as he trod on the fallen leaves. "Where do I go from here?" he wondered. "Nanjing, maybe, or Suzhou."

He had friends in both cities. Admittedly, it had been a long time since he'd last written any of them, but he was confident they'd put him up if he arrived as a refugee. Should these two cities prove impossible for any reason, there was always Hankou, where one of his father's friends lived. That was a sure bet. Everything hinged on the fundamental problem of Qingdao's refusal to be attacked. Every other consideration was academic, as long as his wife remained where she was. He was reminded of the appropriateness of the old maxim, "It's all right to be poor at home, but travel requires coin of the realm. Cars, boats, shops, porters, red tape—the bane of the working man."

He became so engrossed in his thoughts that he very nearly uttered aloud the burning question on his mind:

"How can I live the life of a refugee without money?"

He spotted a crowd milling around a truck from which they seemed to be lifting something down. Then he noticed the emblem displayed at the intersection, and realized that it was a Red Cross first-aid station to treat wounded soldiers.

Losing interest in what was going on there, he strolled down another lane. He hadn't taken more than a few steps before another van laden with wounded soldiers bore down on him. "How can there be so many wounded soldiers?" he wondered. He turned and headed back, but too late to avoid the van, which whizzed past, so close he could nearly touch it. There, in front of his staring eyes, were glorious, blood-soaked warriors of the Chinese nation. Was this a sign that the battle was going badly for China? If so, the need to flee became even more pressing.

He was terrified by what was going on around him, sensing desolation everywhere, a feeling intensified by the overcast sky and drizzle. There was good reason to feel gloomy. The street cleaners apparently had not been out over the past couple of days, and the gutters were filling up with fallen leaves. All around him were clusters of refugees running through the rain, carrying children and an odd assortment of belongings. Their hair was tangled, their feet bare. More refugees clustered under the protection of gateways, most of which were flooded out by the rain, forcing the people to sit or lie in puddles.

Such sights saddened Ma Bo'le, who was thinking: the suffering Chinese must unite in resistance!

After passing one gateway crammed with refugees, then another, he imagined joining their number if his wife did not come. He was shaken by this thought. Never the apple of his parents' eye, he had always still had enough to eat and warm clothing to wear. It had never occurred to him that he could be reduced to such straits. He returned to his room with growing fears, exhausted and impassive. He smoked a cigarette, then another. Being depressed is much like being sick, especially for someone like Ma Bo'le. The moment he became disheartened for any reason, he grew as weak as mud. It was worse than being sick, for when that happened, all he had to do was smoke a few more cigarettes. But they provided no respite from depression. To his way of thinking, illness wasn't a catastrophe; the true catastrophe in a man's life was the intrusion of sorrow, for that was impervious to resistance and can lead only to despair.

Ma Bo'le was convinced that his wife was not coming. Other considerations paled into insignificance.

The tip of his cigarette glowed brightly, for he took a puff on it every two or three seconds, until his pillow was covered with ashes. After all, who can worry about sanitation during refugee times? With that thought to guide him, he brushed the ashes off his bed with his shoe.

He puffed so violently on his cigarette that before long the swirling ashes blinded him. He rubbed his eyes, then dug at their corners with his fingernails. This practice usually succeeded in clearing his eyes of foreign matter. It did so again.

Ma Bo'le had not slept well, except for that one night. His appetite and his menu, on the other hand, remained unchanged—fried rice every day. Sleep had a way of interfering with his thoughts, but eating did not. He could think as he ate; in fact, that seemed to him the best way to go about it.

Once he'd cleared the ashes from his eyes, he lit a fire and began preparing rice. In hardly any time, sparks flew from his little stove. Then he stripped down until he was standing there clad only in a pair of wooden clogs, sweat oozing from every pore in his body.

The wok began to smoke, so he threw onions and the beaten eggs into the crackling oil.

Fried rice is an unbeatable dish, and Ma Bo'le could not imagine ever tiring of it. On the contrary, he enjoyed it more each time. If not for the bad times, he'd have enjoyed it with five eggs at every meal. But that was impossible now, since his prime concern had to be frugality.

"These are refugee times," he said every time he reluctantly laid down his bowl. This reminder of hard times always worked, for even though he might not be as full as he'd like, he accepted the situation stoically. After all, he reasoned, once he was on the run, starvation might be his lot. If he remained a stranger to the pangs of hunger, how would he stand it when they truly arrived? No, it was better to get in a little practice just in case. He could face the future without fear.

This day's fried rice was unusually aromatic; the room filled with the fragrance of fried onions. With a full rice bowl in his hand, he felt himself to be the luckiest man on earth. But just as he was about to take his first mouthful, there was a knock at the door. This rarely happened, for he had few friends who might come calling. No more than two or three, and that had been a long time ago. No one had come by recently.

He did not move. The rice bowl was still in his hand.

Unlike most people, who would go to the door to see who was there, Ma Bo'le, being both intelligent and quick-witted, prided himself on his ability to predict things before they happened. Even if he was wrong, it was still fun to guess.

For some reason he was having difficulty figuring out who was knocking at his door now. Was it Big-eared Zhang? Or could it be Chen, the one-time bookkeeper? Or maybe . . .

He'd run into Big-eared Zhang on the street a few days before, but it had been a long time since he'd last seen Chen. It had to be him. He always knocked slowly, while Zhang would have burst in unannounced.

It was only after he had thought the matter through from every angle that he finally walked over, placed himself squarely behind the door, and opened it a crack, as if he expected to find trouble on the other side. He saw that his caller was Chen—just as he'd guessed. He could not have been happier.

"I thought it was you, and I was right!"

Once Chen was inside, he talked of almost nothing but the war situation, but Ma Bo'le seemingly heard none of it.

"How do you think I knew it was you and not, say, Big-eared Zhang? Because he has no patience. He'd have kicked the door open and stormed in. But you're different. You're like a shy young maiden with your dainty raps. Now, is that what you're like or isn't it? Think about it and tell me if I'm right."

Bo'le picked up his bowl of fried rice and commenced eating. It wasn't until he'd nearly stuffed himself that he thought to ask his visitor:

"By the way, have you eaten?"

Before the poor fellow had a chance to respond, he continued:

"There's nothing decent to eat here, anyway. Fried rice, day in and day out . . . do you have any idea what all this fighting has done to the price of eggs? They used to be seven fen apiece, but today I heard they've gone up to eight. I'm afraid they're too rich for my blood. I bought these the day before fighting broke out at three for 10 fen. But when they're gone, I don't plan to buy any more. My digestive system isn't so pampered that it has to be treated to fresh eggs every day. Have you seen what's going on out there? The streets are crawling with refugees. And what do you think they're eating. Nothing! They're going hungry while we're in here stuffing ourselves with fried rice and eggs. It's not right, and I repeat, when these eggs are gone, that's it for me. But you haven't answered my question—have you eaten? If not, help yourself. Slice some onions, break a couple of eggs, and make yourself a bowlful. Fried rice hits the spot. But maybe you've already eaten. Why don't you say something?"

Chen told him he'd already eaten.

It would be an overstatement to say that Ma Bo'le looked upon Chen as a true friend; rather, it was a friendship initiated by Chen, to which Ma Bo'le offered no opposition, since needy friends were easier to handle, and it made little difference if he had many of them or few.

He paid little attention to whether anything he said to Chen made any sense, since they had little in common, intellectually or professionally. The only link was that they were both urbanites living in the city—that and the fact that they were both broke. Chen had no money at all, and although Ma Bo'le did, it was under his father's control and beyond his reach, which was the same as not having it in the first place.

As it turned out, Chen had come with hopes of borrowing some money. He hemmed and hawed without broaching the subject, for his first glance at Bo'le's way of living pretty much dashed his hopes. On second thought, he was well acquainted with Bo'le's eccentricities and knew that appearances were deceiving where his friend's financial solvency was concerned. Ma was despondent when he was broke; but then he was just as despondent when he was well heeled.

Chen had put a lot of effort into analyzing Ma Bo'le's thought processes. Finally he blurted out his request:

"Say, old Ma, have you got any money? I need a couple of yuan."

His question was met with silence. Ma Bo'le merely walked over to the bed, picked up his trousers, and fished out every coin in his pockets. As he held it up for Chen to see, he said:

"No one will ever accuse me of holding back. I'm as strapped as you are, one step removed from being just another refugee myself."

He stuffed the change back into his pocket and tossed his trousers onto the bed, causing the coins to jingle momentarily. "Hear that?" he said. "That's the sound of poverty—the singing coins."

To look at him, one would think he had no use for coins, that they were beneath him. But that was just his way of reminding those around him of his elite background, that although he may be down on his luck at the moment, it was a temporary setback and not a problem of family status.

As soon as he saw Chen out the door, he rushed over to pick up his trousers and carefully counted the coins in his pocket. He knew there was little buying power in those few bits of metal, but they were, after all, money. They only presented a problem in their scarcity; he could be a rich man if he had enough of them.

A knock at the door interrupted his concentration on the task of counting his money. No one ever came to visit Ma Bo'le at home. Now two visitors on the same day. He was, quite frankly, puzzled.

"Now who can that be?"

He thought and thought.

Following his standard routine, he walked over slowly and positioned himself safely behind the door, as if expecting trouble. He opened the door a crack.

It was his landlady. She asked if he planned to stay on for another month, since she was going to raise the rent.

"People are lining up to rent rooms these days."

She was wearing a black silk top, matching pants, and shiny black embroidered slippers that Shanghai shopkeepers' wives and others of that type favored. She rambled on and on in a mixture of Northern and Southern Chinese before she left.

Rents were going up and the price of food had skyrocketed. But even that became moot as he fretted over the course the battle was taking.

The pounding vibrations from artillery fire felt like an avalanche. Granted, his room was impervious to airborne sounds, but he could sense the pulsations of the floor as each shell landed, making his bed shake. He could not escape this irritating rhythm; it was as if a great boulder were thudding around in his brain. His head swam; anxiety gripped him. He was driven nearly to distraction.

He had written to his wife several days earlier, and even though he suspected that she hadn't yet received his letter, he already found himself in the depths of despair.

"She's not going to come," he moaned. "I just know it. She's a damned block of wood, that's what she is . . . she won't come." Since he knew she wouldn't come, why write? Actually, he had no way of knowing if she would come or not, but whenever he was caught up in his own problems, he invariably traveled down the road of pessimism. You see, his self-love was greater than his love for anyone else. As far as he was concerned, this was more a personality flaw than an odious trait.

The news that his landlady was raising the rent threw him into a deeper funk. Life had suddenly lost its meaning—his time on earth was being wasted, one day after another. When would it all end?

Now that the landlady had gone back upstairs and his door was securely shut, Ma Bo'le hurried over to his bed and lay down. He stared at the overhead light until it affected his vision.

"That light is brighter than the sun," he thought. "But it's not the sun.

"Artillery fire is, after all, artillery fire—different from everything else.

"With all this trouble in the country, life has lost its meaning.

"Whenever someone is gripped by sadness, sorrow is what he must feel."

As was his custom, Ma Bo'le let his thoughts continue for some time:

"As soon as you turn on a bulb, the room lights up.

"As soon as the nation goes to war, the people turn into refugees.

"Fleeing from war is no hardship if you've got money.

"If the Japanese don't attack Qingdao, my wife won't come.

"If my wife doesn't come, fleeing is going to be nothing but trouble.

"Without money, nothing I say means anything.

"Without money, I'm finished.

"Without money, everything is so near yet so far away.

"Without money, I can't move an inch.

"Without money, I'll have to go home."

The thought of going home was almost more than he could bear. How could he return to a home like that? Everyone—from his father, mother, wife, his own children—was cold and heartless. Even little Jacob. No one in his family would welcome him back. A lowly cat or dog would find this state of affairs intolerable. For him, a human being, it was much worse!

Tears welled in his eyes. Where was the meaning in life? The tears threatened to roll down his cheek, so he took several puffs on his cigarette to drive them back. Once his sorrow had scaled the heights, his troubled heart began to calm down. He got out of bed, splashed some cold water on his face, and decided to go for a walk. But when he opened the door, he discovered to his annoyance that it was raining, however slightly. If his clothes got soiled there was no one to wash them for him, and since he didn't have the money to buy new ones, he had better stay indoors after all.

Having briefly forgotten about his financial problems, he was now reminded of them all over again.

He was so mad he pounded the table with his fist, causing hardened kernels of rice to bounce into the air. Since he never wiped his table clean, among the grains on the table were kernels from yesterday, the day before, and quite possibly from several days before that. Some had been lodged in cracks in the table, and the force of his blow had caused them to join the others in flight, as if suddenly coming to life. He hurriedly brushed the lot of them onto the floor, as though fearing they might scoot away if he moved too slowly. He clapped his hands together to loosen the pieces that had stuck to his palms.

There was a knock at the door.

"Damn," he said, "how come everything's happening today?"

His rising anger removed all his defenses. Instead of positioning himself behind the door and acting as if someone were out there to arrest him, he called out:

"Who's there, damn it?"

He'd barely gotten the words out before the door flew open and the visitor entered.

It was Big-eared Zhang, another of Ma Bo'le's "fellow students" during his university auditing days and an employee at the publishing house. This so-called employment, for which there had been no title, was, in reality, free room and board. He and Ma Bo'le were on good terms—he was, in fact, another of Ma Bo'le's needy friends. Zhang had a booming voice and walked with a rhythmic, swaying motion. He actually shook as he walked, as if someone had outfitted his joints with springs. His every action, his every motion, was coordinated with the natural rhythms of his body.

The first thing he asked Ma Bo'le was:

"Have you seen the dogfights over the Huangpu River?"

Ma Bo'le said nothing.

"Were you able to sleep last night with all that gunfire?"

Ma Bo'le still said nothing.

"Are you in a funk, old Ma?" Zhang asked. "Don't you find it interesting that we're passing through such a glorious age? Has it escaped you that this is the opening page of the most spectacular chapter in the history of the Chinese people?"

Even this was met with silence from Ma Bo'le, who merely smiled and flicked his cigarette ashes.

Being an impulsive fellow, Big-eared Zhang launched into an animated and blunt criticism of his friend:

"What's up with you? You weren't like this when we met on the street. You were fuming then, walking around inspired by the passions of an entire nation. No one else could see what was going on around them. They barely sensed—no, you could say they didn't sense at all—that Shanghai would soon be what it is today, a city wracked by the constant sound of gunfire. You alone guessed that Shanghai's predicament was unavoidable. And sure enough, your prediction came true before a month had passed."

Zhang paused for a moment to observe the expression on his friend's face.

Bo'le's disdainful look gave way to a pained smile, then a look of agony. Big-eared Zhang tapped his foot on the floor until he shook.

"Old Ma, you're not lovesick, are you?"

That did it—Bo'le blew up.

"Bloody Chinese!"

"The country's falling apart," he was thinking, "and that bastard goes and says something like that!"

He stopped short of blurting out what was really on his mind.

"I don't understand you," Zhang said. "If all China's youth were like you, we'd be in big trouble. One day you're all steamed up, the next day you're lukewarm, and on the third day, you're burned out. I can't believe the way you are! Is this how China's young men are supposed to act? Can't you see the light shining in front of you? Has the sound of Japanese artillery made you deaf?"

Ma Bo'le finally broke his silence. He was furious.

"You think I can't see, that I'm blind? You think I can't hear, that I'm deaf? You think that just because your ears are bigger than everybody else's you're the only one who can hear? Well, I heard these things before you did. I heard them when you couldn't hear a thing! You can say I heard it before the first shot was fired. You've got some nerve, running over here to shake people up like this. In the few days since I last saw you, you've turned into quite a hero! A person would think that fighting the Japanese was all under your leadership."

Zhang listened to this tirade with a broad grin.

"Are you aware that your 'old Ma' doesn't have two coins to rub together? Dogfights over the Huangpu River! I can't fill my belly with those. 'Old Ma' is about to become a refugee—he's pretty much done for!"

Ma Bo'le's benign expression never changed. He was smiling, true, but it was an empty smile, devoid of substance or significance. It was agony to maintain it.

Darkness had fallen by the time he saw Big-eared Zhang out the door.

He waited a while, but there were no more knocks at his door, so he went to bed.

# Chapter Seven

Two months after the August 13th attack on Shanghai, Ma Bo'le's wife arrived from Qingdao. She had wired him before leaving.

He had lived in unfathomable poverty during those two months, leaving him with the spindly legs of a crane and the thin, elongated neck of a giraffe. His diet no longer included fried rice. He'd long since given up his rented room and was living with Chen in a small garret, where they placed their bedding on the bare cement floor. Bo'le's bedding was filthy beyond recognition; his comforter and pillow were so soiled they blended in with the dirty floor. Chen's were even worse: his bed sheet had turned black, his pillow shone with grease and other filth. It had only been a couple of months since Bo'le had last washed his bedding—certainly no more than three—whereas Chen's bedding hadn't seen soap and water for at least six months. Like a piece of cowhide, it was so stiff and shiny it appeared indestructible. Bo'le's pillow was shamelessly filthy, no question about that, but at least it retained the shape and appearance of a pillow. Chen's had been transformed, until it resembled nothing at all. If a description is necessary, owing to its stiff and shiny appearance, it might have been mistaken for a little leather drum.

By rights, since they shared this garret, upkeep should have been their joint responsibility. But in point of fact, neither of them cared how the place looked.

They left the window open when they went out during the day, so when it rained, their bedding got soaked and lay there in puddles. When they returned home and saw what had happened, they'd comment:

"Now what? Where will we sleep?"

Their room was matchbox size, with barely enough space to make up two beds. Not even enough room to stow their shoes when they took them off at night. If they put them by their pillows, the stench was overpowering; if they placed them alongside their bedding, they might flatten them when they rolled over in their sleep. And if they put them at the foot of the bed, they wouldn't be able to stick their legs out straight.

On one particular rainy day, the floor was a mass of puddles, and their bedding, not surprisingly, was waterlogged. The two roommates stood outside the door looking at one another.

"Now what?"

They had identical thoughts, though neither moved a finger to remove the bedding or mop up the water on the floor. No grumbles, no fault finding. Since Heaven had sent down the rain, who was there to blame? They exchanged glances and grinned, as if the disaster had been visited not upon them, but upon someone else.

That night, after pushing their wet bedding to the side, they curled up on the damp floor and slept the night through in complete peace.

Sometimes it rained as they slept. As soon as the rain fell on Bo'le's feet, he buried them under his bed sheet. Chen did the same. Bo'le would not get up to close the window, nor would Chen. They let the rain pour in—two men sleeping in growing puddles, but oblivious of the fact.

If Bo'le had gotten up to close the window, he'd have felt imposed upon, for it wasn't his alone to close. If Chen had gotten up to close it, he'd have felt the same way. Getting up to close it together made as much sense as two people lifting a teacup. So it stayed the way it was—open.

Chen was broke, having been unable to find a job in the two years following his stint as a university auditor, not counting his brief "employment" in Ma Bo'le's publishing house. During the first year he'd blamed his bad luck on not having a degree. But his observations soon revealed that university graduates were just as unemployable. From then on, he harbored no more illusions and was content simply to get by in Shanghai the best he could. Sometimes he moved in with friends, at other times he rented a place by himself. Although he had no observable income, he was never without cigarettes, always wore a tie, had shoes on his feet, and did not go hungry. After every meal he took a stroll in the park. As far as Bo'le was concerned, that was a lifestyle fraught with danger. How could a person live only for today? With no food on the table tomorrow, wouldn't he starve?

Bo'le had originally been better off financially than Chen, who, if he was able to wheedle a yuan or two out of one of his friends, would happily treat Bo'le to a meal of stuffed dumplings or lamb stew. Money burned a hole in his pocket. With Bo'le it was different: Even when he managed to put the touch on one of his friends, he acted as if he'd been turned down. He stuffed the borrowed money into his pocket and no one was the wiser.

As soon as Bo'le finished reading his wife's telegram, he dashed out of the garret, flew downstairs, and ran to a barbershop, where he sat in front of a large mirror, a white barber's smock around his neck. "Tomorrow's certainly not going to be a repeat of today," he mused. "By then my problems will be a thing of the past. My tasks for today are to get a haircut, take a bath, run out and buy a new shirt, change my socks, and shine my shoes."

His eyes remained shut even after his hair was cut, and five minutes after a lathering, he was cleanly shaved. Opening his eyes to survey his new appearance; he was satisfied with what he saw, though he had a bit of trouble recognizing himself. Thinking back, he realized that he'd gone three months without a haircut. What frightful times they had been: his days spent aimlessly wandering the streets, his nights even worse, as he wordlessly curled up on the floor to sleep like a mongrel.

The next day he welcomed his wife and children to Shanghai and took them to a hotel room he'd reserved for the occasion.

"Paul, you look terrible!" she said the moment she saw him.

He nearly burst into tears. He bit his lip to regain control, but to no avail. He turned away and looked at the framed rate schedule hanging on the wall to forget the sadness in his heart. It did not work. Thoughts of his experiences over the past months came back to him, one after another: his experience in the dark hole that had been his room, a life filled with fried rice, the looks on people's faces when they refused to lend him money, the unanswered letters to his wife . . .

He finally regained his composure after his wife walked up and rubbed his shoulders tenderly. That evening he went back to Chen's garret to fetch his bedding and move it to the hotel. When she opened the door on his return, she exclaimed:

"My God, Paul, where have you been staying? How did your things get like this?"

His sadness returned in a flash, and he came within a hair's breadth of crying again.

His wife brought him up to date on news from home. Everyone was in decent health, though his father spent less time on business ventures, turning over much of the day-to-day responsibilities to his younger son. Younger Mistress was delighted that her sister-in-law had left to join Bo'le, but Lao Taitai had assured his wife that she needn't worry, that Bo'le was still the heir to the family fortune, which, unfortunately, was dwindling. Pastor Ma had returned home, so Father was without his spiritual adviser. The city, she said, was tense. To all this, Bo'le responded with grunts or laughs, as appropriate. His eyes were not dry for a moment, and he seemed to be in deep reflective thought. His gaze shifted from the bed frame to the mosquito net above the bed. His hands seemed lost as they moved from place to place: if he wasn't stroking the edge of the comforter, he was grabbing hold of the bed frame or tapping it noisily with his fingernail.

She asked him if he wanted a cup of tea.

He nodded.

After taking the cup, he held it for the longest time without taking a sip. He appeared engrossed in recapturing a thought that had somehow vanished.

The reunion of Ma Bo'le and his wife accomplished what is known as the fusing of a broken mirror. He was alternatively happy, disconsolate, grateful, and deeply pained. He could not escape his sense of loneliness, feeling whole and empty at the same time. His eyes brimmed with tears, which threatened to spill down his cheeks the moment he let down his guard.

"How much money did you bring with you?" she asked him. He merely shook his head. "Father said it was over two hundred."

Once again he shook his head.

"If you were that short on cash when you got here, even if Father was unwilling to help out, I'd have found a way to send you what you needed."

Ma Bo'le's eyes sparkled with the accumulation of tears.

"Just how much did you bring?" she demanded.

"How much? I arrived in Shanghai with thirty yuan."

"No wonder we received such a flood of urgent letters and telegrams. How in the world did you manage to get by for three months on thirty yuan?" Ma Bo'le took her hand in his and buried his face softly in a pillow.

The first thing the next morning, he went to the Fanwangdu West End Station, the last remaining point of departure for trains bound for the interior. At the ticket window he asked the price of a ticket and whether children traveled for half fare or for free.

He planned to go first to Nanjing, and from there to Hankou. That is where his father's friend lived. Instead of discussing his plans with his wife, he had decided to let her take it easy for a couple of days in the hotel. There was plenty of time to talk things over when she was well rested. So he had kept his thoughts to himself. Besides, he knew she would agree with whatever he recommended.

He was pleased that she was treating him better now than she ever had at home. Warm and considerate, she seemed to have grown younger, looking more and more like the girl he'd married, once again a paragon of docility and patience. Confident that she would approve of his plan to travel to Hankou, he had taken the liberty of scouring the train station, so he'd know his way around when the day came.

An exit strategy was his first priority.

Just then some Japanese airplanes threatened the train station. The crowd scattered. Ma Bo'le started running toward the British Concession at full speed, but before he'd taken more than a few steps, the airplanes were directly overhead. Everyone around him hit the ground. No bombs fell—they were recon planes—though you would not have known that if you'd been watching from a distance, where the scene below looked like a colony of ants on a hot skillet. It was instant chaos.

Ma Bo'le watched travelers scurry aboard the train, and continued to watch as it began to pull out of the station. Before long he would be part of a similar crowd of people, packed into a train carrying him to a place he'd never been. There he would begin a new life. What this new place would be like, he could not begin to imagine, but he knew that adapting to yet another new environment was not going to be easy.

He looked after the slow-moving, smoke-belching locomotive—*chug-chug*—as if its load were too great. Possibly, he thought, these refugees would be thrown out once the train passed through the suburbs and reached the countryside, where they would be left to their own devices.

He sighed, then turned to head back. Expecting that his wife would be waiting with breakfast for him, he hailed a rickshaw (that bourgeois luxury), and twenty minutes later was bounding up the hotel stairs.

He met his wife coming out of their room carrying a basin of laundry, her hands covered with soap bubbles. She was on her way to the roof to rinse out the children's clothes, but changed her mind and went back inside upon her husband's return. The moment he entered the room, Bo'le spotted his three children playing together. He had not seen them in many months, and felt almost as if he'd never laid eyes on them before.

Bo'le's oldest son, eight-year-old David, had spent most of his time in school in Qingdao standing in the corner as punishment. One day back home he had burst through the door, thrown down his schoolbag, and rushed into the kitchen to announce:

"I didn't have to stand in the corner today!"

"Good boy, that's fine. Would you like something to eat?"

"I want some fried rice!"

Like his father, David could never get enough fried rice.

"Shall I add some onions? Or would you prefer dried shrimp?"

"Which tastes better? I know onions are good, but how about dried shrimp?"

"You can't have both. Shrimp has a fishy taste. Eggs, which come from chickens, taste different. Shrimp and eggs make two different flavors, and if you add onions, you'll have three. With all those different flavors in one dish, it will be too strong. Why not settle for eggs and dried shrimp?"

He clung to his mother's leg and made a fuss, pouting, grumbling, and bawling, insisting that she put them all in, that it wouldn't be too strong for him.

She pushed him away gently.

"My little pet, don't carry on like that. Mommy will chop up some ham and put it in. Isn't ham one of my little David's favorite foods?"

She picked up a handful of ham slices the cook had prepared. David stood by her as she chopped it, telling her to make smaller pieces and coaxing her into chopping up a bit more.

He was still standing next to her as she fried the rice.

"Use more lard," David said. "That'll make it better."

She scooped another half ladleful of lard out of the jar, and when the rice was finished, it glistened like shiny pearls.

David never ate fried rice when his mother was out. He didn't like the way the cook, who was deaf to his childish entreaties, made it. He used as much lard as he thought appropriate, paying no attention to David's entreaties. He had his own opinion regarding how much was required, and David was not brave enough to object. All the cook had to do was scrape his ladle against the pot and glare to frighten the boy away.

David, who was prone to stomach problems, seldom ate vegetables. As far as he was concerned, he could live on fried rice.

At six years old year he lost his baby teeth and had trouble chewing, yet he still had fried rice at nearly every meal. His mother took pity on him by steeping it in hot water and spoon-feeding him, one mouthful after another, all the while saying:

"My poor little David, let's add a little more soup, okay?"

Owing to David's stomach problems, his mother often gave him Epsom salts when no one was looking. Why wait until no one was looking? Because her father-in-law placed no faith in medicine, relying instead on the power of the Lord. No one in the family was permitted to take medication for any ailment. The one all-purpose cure was prayer. Also, as we know, his father's preferred remedy for childhood sickness was cookies.

David's finicky stomach was the main reason why, even at the age of eight, he was no taller than his younger brother, who held him in contempt. Friends and relatives often remarked that Joseph was overtaking his elder brother. Stronger than David, he disavowed his brother's elder status and often fought with him, pinning him to the ground and straddling him until David called him "General."

Even when they sat down to eat the same food, Joseph always filled his bowl first, choosing what he wanted and leaving the rest for his brother. If David defied him by filling his bowl first, Joseph would rush over and slap it out of his hand, sending it crashing to the floor.

David soon learned to let his younger brother have his way.

David was a mama's boy. His mother did his math homework for him. She felt sorry for her son, helping wherever she could in order to keep from tiring him out. This included a Saturday handicraft class, for which she folded all the colored paper figures—pagodas, carts, and lotus blossoms—at home, and then put them into his schoolbag before he left for school. Once seated in the classroom, he busied himself with folding a piece of paper for the teacher's benefit, stopping his charade when she walked off. As soon as she returned, he set his hands flying again. This would go on until the end of the class period. As soon as the bell rang, David would jump to his feet and hand in the pagoda or cart his mother had made for him.

This hour-long handicraft class seemed to David to last forever— it was all he could do to get through it. Nearly every week he was so exhausted by the class he yawned until his eyes watered.

The teacher would stand at the front of the classroom and give the students' class projects the once-over. David was always on pins and needles, fearing that she would spot someone else's hand in his work. He was a very timid pupil. If, when the teacher was lecturing from the podium, she raised her voice to make a point, David grew pale from fright, assuming that she was going to make him stand in the corner. When he was walking in the schoolyard and one of his schoolmates came up from behind and patted him on the shoulder, he quaked from fear that he was going to be beaten up.

David was a nervous boy. But, like his father, he was intelligent and always had his wits about him.

He was forever pulling stunts that should have gotten him into hot water. For example, if he was watching his mother make fried rice, and the old cook walked out of the kitchen, he'd rush over and put his hands all over some cucumbers the cook had just scrubbed clean. If the old cook walked back into the kitchen just then, David would be scared stiff. Or if the cook was out of the room, David might stuff some raw sliced cabbage into his mouth and begin chewing on it, but when the food was cooked and placed on the dinner table, he would not give cabbage a second glance.

When David was alone he amused himself by digging through other people's belongings. If he was first to arrive at school, he rummaged through his classmates' desks, removing anything he found, even scraps of paper and peanut shells. He knew there would not be anything worth seeing, but he looked anyway. Since he was alone, it would have been stupid not to.

At home, when Mother and Father were out and Joseph was nowhere in sight, David opened drawers and cupboards, removing knives and scissors, and then using them to carve on tabletops or chair legs. If he found colored thread, he rolled it into a ball. He knew there could not be anything in the cupboards worth playing with, but he was powerless to keep from scrounging around inside. He was, after all, alone, so what else was there for him to do?

Once Mother and Father came home, he would have to stop. They would not let him keep doing it.

If he happened upon Joseph's schoolbag when his brother wasn't around, he opened it without a second thought, wanting to see things that were kept from him. Actually, there was never anything remarkable inside, but again, that was no reason not to look. His sister Jacob was the only one David did not have to worry about; he could look through her things anytime he wanted. It really was like taking candy from a baby. If he'd finished his peanuts and she still had some, he'd say:

"Hey, Jacob, look at the butterfly up there in the rafters."

Then, while she was searching the rafters with her eyes, he'd snatch away most of her peanuts.

Later, as Jacob grew older, she wised up to David's tricks, so when she was eating something and David walked by, she quickly covered it up and screamed:

"Mommy, David's coming after me!"

David's status at home differed from person to person: the cook hated him, his mother pitied him, Joseph beat him up, and his sister feared him.

Ma Bo'le's second child, Joseph, was nothing like his father. He had the pluck of a warrior; he thumped his chest as he walked and gave a cocky thumbs-up when he spoke. He kept his eyes fixed straight ahead, like a bull.

Joseph's hair was a burnt yellow. He was the favorite of his grandfather, who said he had the hair of a foreigner—golden locks, which were described in glowing terms in the Bible.

Joseph was taken to nursery school and picked up every day by a governess, who never left him alone for a moment. Even if he was playing in the schoolyard, the moment she took her eyes off him, he started beating on other children, the same way he beat on his brother at home. He would wrestle the other kids to the ground and sit on them. He didn't care if his opponent was bigger than him; once he got angry he fought, no matter who it was.

"Ah, Joseph, my little hero," his grandfather would say when that happened, "what are you going to be when you grow up?"

Joseph would tug on his grandfather's beard and say:

"When I grow up, I'm going to be an official."

With that he'd jerk some whiskers out of the old man's beard.

"That's some boy we've got here!" Grandfather would laugh and say proudly. "He's not an official yet, and already he's bearding his grandfather. Just think, if he were an official . . ."

When guests dropped by, Grandfather called Joseph over. "What's Joseph going to be when he grows up?"

"When I grow up, I'm going to be an official."

The guests would praise the boy, saying that he was as strong as a lion, that he had the features of a wise and just person, that all the signs pointed to a life of riches and honors, a boy fated to be a great military officer. His grandfather nearly popped his buttons with pride.

He stroked his beard, content in the knowledge that the praise was warranted. Yes, he was a special child, strong and robust, brave as a dragon and lively as a tiger. See the strength in that chin, look at the fullness of that hair and the sparkle in those eyes! If he doesn't grow up to become another Guangong, the God of War, he'll be another Yue Fei, the Song Dynasty patriot.

To tell the truth, anyone who saw the boy out walking would not automatically assume that he was a future Guangong or a Yue Fei in the making. No one had ever come up to him and sung his praises, even at nursery school. To take it a step further, he was actually the frequent target of harsh criticism. Joseph Ma was characterized as a mean, vicious, arrogant boy. It was difficult to reconcile the two views of Joseph—one completely positive, the other totally negative. In his grandfather's presence Joseph was a great official; away from him, he was a little thug.

That is not to say that the old man forced his guests to sing his grandson's praises—no one could accuse him of that. They did so willingly.

A few, however, could be too candid for their own good. David's appearance, for example, did not promise good fortune in the eyes of his grandfather or the average Chinese. Yet one friend of the family, a man who had studied in Germany and was currently a deacon in the church, used scientific methods of calculation to predict that David, too, would grow up to be an official.

This did not please old Mr. Ma. It wasn't that he'd be unhappy to have both of his grandsons become officials, but the deacon had clearly erred in his judgment.

To recoup his losses, the man quickly declared that Joseph had a countenance that placed him in a category all by himself.

Ma Bo'le's third child, Jacob, requires no introduction, since from the day of her birth she was an ideal, if unspectacular child. She was totally unlike her brothers, neither as timid as David nor as uncontrollably wild as Joseph. Her nature placed her about midway between them. She did not take after her mother, whose nature was in the same mold as Joseph's, nor after her father, whose temperament was like David's. Her sole distinguishing feature was that, thanks to her grandfather's limited knowledge of the Bible, she went through life with a boy's name, though most Chinese would not have known that.

• • •

Now their mother had brought all three of them to Shanghai to be with their father in a hotel room, where they were bouncing on the bed as if they wanted to send it crashing to the floor; the springs creaked loudly and the mosquito netting swished violently in the air above them. The pillows and bedding were in a heap, while the children laughed and shouted for all they were worth, totally out of control.

"What's going on here?" Ma Bo'le demanded.

David jumped off the bed and sat meekly in one of the chairs. Jacob stayed where she was, but quieted down and stopped jumping. Only Joseph paid no attention to his father. He did not skip a beat in his game of hitting Jacob over the head with a pillow.

"Joseph, you little brat, what are you doing!"

He yelled so loudly that poor David nearly leaped out of his chair. But Joseph, who was far too unruly to be afraid of his father, showed his defiance by jumping off the bed and wrapping his arms around his father's leg. He could not be pried loose no matter how hard Bo'le tried. Leaning backward until his head nearly touched the floor, he shouted and laughed as if crazed.

Ma Bo'le was disgusted with the whole scene, but he could not break the boy's grip on his leg and was not about to hit him, since his wife was nearby. Normally, as a henpecked husband, he would simply walk away from such a situation, but with Joseph clinging to his leg, he couldn't move.

His wife, who thought the whole thing was hilarious, stood there laughing, which made Joseph even bolder; he rubbed the soles of his shoes on Ma Bo'le's pants. This, of course, placed an even greater strain on his father's patience.

"Bloody . . ." he shouted, checking himself in the nick of time.

His wife really laughed now. Under normal circumstances, that would have been all Ma Bo'le needed to start an argument. But not today, for these were dangerous times, during which a family must stick together and be forgiving. So he laughed along with her, seemingly as carefree as if all of this were happening to someone else.

That evening he discussed with her where they should go next. He reasoned that they could not stay on in Shanghai, for sooner or later the foreigners would hand the International Settlement over to the Japanese. By then it would be too late to get out. So, should they head for Nanjing, and then move on to Hankou? Or maybe go directly to Xi'an? He had a friend there, a middle-school principal, so he could probably find a teaching position. But if that didn't suit her, they could go first to Hankou, where a friend of Father's would surely come to their aid.

Actually, there was no aid to come to, since his wife had brought money from home. Money, as he was fond of saying, makes everything possible and eliminates all problems.

She thought they should go to Xi'an, considering his prospects of landing a teaching position. But Ma Bo'le wanted to go to Hankou. He looked forward to running into friends there, which would make their stay livelier and more interesting. Many people had already left for Hankou or were making plans to leave, but he hadn't heard of anyone heading for Xi'an, which was why it appeared so unattractive to him.

He and his wife had a minor squabble over this—not an argument, just a difference of opinion. Unable to resolve the issue, they decided to put it off for the time being. Ma Bo'le did not want to press his views too strongly, since he had yet to catch a glimpse of the money his wife had brought with her. The last thing he wanted was an argument before the money issue was resolved. So all he said was:

"Xi'an sounds all right, too. Let's think it over, we've still got time. We'll get a good night's rest and talk about it tomorrow."

They rolled over and went to sleep.

Early the next morning, they woke up and continued their discussion.

They could not put off a decision, since people were leaving the city in droves. Ma Bo'le had originally intended to let his wife have a few days to recover, concerned that the long, hard trip might have worn her patience thin. This was not the time to go overboard in discussing their predicament or to force her onto a train before she was rested. That would ruin everything. But it was necessary to make a decision before the final rail link was cut. Once the Japanese eliminated this last avenue of escape, they were stuck.

His wife held steadfastly to her opinion of the night before—reason dictated that they go to Xi'an. One by one she listed the advantages, until it seemed the only logical choice. She made it clear that it was useless for him to even consider anywhere else.

When he mentioned Hankou as an alternative, she reacted as if she hadn't heard him:

"My mind is made up—we'll go to Xi'an."

Ma Bo'le could have kicked himself for mentioning the possibility of landing a teaching job in Xi'an. With her eye for money, she never passed up an opportunity to add to the pot. Then once it was in her grasp, convincing her to part with it was an impossible task.

He got up and paced the room, feeling increasingly despondent. He should have packed up, bought the tickets, and taken the train to Nanjing. There they could have boarded a ship to Hankou. He had only himself to blame.

Now what?

As long as she held the purse strings, she called the shots.

Three more turns around the room, as Bo'le grew so anxious his eyes nearly popped out of their sockets. He did not know how he was going to deal with her on this. Since they had to leave, they ought to be going as soon as possible. Nothing was gained by stalling. Every day they waited made things that much worse.

But what counter-arguments could he make to change her mind? Her stony silence told him she was already starting to fume. He looked at her out of the corner of his eye. She was angry, all right. Her pursed lips made her mouth look like a cherry; her cheekbones jutted out like little dumplings. She was wordlessly folding the children's clothes.

He burst out the door and ran down the stairs. Once outside the hotel he just sort of stood around. The streets were thronged with pedestrians, automobiles, trolleys, and rickshaws. The war had raged for more than two months and people were still in the process of moving their things back and forth. Crates, baskets, bundles, children, and womenfolk . . . some people were moving from the International Settlement to the French Concession; others were moving from the French Concession to the International Settlement. Some had moved from relatives' homes to the homes of friends and from there back to their relatives' homes. Then there were those who moved from one street to another, only to vacate their new residence and move back to where they had come from. No matter how often they moved, it seemed, they were incapable of finding a place that suited them.

He paced the street for a while, growing increasingly restless. To delay any longer was unthinkable. There must be no more stalling. He walked back to the hotel, determined to go upstairs and confront his wife. But when he entered the room, he was not emboldened by the cold, forbidding look on her face. Each time he opened his mouth to deliver his prepared speech, the words stuck in his throat. He made a turn around the room, then another, three or four in all, but could not muster the courage to speak. He had a feeling that his speech would not be well received, that it would probably anger her more. With her unreasonable love of money, she would interpret his behavior as the first step in relieving her of what she had brought. That was a recipe for disaster.

In the end, the fear of speaking his mind was greater than the imagined horrors of staying in Shanghai.

That night in bed, he showed how anxious he was by persistent coughs and long sighs. His wife had experienced enough of this behavior to know what he was up to, so she did not concern herself with it. After living with him for more than a decade, nothing he did ever caught her by surprise. The moment he opened his mouth to speak, she knew what

he was going to say, whether it was a request for money or something
else. At one time or another she had fallen prey to every trick in his
repertoire.

For the several nights that Ma Bo'le and his wife slept in their hotel
room, he sighed deeply every time he rolled over.

His sadness had begun the day he was born. A hangdog look was
stamped upon his face; even his smiles gave no hint of happiness—they
were sad smiles, smiles of despair. Anyone who saw him smile would be
pained and distressed instead of pleased; he gave the impression that life
was little more than submitting to adversity.

In three days and three nights of hotel living, Ma Bo'le's primary
activity was sighing. Whenever he screwed up the courage to ask his wife
how much money she had brought, it was gone before he could get the
words out—her stern countenance stopped him every time.

"We . . . ought to . . ."

The look on his wife's face seldom allowed him past the first three
or four words.

"We can't keep on like this, we . . ."

On those rare occasions when he was able to force out a few irrelevant
words, he was even more aware of the disagreeable look that confronted
him—he grew fearful that she would lash out at him. That's all it would
take to send him flying out the door and down the stairs.

By the fourth day he had gained a newfound determination. "Something like this just cannot continue," he thought. "She came all the way
to Shanghai from Qingdao with the children and . . . for what? Stupid woman! Did she come thinking it was going to be her new home?
Shanghai is no home for the Chinese! Sooner or later she's going to be
sorry!"

This time he was determined not to let matters take the same course.
He was going to have his say without beating around the bush. This time
he was finally going to ask her how much money she had.

He strode into the hotel with the airs of a man determined and
headed upstairs. Up ahead was number 32—his room. He approached

it with the single-mindedness of a shark on the prowl. "If a man has no character," he reminded himself, "what good is he?"

Strengthened by this thought, he continued on until he was standing directly in front of number 32. He pushed the door open, displaying the courage of a man bent on confrontation.

He entered the room boldly—his wife wasn't there.

She returned shortly with the children in tow. He heard them clamoring in the corridor, the sound drawing progressively nearer. When they reached the door, Joseph kicked it open so hard that the glass rattled. He burst into the room, followed by David, then Jacob, and finally their mother.

The room was immediately engulfed in an incredible din. Bo'le's wife launched into a virtually endless report on what she had just seen—refugees, beggars, wounded soldiers. "There were truckloads of wounded soldiers!" she said. "A nurse on every truck, all flying Red Cross flags. And refugees, there were truckloads of them too—old folks, youngsters, even newborns." On and on she went, obviously pleased with herself. Looking like someone who had been reminded of a strange and miraculous occurrence, she held up her hands, lowered her voice slightly, and said:

"Some women are out there under covered gateways having babies! When they hear those babies cry, people gather to see what's going on . . ."

While she was telling her story and Ma Bo'le was listening attentively, Joseph bounded over, hopped onto his lap, grabbed his ear, and held on as if for dear life.

Bo'le asked him what he wanted, but the boy held on without a word.

Bo'le's temper flared up again. His first reaction was to shove his son off his lap, but the presence of his wife changed that.

"Joseph, why don't you get down and play?" he said. "Go play with Jacob." The absence of anger on his face was all Joseph needed to stick his fingers into his father's nose and bite his ear like a rabid dog.

Bo'le saw his wife's monologue as the perfect opportunity to bring up the subject of their escape plans, but the scene with his son had ruined that. Meanwhile, his wife had lost her enthusiasm; she lay down on the bed and shut her eyes from what appeared to be fatigue.

A moment later, Bo'le looked over at the bed—his wife was asleep. Meanwhile, the children were happily climbing all over the furniture. He stared at them until he no longer felt any anger and averted his eyes; then he lit a cigarette and sat down in a chair from which the paint had worn off. It was one of those old Chinese armchairs called an "official's chair." Big, boxy, and sturdy, it probably weighed more than twenty pounds. In the olden days, the Chinese weren't so peripatetic, so they made their furniture out of the densest wood they could find. Even their tea tables were made out of hardwood.

It was just his luck to be staying in a hotel that catered exclusively to Chinese, mainly small-time businessmen visiting Shanghai. After a few days, they would be off to some other place. Since most were in the unfamiliar city for the first time, they chose a hotel at random, staying for two or three days before moving on. The cost was low, so no one cared whether the service was good or bad. No one, that is, but Ma Bo'le, who could barely contain his dissatisfaction with the hotel and the people who worked there. He reserved his greatest irritation for the fat hotel attendant, who walked around in sandals with no socks, his feet understandably filthy. His stomach bulged out in front of him, his feet splayed outward.

If a guest called for the attendant, he had to plan on a five- to eight-minute wait before the man dragged himself up to the room. Some of the more impatient guests called for him several times, but it made no difference—they still had to wait five to eight minutes, like everyone else.

"I need a pack of cigarettes—Saber Brand," a guest might say. He'd hand over the proper amount to the fat attendant, who would stand there for a moment without turning to go, as if only half awake. Then he'd rub his eyes, yawn, and walk off slowly and laboriously, his enormous belly propelling him down the stairs.

It would be a full half hour before he came back. Forced to walk at a snail's pace, he deserved a bit of empathy—he couldn't help it.

Another guest might ask for water to wash his face. Five minutes later, another attendant, a skinny one this time, would show up with a basin of water. The man's legs were as long and thin as a grasshopper's, and one might assume that he could make it downstairs in a single leap if he wanted to. But no, as it turned out, he was easily distracted and often forgot what he was asked to do.

Meanwhile, the guest waiting for his water would have run out of patience.

"Attendant," he would shout, "bring the hot water, and be quick about it!"

Only then would the attendant pick up the basin and go to fill it. Once filled, he would head back, but be stopped at the foot of the stairs by the washerwoman, whom he would follow upstairs to the rooftop.

There on the rooftop, the skinny attendant, in his customary vest, and the washerwoman would carry on passionately for some time. The basin, which had been set down on the roof, would be nearly kicked over during their cavorting, the water splashing around precariously before settling back down.

"Attendant! Attendant!"

The guest waiting for the water has walked out of his room and is screaming down the stairs. There will be no one down there to hear his screams, and he can only wonder what has happened to his basin of water.

For Ma Bo'le, whose only thoughts were of moving on, poor service was the price to pay for being a refugee.

# Chapter Eight

That, then, was the sort of hotel Ma Bo'le and his family were staying in. It wasn't large—no more than forty or fifty rooms, twenty or so of which were occupied at any given time; the rest stood vacant. That kept the room rate lower than many of its competitors, which was a prime reason he had chosen it. Given some of his children's often-destructive behavior, he needn't worry if something in the hotel was broken or put out of commission. Reason number two. And that was enough for him; everything else was secondary.

The hotel was crawling with bedbugs, and although the guests did not belong to the upper crust—the rich, the noble, the officials—they were at least in possession of sound bodies when they moved in. Not so when they moved out, for by then their afflictions ran from a slight blood loss to a mass of bruises, all bedbug-related.

Just inside the hotel lobby stood a large mirror, some four or five feet tall. An old-fashioned wooden chair had been placed on either side of the mirror, as in the standard sitting room. The walls were hung with scrolls, which lent the room a touch of class, though the total effect was spoiled somewhat by the age of the chairs.

Leaving the lobby, one passed through a small courtyard in the rear of the building before going upstairs. All the corridors around the enclosed courtyard were decorated with carved ledges that had not seen a coat of paint in years. The more they were buffeted by the elements, the older they looked and the greater the quality of simple sophistication.

Two staircases led upstairs from the courtyard: one to the east, another to the west. A potted hydrangea had been placed at the foot of each staircase. They had not flowered for years—the leaves were yellow, the stems withered—but no one bothered to remove them, so there they stayed.

The upstairs was dark and gloomy, the windows covered with soot and dust after years of neglect. It was impossible to see out of them. This made it unnecessary for the owner to hang curtains, and one by one he had removed most of those that had been in place when he bought the hotel, and turned them into rags for the attendants' use. The few that had not been taken down hung or lay in tatters on the windowsills. The rooms were dark enough without the addition of curtains. Some of the windows no longer had any glass, but were covered with newspaper or red-lined Chinese writing paper. Even worse, a few were left uncovered altogether; since those rooms were never given out to guests, they were repositories for all the dust and dirt that blew in.

The banisters were rickety and the flooring in the corridors was not only scuffed clean of color and badly warped, but had shed many of the nails used to hold it down. Guests had to walk carefully so as not to hook a shoe on an exposed nail.

When you entered a room—whether occupied or vacant—your nose was assailed by one of several hard to identify and peculiar odors. Some had a sour smell, others a scorched smell; still others had an acrid smell, while a few had the sickening sweet odor of rotten fruit.

Each room, regardless of size, was illuminated by a naked, fifteen-watt light bulb suspended from the ceiling by an electric cord.

The hotel was cold and cheerless. Sometimes there were no more than three or four families staying there, and at such times the place was so quiet, upstairs and down, that the sounds of automobiles and other street noises seemed to emanate from the rooms themselves. When a heavily laden truck rumbled down the street, the building shook.

In the afternoons, when all the guests were out, the attendants bedded down for a nap. Their snores carried from the street-level rooms up the stairs and down the corridors to converge in the courtyard like a swarm of crickets. The noise was deafening, as the fat attendant, the skinny attendant, and the young apprentice echoed one another's nasal greeting.

This was the state of the hotel prior to the August 13th attack by the Japanese.

The outbreak of war changed everything: people of every conceivable stripe began moving in to the hotel, creating a virtual refugee camp. The courtyard was a dumping ground for broken and discarded furniture. Cook stoves made their appearance in the hallways, turning them into makeshift kitchens; they were soon so cluttered that guests could barely squeeze through. Pots, bowls, ladles, basins, cooking oil, soy sauce . . . bedpans stuffed into wash tubs, basins filled with tattered shoes, it was sheer chaos. Children bawled, adults screamed—the noise level was ear-splitting. There were never-ending shouts for the attendants, resulting in bickering and cursing, even leading to guests' confronting the hotel owner in his cashier's cage with complaints of poor service. He ignored their grievances; with a large fan in his hand and a broad grin on his face, he showed no willingness to aid his countrymen.

People flooded into the inner city from the surrounding areas— from Yangshupu, from the east side of the Whangpoa River, and from Shanghai's Nanshi District. Fortunate ones moved in with friends or relatives, the rest simply set up housekeeping on sidewalks or in lanes and alleyways.

Ma Bo'le's hotel filled up immediately after the outbreak of hostilities, leaving no vacancy, as was the case with every other hotel in the city. A few people moved out from time to time, but before they left they turned their rooms over to friends or relatives. It was a foolhardy soul who tried his luck at finding a vacant room anywhere without any connections.

Some of the former tenants had left for the interior, the more far-sighted among them heading west for Sichuan province. There were even people who fled to places like Suzhou and Hangzhou, which were quite near. Those with families in those places went home, those who didn't moved in with friends or relatives. No one wanted to stay in Shanghai. People who left early worried about those left behind, while those who were left behind envied the ones who had already left, as if to say:

"Well, you've made your escape."

Everyone approved of fleeing from Shanghai, although they secretly held those headed for Sichuan, in particular, in some measure of contempt. They were a little too chicken-hearted, they felt, had started making plans a little too early, and were overreacting.

"Why do you have to go so far? What a joke! You don't really believe that the war will reach Sichuan, do you?"

Ma Bo'le had been among the earliest to broach the subject of escape, but as far as implementation was concerned, he was afraid he might be among the last. Now here he was, living in a hotel, his every thought focused on his precarious situation, wanting to leave but having to stay, which caused him no end of pain and anxiety.

Joseph and David went wild until their mother, who had returned to the hotel with tales of refugees and wounded soldiers, took a nap. So they went downstairs into the courtyard. After playing with her brothers, Jacob climbed up onto the bed and fell asleep next to her mother. Bo'le sat in the wooden chair to smoke a cigarette. He had thought about the matter of escape from virtually every angle, until there was nothing more to think about. Continuing to rack his brain over the matter would only result in a headache. He could not conceivably improve the situation now.

The last thing he wanted was to do was anger his wife, since she might pack the kids off to Qingdao. He did not think much of her at the moment, but having her around was better than having no one at all.

She might not be in a hurry to tell him how much money she had, but it was comforting to know that she was there if he needed her.

But she had not brought up the subject of going to Xi'an over the past few days, and he wondered why. What did she have up her sleeve? He was struck by the fearful realization that he might have lost his chance of going anywhere, even to Xi'an.

"Every day we hang around Shanghai is one day closer to danger!" he said to himself, as he felt himself growing red in the face; his hair stood on end. He jumped to his feet in an effort to calm down, and then opened the door to go out into the corridor. But the moment he set foot outside, he kicked over a tin pot, which clanged noisily and woke his wife. She got up and peeked into the hallway. When she saw it was Ma Bo'le making the racket, she glared at him.

"I've never seen a grown man stumble around like you do . . ."

Seeing that she was awake, he fell all over himself in his haste to say:

"I got a little careless . . . besides, this hotel is a disaster area."

"If you can afford to be picky, then move to a better place!"

Since his purpose in complaining about the hotel had been a sideways apology, his wife's angry reaction caught him by surprise. More than that, he was stumped for a response. Being respectful and submissive was out of the question, as was taking a hard line. Finally, he settled upon a meaningless, if incontestable, comment, which he delivered with a smile on his face and an ache in his heart:

"Being at home is better than being on the run."

A quick glance at his wife told him that her anger had not abated. Fortunately for him, David chose that moment to bound up the stairs and into the room, where his mother lashed out at him for no apparent reason:

"Damn you, have you gone crazy . . . !"

David didn't wait to hear any more, but made a fast sweep through the room and bolted right back out.

Knowing that he had been the real target of this outburst, Bo'le brooded for a long while—neither he nor his wife said a word.

Just then, Jacob woke up. Bo'le went over to pick her up, but was stopped by a shout from his wife:

"Leave her alone!"

He let his daughter be, left of the room, and went downstairs, his eyes brimming with tears. He walked the streets for two or three hours.

Ma Bo'le seldom took walks when he was feeling good. But when he was glum, walking was about all he did, though the walks did little to comfort him. Everything he saw angered him—telephone poles, streetcars, women out for a stroll . . .

He was still angry when he returned to the hotel. He opened the door and saw that the table was set for dinner.

Joseph and David were already at the table, one kneeling, the other standing on his chair. Jacob was sitting on the table. They were fighting over the food and making a mess.

"Where's Mother?" he asked.

His second born, Joseph, sprayed a mouthful of food as he said:

"She's out making me some egg fried rice."

He sat down to eat with the children, feeling greatly relieved, as his wife walked in with a heaping platter of steaming fried rice.

"Be careful," she said, "it's hot!"

She was carrying the rice in her left hand and a bowl of soup in her right, so he jumped to his feet to take the soup from her, and spilled some over his own hand. It burned so badly he had to clench his teeth and grimace for all he was worth. But he didn't dare say a word, since he needed to get into his wife's good graces. So, putting on a happy face, he merely dried off his hand with his handkerchief.

"Let's see that," she said. "It might be a bad burn. Hurry up and put some salve on it. I brought some with me."

She walked over and opened her trunk to look for the salve.

"That's all right. I'll be okay."

He went over to bring her back to the table, but she remained steadfast.

By the time she found what she was looking for and brought it over, a blister had started to form. But, strangely enough, he experienced no pain. On the contrary, he was consoled when his wife gingerly rubbed on the salve. Moved beyond words by this display of affection, he was nearly in tears.

"What a wonderful wife!" he thought. "Just look—she brought salve, iodine, and aspirin, proving she meant to go wherever I went . . ."

He'd also noticed some sweaters in the trunk. It was only autumn, but she'd looked ahead to their winter needs. More proof. Once again he was moved nearly to tears.

Like a man snatched from the jaws of death, his gratitude was tempered by a sense of foreboding. He was in an agitated frame of mind, feeling happy one moment and sad the next. It was almost as if something were dancing in front of his eyes, just out of reach, like drifting clouds. He didn't know why he was feeling sad or what was causing this anguish. His eyes again filled with tears, but he was powerless to stop them from rolling down his cheeks. There was a lump in his throat.

He lay down without eating a bite of food.

His wife asked him if he had a headache.

"No."

She asked why he wasn't eating.

"No reason."

At this point she stopped asking questions and sat down to eat with the children. She drank some soup and ate some of the fried rice.

During the nearly two weeks she had been in town, she had eaten nothing but hotel food—fried bean curd, fried rapeseed . . . neither sour nor spicy, it was all indescribably bland, and she could barely get it down. On this day their neighbor, Mrs. Zhao, had been good enough to let her use her briquette stove to fry the rice and had even made her a bowl of watery soup, into which she'd put some MSG and soy sauce. Mrs. Zhao, who lived next door in No. 31, was a thin woman who spoke in a whisper and had a pockmarked face. The mother of five children and only in her forties, her face was already cobwebbed with wrinkles. Her speech was barely audible.

She said to Ma Bo'le's wife:

"This hotel food is inedible. We tried it our first few days here, but I could see that long term we had to think of something else. So I bought this little stove . . . actually, I had the attendant buy it for me . . . I don't know if he profited on the deal, but it cost over one yuan. This is my first time in Shanghai . . . just think, a briquette stove selling for more than one whole yuan!"

"This is my first time in Shanghai too," Ma Bo'le's wife volunteered.

"See what I mean!" Mrs. Zhao continued. "I wanted no part of the city, but their daddy said we had to come. I didn't think Nanjing would be in immediate danger."

"Men are all alike," Ma Bo'le's wife said. "My husband said we had to come to Shanghai. So what do I find when I get here? That the city is going to fall any day and its residents are leaving in droves for places like Hangzhou, Hankou, and Sichuan.

"Aren't you folks leaving?" Mrs. Zhao asked. "We are, though not right away. Around the end of next month. Their daddy's job in Nanjing keeps him too busy to come for us, and there's no way I could handle these kids alone. Someone said that the Song River Bridge has been bombed out, and trains can't get through. The people have to get off at night and feel their way across the bridge on foot. They say it's so chaotic that children have been pushed into the river. Ah, so tragic . . . I heard there was an old man who tried to carry his grandson over on his back, but the boy was shoved into the river. By the time the old man got to the other side, he had already lost his grip on reality. He just sat on the riverbank like a statue, not crying or saying a word. Whenever someone asked him why he didn't get onto the train on the other side, he said he was waiting for his grandson so they could board together . . . isn't that the most bizarre thing you ever heard? You'd think his grandson would be climbing up out of the river any minute. Before long, the old guy was a certified lunatic!"

"Where do you folks plan to go?" Ma Bo'le's wife asked.

"We're going to Hankou."

"You have family there?"

"Friends."

By the time this casual conversation had run its course, the rice was fried and ready to go.

"Fried rice goes best with some broth." Mrs. Zhao poured water into the pot that had been used for the rice. Before long, it was bubbling nicely, and the oil clinging to the sides of the pot sizzled. As soon as the water was at a full boil she drizzled some soy sauce into the pot. The water turned dark from the bottom up. She then added a pinch of Celestial brand MSG.

Ma Bo'le's wife spotted a layer of dust around the mouth of the soy sauce bottle. The stopper was made from an old newspaper. It could not have been high quality soy sauce. When she saw that Mrs. Zhao was using Celestial brand MSG, she said:

"In Qingdao we used Ajinomoto brand . . ."

This gave Mrs. Zhao an immediate sense of inferiority, so she quickly replied:

"That's what we used. I only started buying Celestial after I came to Shanghai. Since Ajinomoto is a Japanese product, we probably shouldn't buy it now."

The broth was ready. As Ma Bo'le's wife was about to walk off with it, Mrs. Zhao rushed up and sprinkled in a few drops of sesame oil.

Back in their room, Ma Bo'le's wife was prepared to tell her husband all about their next-door neighbor, Mrs. Zhao, paying particular attention to the poor quality soy sauce she used. But she never got around to it, owing to the injury to Ma Bo'le's hand.

She didn't think about it again until that evening, when she turned to Bo'le, thumped him on the leg, and announced with a laugh:

"That next-door neighbor of ours, Mrs. Zhao, is funny . . . she's become a true patriot . . . doesn't use Ajinomoto. She said . . ."

She talked on and on, but Bo'le did not move, and she assumed that he was asleep. He had covered his face with a handkerchief, which she tried to remove, without success, because the corner was clenched between his teeth. Even this did not prevent her from seeing that his eyes were red from crying.

"What's the matter?"

He did not answer. All his pent-up frustrations had burst into the open:

"Life is nothing but meaningless hustle and bustle."

By the time his tears had taken him to the depths of despair, he had forgotten his desire to flee Shanghai and his inability to do so. He was too wrapped up in life's great illusions.

He cried off and on for a while. When Ma Bo'le cried, he did not wail like those people who let fly with earsplitting screams no matter how many people were around. He never cried in public. Whenever there was anyone around he stopped—he simply could not cry. He had to find a quiet spot where he could cautiously and quietly weep over his thoughts, for he was afraid that he might be crying for all the wrong reasons. This was a habit carried over from childhood.

At this moment, he was crying sorrowfully, curled up in the fetal position. Nothing his wife asked him elicited any response, and he sobbed late into the night. Fortunately, she had taken a nap earlier and was wide-awake, so she was able to stay up with him. Not since her arrival in Shanghai had they had a real argument, and if this were to be considered an awkward moment, it was their first in a long while. She displayed uncommon patience in staying up with him—normally, she'd have fallen asleep long before.

"Is there something you want to buy?"

"No."

"Would you like to have some friends over?"

"No."

"Want to go dancing?"

"No."

"How about a new . . ."

"No."

These were things that had made him cry in the past. But this time it was different—he seemed to want nothing. This got her thinking: not only had she brought all his suits with her from Qingdao, she'd also brought his white shoes, his brown leather shoes, even a pair of patent leather shoes he'd bought in a Qingdao boutique. His suits were in good shape, but the shoes were old, and that was probably why he was crying. His neckties were getting old too—he hadn't bought a new one in a year or more. Day in and day out he had to wear his old ties. Was that what he wanted? She nearly laughed out loud, but managed to hold back and ask with feigned calm:

"Do you want to buy a new tie?"

To her surprise he answered indifferently:

"No."

Having run out of ideas, she fired off a series of random questions, though with little hope of getting to the heart of the matter:

"Do you want a new pair of shoes?"

"Is your hat worn out?

"Would you like a good cigarette?

"How about a pack of Front Gates?"

He answered "No" to each question.

"Is it money you want?"

The mere mention of the word "money" made him quake. He was so overcome with emotion he nearly burst. It was as if his heart had become a congested mass in his chest. At this moment in time, a good man was perilously close to falling apart.

In his semi-delirious state he mustered the courage to say:

"I want to go to Hankou!"

His urgent plea was met by laughter, as his wife leaned over and laid her tightly curled head on his shoulder.

"Why didn't you say so? I thought something terrible was bothering you. All this because you wanted to go to Hankou! Then let's go."

She sprang nimbly off the bed. Dragging the trunk out from under it, she opened it and took out a red bankbook with gold lettering. She tossed it to him.

He did not jump up happily or snatch up the bankbook, as most people would have done. Concerned that someone else might see the bankbook, he gave his wife a cautious look and said:

"Draw the curtains."

No one could possibly have seen into the room through the soot and filth covering the window, but she did as he asked, not so much to carry out his wishes, but because she felt sorry for him.

When she turned back to face him, she saw that the mosquito netting had been drawn tightly around the bed. It was almost as if things like bankbooks were not meant for her eyes.

She heard him count: "One thousand two hundred thirty . . ."

Three days later they packed up their belongings and left Shanghai.

# Chapter Nine

Ma Bo'le was overjoyed when he arrived at the Fanwangdu Station.

"You carry Jacob, and hold her tight," he said to his wife. "And keep a close eye on Joseph," he added.

Then a moment later:

"David, sit there and behave yourself."

He and his family had come in three rickshaws, one for bedding and luggage, the other two loaded with human cargo. The sun was shining brightly in the western sky and had been all day, its dazzling rays looking like a million sparkling fingers, a sign of good fortune. He was finally making his exit out of Shanghai, and that was all that mattered—what happened to the city now was no concern of his.

The family's belongings were in the first rickshaw. Ma Bo'le's wife rode in the second, carrying Jacob in her arms; Joseph was on the floor squeezed up against her leg. Fearing he might fall out, she held him fast across the stomach, so that by the time they arrived at their destination his face was bright red. Ma Bo'le rode in the third rickshaw, which had the most room, since it carried only him and David, who was seated on his father's lap; eventually his weight and the bouncy ride cut off the circulation in one of Bo'le's legs.

But no matter—it was only a leg. It had no effect on his good mood. He wore a determined smile, a curled lip that looked like a sneer, since only the right side of his mouth was curled—always the right side.

According to his mother, this trait of curling the right side of his mouth had begun with his nursing habits as a baby. A boil on his mother's left breast had caused it to dry up, so Bo'le had been forced to nurse only at her right breast. Whenever he tried the left one, he sucked futilely out of the right side of his mouth. The result was a life-long unconscious habit that had caused him no end of grief during his middle-school days: his schoolmates had mocked him by calling him a "rightist," when in fact he'd been a radical leftist. During every student strike he had aligned himself with the students, never once throwing in his lot with the school authorities. At every demonstration and protest march, and during every anti-Japanese campaign he'd always stood on the side of the Chinese, steadfastly refusing to stand with the Japanese or their supporters.

Yet, the "rightist" moniker had stuck. Whenever he smiled, and his lip curled to the right, his schoolmates taunted him: "Ma Bo'le, the rightist."

These episodes, of course, had occurred long ago, and even he had forgotten them—it had been years since he'd last heard anyone use this moniker. But at night, as he slept, they occasionally crept into his dreams.

Today, however, he was delighted with everything. Admittedly, his leg had fallen asleep, but he shrugged that off when he thought about soldiers at the front, who suffered not from numb limbs but from shattered ones. And so he smiled happily, his eyes fixed far off into the distance, all the way to Fanwangdu Station. There were actually several blocks to go before he reached the station, which had not yet come into view. But when he heard the train whistles, he turned his smiling face in their direction.

When all three rickshaws arrived at the station, they were prevented from proceeding any further because the platform area, some twenty paces away, was cordoned off. Ma Bo'le did not notice the rope barrier at first and refused to climb down from the rickshaw.

"Take me all the way!" he shouted. "Or you won't get paid."

He had half a mind to give the rickshaw puller a kick in the pants, for he was jabbering in the Shanghai dialect, which Ma Bo'le had trouble understanding. He thought the fellow was being a troublemaker and deserved that kick. But it was no use, since his leg had fallen asleep.

As luck would have it, a policeman walked up, waving his nightstick. "Move back . . ."

Ma Bo'le needed no more encouragement to climb down. But once he was on the ground, his still numb leg immobilized him. He thumped it, but the improvement, if any, was slight.

Meanwhile, the rickshaw puller glared at him, demanding payment.

Bo'le paid him as soon as the circulation had returned to his leg.

The man walked off with his money, pulling his rickshaw behind him and cursing at Ma Bo'le, whose happiness had already shrunk by some seventy or eighty percent. Seething with anger, he walked up to the platform to take a look. It was a sea of black hair—men, women, old, young—and personal belongings—crates, baskets, and bundles that looked like great boulders balancing precariously atop a lonely mountain. It was virtually impossible for latecomers to squeeze onto the platform.

It took only a glance at this scene for Bo'le to abandon all hope. He shut his eyes and was visited by the image of his children trampled under the feet of this mass of humanity.

Ma Bo'le despaired not for the present, but for the future. In other words, it had nothing to do with the fact that there was no room on the platform for his belongings, nor that his family might be denied space on the train, not even that the train was so overcrowded they might be crushed to death. His despair went far beyond that—he was thinking only of the Song River Bridge. Anyone traveling from Shanghai to Nanjing had to cross it. But soon after the August 13th attack, it had been bombed out by the Japanese. In fact, it had been bombed on several occasions, each run leaving greater destruction in its wake.

Newspapers ran stories on the bombings daily, including photographs of burnt corpses, alongside which ran captions like "Inhuman brutality!" The sight of all the people on the platform sent the blood rushing to Ma Bo'le's head. Yes, he had made it to the train station, but the Song River Bridge was still a long way off. Since he always calculated the completion of a trip not in distance but in time, in these terms the Song River Bridge was half a night's ride from Fanwangdu Station.

His foreboding intensified. He could sense disaster looming, seeming to know that Japanese airplanes would once more bomb the bridge the moment he reached it, as if they were on a specific mission to destroy him alone. Trains from Shanghai went as far as the bridge but no farther because the track had been demolished. The passengers had to scramble across in the dead of night. Even then, the Japanese occasionally made night runs, which proved catastrophic, with many people falling victim to their inhuman acts.

To avoid becoming sitting ducks for the Japanese airplanes, trains from Shanghai departed after nightfall, arriving at the Song River Bridge well after midnight. Moonless nights were the best, for the Japanese planes seldom came then.

As they crossed what was left of the bridge, which was several hundred feet long, throngs of refugees raised a tremendous din with their shouts. In the darkness beneath the bridge flowed a great river of white water in which crossers could see the reflections of stars on moonless nights. The people made their way across with caution, assisting their elders and carrying their young, calling out endlessly and holding tightly onto each other's clothing to keep from falling into the water below or losing track of family members.

Whatever bridge flooring remained was perilously narrow, one row of planks laid end to end, making it necessary to cross single file. One careless step was all it took.

Each train disgorged darkened car after darkened car of passengers when it reached the bridge. Roused from a sound sleep, the refreshed people sprang into action, especially the young, who walked at the fastest pace they could manage, running whenever feasible. If it was possible to get ahead of others by knocking them to the ground, they did so with a clear conscience—it was a classic case of the survival of the fittest.

The hardy ones forged on, clawing and scratching their way ahead without a thought for anything or anyone. It was the same every night—shouts punctuated by weeps and wails. These were not the normal, crisp sounds of crying, but stifled wails, wrenched from throats with the greatest reluctance. They were heavy, powerful sounds, like a single musical instrument played by a thousand people. The old and less agile fell into the river and drowned. Children, too, were occasionally pushed off the bridge and into the river, where they met the same fate. No wonder there were so many frightful tales about the Song River Bridge, and why it was viewed as the arbiter of life and death.

Women, young and old, climbed onto the new trains with difficulty, only to find no seats and virtually no standing room. They stood with sweat- and tear-streaked faces, carrying babies in their arms and bundles on their backs.

The paragons who had gotten to the seats first sat confidently, looking as if a bright future was virtually assured. None ever stood for the women with children, nor did they bestow a sympathetic look. The first to make it to the other side were first aboard the waiting train, where they occupied the available seats. They treated those who came after them, whether gray-haired oldsters or newborn babies, as inferiors. "If you can't cut it, it's your own damned fault!" was what their expressions signified.

Meanwhile, Ma Bo'le's foreboding increased as he stood at the station pondering the terrible prospects of what awaited them.

"Papa, Papa . . ." It was Jacob.

He ignored her.

"Papa, I'm hungry. I want to buy a tea egg." That was David.

"Move over here by me, you little brat!"

Joseph was running up and down the platform, kicking people's bundles, pulling children's hair, and getting into scuffles with other kids.

"Go get your son," Bo'le's wife said, sounding ill-tempered. "I don't know what's gotten into him. He's already fighting." Even after she finished, Bo'le hadn't moved. It was getting dark, and the train still had not arrived at the station. Meanwhile, the crowd was swelling by the minute. She was fretting over their prospects of boarding once the train arrived, and worried that the children and the family's belongings would get lost or ruined in the mob. Already in a bad mood, the sight of her husband standing like a statue infuriated her. She had no choice but to dash over and spank Joseph, who began to bawl. She dragged him back roughly by his arm.

In Qingdao he'd had free rein, kicking or hitting whatever and whomever he liked. If he saw a little sapling that somehow got his pique, he uprooted it. In his nursery school class, if he felt like punching one of his classmates in the nose, he did it. Walking around with a pocketknife, he cut and scraped anything he wanted, including his grandmother's fox skin coat, in the back of which he carved out a big hole.

This was the boy's first trip away from home, and now he was just another refugee. Who could have imagined that at this place and at this time his mother would be trying to change his nature! Screaming and bawling like a baby, he kicked and clawed until he had broken her watchband. She was holding him with both hands, but could not stop the wild thrashing of arms and legs. Yet she held on, knowing that the moment she released her grip he would rush back and start fighting again. How long they kept this up no one could say, but they were still at it when the sun had set.

She finally succeeded in quieting him down, and then dragged him back to her husband, who had been standing there thinking about the Song River Bridge for so long he did not know where he was.

"Are you nailed to that spot?" she nearly said. "Have you forgotten how to move?"

But before she could get the words out, an airplane emerged from the clouds. The crowd on the platform erupted into shouts:

"A Japanese airplane!"

As if on signal, the thousand or more people scattered to the four winds. Gripped by panic, Bo'le's wife shouted for David and Joseph. Then, turning to look at her immobile husband, she discovered that he was nowhere in sight. "Paul!" she shouted. "Paul!"

The airplane circled without incident, and left.

After it flew off, Mrs. Ma finally managed to round up her husband and three children. Bo'le's face was covered with mud. His wife asked him how he had gotten so filthy. To her surprise he just stood riveted to the spot, staring as if in a dream world.

"Do you plan on leaving today?" she asked impatiently.

No answer.

"What are you thinking about?"

No answer.

"Do you have a headache?"

"Have you lost something?"

He answered none of her questions. She found his attitude mystifying. Just then the train pulled into the station.

"Let's go!" he shouted.

Without losing a second, they barreled toward the train. Needless to say, he led the way, his wife and children bringing up the rear.

It immediately became clear that they would fail. He knew what he was doing, but his wife had no experience in this sort of thing. But then, she could not be faulted, since she was holding David with one hand and dragging Joseph with the other, not to mention Jacob, who was more or less in her arms. How could she be expected to get onto a train that way? More to the point, the crowding was so fierce they were almost immediately separated. Still holding onto Jacob, she looked around for her sons, but they were gone. She was a perceptive woman, and knew when to quit. As she backed off she shouted for the children:

"Joseph, David . . ."

Eventually she found them. They were both in tears. David had always been a crybaby. He cried if he lost a piece of candy, and he cried if he nicked himself while sharpening a pencil. But Joseph was her little hero, who had never been bullied by anyone. What was going on here—three or four tears had already rolled down his cheeks, and a large one hung precariously from the corner of each eye.

"Let's go home!" he said.

That nearly broke his mother's heart.

"My poor, poor little hero . . ."

She put Jacob down and dried Joseph's eyes with her sleeve. But before his face was dry, Jacob, whose feet had barely touched the ground, was knocked over.

She lay on the ground, arms and legs sticking up like an overturned turtle. Fortunately, her mother managed to scoop her up before she was trampled.

Admitting defeat, she retreated as far as she could, trying to keep her children out of the way of people rushing toward the train. But the violence of the surging crowd made it nearly impossible to buck the tide. For every two or three steps she managed, the opposite motion of the mob more than negated her progress, and by the time she was free of the crowd, the train was about to leave the station.

Bo'le's wife wore a pair of pearl earrings the year round. Each with a soybean-sized pearl encased in a gold setting, and dated back to her wedding day. Every time Bo'le was strapped for cash, he tried to get her to let him pawn them. Her thoughts on the subject were clear: nearly all her jewelry had gone a glimmering, including her gold bracelet (sold), ten or more gold rings (pawned), and a diamond ring (also pawned), and she was determined not to let that happen to this pair of pearl earrings. She would not be swayed by any of his arguments to part with them. Reaching up to touch her ear, she was horrified to discover that one of them was missing.

"Paul! Paul! My pearl earring's gone . . ."

All this time she had been struggling to get to the train, concerned only about the three children, forgetting Bo'le until she called his name. Suddenly, she realized that she hadn't seen him since the train pulled in.

No one knew her husband better than she. When faced by a tense situation, he lit out for the safest place he could find to weather the storm.

Once, as a child, he'd made a trip to the countryside with his father and encountered flooding by the Yellow River. Many had drowned in the disaster, but not Ma Bo'le, who had scrambled up a chimney and perched there until the danger had passed. The floods had also washed away stoves and cooking utensils, so no one had anything to eat. No one, that is, except Ma Bo'le, who had taken the precaution of preparing a string of stuffed buns, which he'd hung around his neck.

This incident was the first thing that popped into his wife's mind. It was followed by more of the same, and these thoughts angered her. If he wanted to leave, he could leave by himself! She and the three children sat down on their suitcases. Luckily, nothing but an earring had been lost.

Everyone was too busy worrying about his own skin to pay any attention to other people's belongings. Nonetheless, she was terrified by thoughts of the bind they would be in if someone else had carried their belongings onto the train; how would they retrieve their winter clothing? Suddenly, her heart skipped a beat as she was reminded of the platinum watchband in the leather purse she had put in the small suitcase. She'd brought it without Ma Bo'le's knowledge as a precaution. If their backs were against the wall, she could sell it for enough to return home.

In Qingdao they'd always had a place to live in and food to eat; but as refugees, where were they to go? So, since everyone else was striking out, they might as well join in. If it didn't work out, they could backtrack any time they wanted to. After all, the door at home was always open.

But this did little to calm her troubled heart. She was exhausted from trying to make the train, angered by her husband's actions, and still quaking from the near loss of her watchband; she was so consumed by anger that she did not look back at the train until it was about to leave the station. Besides, what happened now made no difference. Shanghai, Hankou—they were all the same to her. So was Qingdao, for that matter.

She looked up in spite of herself when she heard the patrolman's whistle. This fortuitous glance was rewarded by a glimpse of Ma Bo'le standing in the open doorway of one of the cars. He was shouting and swinging his arms as if someone had dragged him onto the departing train. His eyes were bloodshot.

"Come on," he shouted, "get on the train, why don't you?"

The train lurched forward.

He continued shouting even after the train began building up speed and headed out of the station. At the last minute he jumped down onto the platform, barely escaping being caught in the closing door; he did not fully realize that he was no longer on the train until he was lying on the ground. By then the train had chugged out of the station.

He picked himself up and massaged the unlucky shoulder that had taken most of the force of his fall as he walked over to where his wife was sitting. He was greeted by silence and a blank expression.

Mrs. Ma kept her head down, as if she hadn't noticed that he had nearly broken his arm in the jump. Joseph, on the other hand, was delighted. He stood on one of the trunks, stomping his feet and clapping his hands as he greeted his father excitedly.

His wife celebrated his return with a single curt sentence:

"Go find my earring!"

This shocked him, not so much by news of the loss of her earring, but by her evident loss of temper. What did she have to be angry about?

They hadn't even gotten close to the Song River Bridge, and things were already worse than he had expected. He stood there motionless, baffled.

When the next train arrived, Bo'le's wife surprised him by an absence of anger. While the train was still some distance away she took charge:

"Paul, you stay with the luggage while I take the children up to the train. After they're settled, I'll come back to help you with our things." She picked up the small suitcase in which she had stashed the platinum watchband.

"Here, let me take that," he urged her.

Her resolve to board the train had moved him—he was, of course, on the verge of tears. Remorse set in—she was a good woman, after all. This was encouraging, and he was determined to carry her suitcase for her.

"No, I can manage."

There was more to this than met the eye.

"Just look at you," he said insistently. "You can't manage all these kids *and* the suitcase. I'll take that for you." Full of enthusiasm and good intentions, he tried to lighten her load by taking the suitcase away.

She would not release her grip.

"I can manage just fine!"

His enthusiasm was not to be denied.

"What do you have in there? Why won't you let me take it?" He tried wrenching it out of her hand.

"Damn you!" she blurted out.

Holding firmly onto the suitcase, she strode off in the direction of the tracks.

"Bloody Chinese. Ingrate!"

Of course he only mumbled this, not having the nerve to say it aloud.

Before long, the train pulled in to the station. The Ma family fought to get aboard for a while. The quantity of their belongings, the number of children, and his wife's lack of cooperation spelled defeat. All she cared about was that damned suitcase, which didn't seem all that valuable to him. Always the pessimist, he yielded to despair and was reduced to standing there transfixed. Seeing that the tide had turned against them and their chances had gone from slim to none, they once more gave up the fight.

How it happened they never knew, but as soon as they stopped struggling, Jacob was propelled over the top of the surging crowd and on to the waiting train, which was readying to pull out of the station; it stirred, exhaling the steam that was its life breath. The platform patrolman was frantically blowing his whistle, a sign that the train was leaving. It had to leave now, for if it waited even a few minutes longer, it would be too late—its seams would burst in the crush of embarking passengers.

The wheels turned haltingly—two or three slow revolutions followed by four or five more rapid ones. People hanging on so determinedly did not know what to do now. Some clung to railings and ran alongside to keep from being left behind. Others managed to get half their bodies aboard, their legs suspended precariously above the platform. Nothing could have held them back. A few were lucky enough to find space on the roofs, where they rested in comparative roominess, breathed fresher air, and were beyond the bounds of the conductors' authority. But this was no place for the faint-hearted—the sloping roof offered little to hold onto, so the few people who dared to climb up to this perch had the space to themselves.

They were actually better off than the hapless individuals stuck in the windows, half inside the train and half outside. They had nowhere to go in either direction. Worst off by far were those whose legs were inside the car and upper bodies—that is, the heavier half—sticking out.

As soon as she saw what was happening, Ma Bo'le's wife cried out: "My little Jacob . . . !"

The train sped up.

Bo'le ran alongside while his daughter was still inside the train, crying. He reached out to grab her arm, but missed. He tried again, this time reaching for her hair, but again he grabbed only a handful of air.

After running for fifty feet or more, he finally managed to rescue her.

She was so terror-stricken as her father pulled her through the window that she was like a timid little rabbit, neither bellowing nor crying. When she was safely in her mother's arms, she cowered without stirring.

"Don't be scared, Jacob," her mother said, "Mommy will take you home and get you into some warm clothes . . . come on . . ."

She rubbed her daughter's head and tried to revive her spirits.

But Jacob remained motionless, her face displaying no emotion. Her silent calmness alarmed her mother, whose tears fell on the child's hair. She told her husband to hire rickshaws to take them back to the hotel. They could try again tomorrow. Both of today's trains had come and gone. They did not realize that one of their suitcases was missing until they were seated in the rickshaw.

"I think I saw it," Bo'le said. "It was shuttled over people's heads onto the train."

"Don't lie to me!" his wife railed. "You threw it onto the train! Didn't you say that every item we got onto the train put us that much closer? The more the merrier, you said. God knows where you got all that energy. Your eyes light up with the mere mention of the word 'escape.'"

Jacob had been rescued at the last moment, and their suitcase wound up making the trip without them.

Ma Bo'le and his family returned to the hotel.

The first thing she did back in their room was check to see if her platinum watchband was safe. Once her mind was at ease on that score, she took out some ointment to attend to her children's cuts and bruises. Jacob had a cut on her ear, there was a nick on David's nose, and Joseph's knee had been badly scraped. One by one she patched up their injuries. Her motherly duties completed, she turned to her husband.

"Paul, it's your turn." She held out the ointment.

He had a nasty bruise on his arm, but he refused her offer to treat it.

"I'm fine," he said. "Take care of yourselves."

He yelled for the fat attendant to bring some water. When it arrived, he washed his face and went out to buy cigarettes. Upon his return, he sat at the table and smoked with a wide grin on his face, the right side of his lip curling slightly. He considered himself the luckiest man alive—Jacob had not been taken away by the train. He had rescued his daughter.

All in all, it had been an eventful day, though little had been accomplished. Before going to bed he said:

"Manual labor is the source of man's greatest fortune."

With that non sequitur he thumped himself on the chest, stretched lazily, got into bed, and fell asleep. His wife did not have the slightest idea what he was talking about.

# Chapter Ten

The Ma family spent the next day making preparations. They would limit their luggage to only those things that could be carried or worn by the five of them. They already had a taste of what it was like to have too many children—they had nearly lost Jacob—and it would be even worse with their bags.

One large thermos, one small thermos, and a military canteen, all of which had originally been placed in the net-covered basket, were now draped around three necks: the large thermos around Bo'le's and the small one around David's. They had planned to give the canteen to Joseph, but Jacob objected. She threw a tantrum, demanding that it be given to her.

"Look here," her mother said. "If you get swept away by the train the next time we're at the station, the canteen will go along with you."

"Then when you get to the Song River Bridge," her father continued, "things will be different. What are you going to do with a canteen when you can't even find your mommy?"

But Jacob refused to listen. She ran around the room with the canteen strapped to her back.

They turned their attention to other things: apples, eggs, and duffel bags—these all went on their backs. David and Joseph carried flashlights. According to their father, they were indispensable, for when they were shrouded in darkness at the Song River Bridge, where family members lost sight of one another, the situation could be saved by these lights.

These had all been Ma Bo'le's ideas. He even made a duffel bag out of a piece of canvas. While he was working on it, his wife tried to take it away from him to do it herself, but he would not let her. "A man must be self-sufficient," he said, "especially during hard times like these."

Seeing how much effort the work was costing him, she again asked him to let her do it. But he stopped her by spreading out his hands and saying:

"I'll do it. Who knows, someday I might join the fight against the Japanese, so I may as well learn how to do this now."

When finished it looked like a child's knapsack, but larger. He stuffed it full of toothbrushes, soap, some changes of clothing . . . even a box of Tiger Balm ointment.

Ma Bo'le wasn't big on medicines—Tiger Balm was the sole exception. This, however, should not be considered a testimony to the ointment's efficacy; he did not really think it did much good, but it was the cheapest thing around (it sold for ten fen a tin), and anything that cheap held an attraction for him. Besides, even if it didn't cure anything, it didn't make you any worse. And it smelled good. So he kept some of it around.

He also put bread and butter into each knapsack.

If, when they reached the Song River Bridge, one of them got lost, was separated from the others, or missed the train, there would at least be something to eat.

He still had some canvas left over after making his duffel bag, so he made Joseph a little backpack, into which also went bread and butter.

Once he had the children dressed and ready to go, they resembled a little platoon, outfitted with thermoses, canteens, and flashlights.

He, of course, was the platoon leader. With him at their head, they marched twice around the hotel room in what he referred to as a military maneuver.

"It's folly to try anything without first practicing," he said. "What do I mean by folly? Something that's not practical. You might get by without being practical in other matters, but crossing the Song River Bridge will be a matter of life and death."

Later that evening he went through his maneuvers again by himself. Wanting to see how strong he was, he strapped the duffel bag onto his back and slung the knapsack over his shoulder; those two objects alone, with everything they held, weighed at least fifty pounds. He added the flashlight and thermos, and then lifted up the large suitcase in which he had packed his suits.

Sweat flowed when he picked up the suitcase. His neck flushed all the way up to his ears. His wife could see he was straining to the limit.

"Put that down," she said, "right now!"

But instead of following her advice, he reached over and picked up Jacob, who hadn't finished eating.

"I can't afford to lose this suitcase," he said. "It's got all my suits. And this has our food in it. And we sure can't afford to lose our darling Jacob."

A determined man, he marched around the room two or three times carrying more than a hundred pounds and saying over and over:

"This is the Song River Bridge, this is the Song River Bridge . . ."

The next morning he started in with his maneuvers all over again. They were going to make another try at boarding a train. The hundred pounds were once again draped over him. His tendons nearly popped out. All the while little Jacob rested in her daddy's arms and laughed happily.

"Is this the Song River Bridge?" she asked.

Bo'le stomped across the floor, making the floorboards of the old hotel creak and quiver.

"This is the Song River Bridge," he intoned.

Jacob's voice was crisp and clear as a bell; Bo'le's voice was so weak you had to wonder where the next breath was coming from.

Just before they set out, he grilled his three children:

"What's your name?"

"David."

"You have to say, 'My name is David Ma.'"

"My name is David Ma."

"What's your name?" he asked his second born.

"Joseph Ma."

Then it was Jacob's turn.

"What's your name?"

"My name is Little Jacob."

"What do you mean, 'Little Jacob'? Say your name is Jacob Ma."

The night before, he'd taught them to give their full names if the worst happened and they were separated after arriving at the Song River Bridge. He never imagined she would get it wrong so soon. So he continued the grilling:

"What's your father's name?"

"Ma Bo'le," David answered.

"What's your father's name?" he asked his second born.

"Ma Bo'le," Joseph answered as he chewed his fingernails.

Again it was Jacob's turn.

"What's your father's name?"

"My father's name is, uh, Paul Ma Bo'le . . ." She was more interested in taking the cap off of Joseph's canteen than answering the question.

"What's your father's name?" he asked her again.

"My father is going to cross the Song River Bridge," she replied. "Joseph . . ."

She lunged for her brother, who kicked her, and before you knew it, they were fighting.

Ma Bo'le separated them and held Joseph down, then recommenced the questioning, starting with David:

"Where's your home?"

"My home is in Qingdao."

He then asked Joseph and Jacob, and both said Qingdao. Everything ran smoothly this time around.

This was followed by the most important question of all—the address of their home in Qingdao.

This time it was like a burlesque show. David said he lived on Observatory Road, while Joseph said he lived on First Avenue. Ma Bo'le had told them over and over that they lived on First Observatory Road, but they kept forgetting. Little Jacob was the worst; she didn't come close. She answered the question with nonsense:

"There's some kind of observatory on the hill behind our house. It's a great place to look at the moon during the Mid-Autumn Festival. Mommy took me there once, but she didn't take Joseph . . . did she, Joseph?"

"Liar!" Joseph snapped. "She didn't take you . . ."

"Liar yourself!" Jacob shot back.

Joseph slipped the flashlight cord off his shoulder and wrapped it around his sister's neck, then pulled her over backwards.

David was the only one who behaved himself while his father quizzed them; his brother and sister had long since given up listening and were raising all sorts of hell. As a result they set out for the train station without getting their stories straight.

They were better prepared than the time before, when they had worked at crossed purposes until all the signs pointed to disaster. They had given no thought to their luggage, utensils, or anything else. But on this attempt, everything went like clockwork; one could say that they were in full battle readiness. They had all the items they needed, from rations and water to flashlights, divided evenly among them, so no one was totally dependent upon anyone else. Even Jacob had a flashlight of her own.

This time they made it onto the train without too much trouble. Most likely they had their training and organization to thank for that. Not only did they manage to get aboard, they never broke rank. Even

1

though the cap on Joseph's canteen got knocked off in the shuffle, he managed to keep the cork stopper in with his hand so that not a drop of water was lost.

Then there was Joseph's flashlight, which somehow lit up on its own, but his father easily fixed that. The little canteen remained on Joseph's back, though it hung upside down. In a word, although there were minor mishaps, all things considered, it was a great success, and their spirits remained high, Joseph's highest of all. He had his sleeves rolled up and fists clenched. But there was no worthy opponent in sight.

The train was not as packed as previous ones had been, but there still wasn't much room to move around, and people were stepping on each other's toes. And there was Joseph, just standing in the doorway.

His mother called to him as he stretched out his foot and flexed his muscles:

"Joseph, come here to Mommy."

Just then, a white-bearded old man climbed unsteadily into the car with the aid of a cane. He was shoved from side to side until he wound up standing next to Joseph. Although he wasn't crowding the boy, he bumped into the canteen slung across his back. That was enough for Joseph to light into him with fists and feet.

Nearly everyone in the car who witnessed what was happening praised our little warrior.

"That's quite some boy there! A real tiger!"

His mother rushed over and dragged him away.

"This isn't Qingdao," she scolded him. "It's all right to have your little fights at home, but not here in Shanghai. Now get over here!"

But fighting was in Joseph's blood, and he was not about to listen to her. He broke free and ran back to the old man, where he reached up and pulled several hairs out of his beard. That took the edge off his anger.

Before long he'd run off again, this time to the head of the car, where a four- or five-year-old girl in a red jacket was sitting in a woman's lap. He pulled the girl to the floor and began hitting her.

When it was over, his father asked him why he'd done it.

"She looked at me!" Joseph said defiantly. "She stared at me."

They had a good laugh over their son's answer. Not only did they not give him a talking-to, they praised him:

"That's some boy we've got here. Talk about guts! He'll fight anyone, big or small."

Mrs. Ma wife rubbed her son's head. She was grinning so broadly her eyes were mere slits.

"If everyone in China was like Joseph," she said, "we'd be invincible."

All that talk obviously gratified Joseph, who calmed down and momentarily forgot about fighting.

Whenever Joseph was in a fight that failed to elicit compliments from onlookers, he figured he must not be doing a good enough job, and redoubled his efforts. On the other hand, when he was complimented, his spirits soared, and nothing could stop him. The only thing that could still his fists was praise from his grandfather or his mother, for that was affirmation of his combat skills from his only true supporters.

But now, having burned off some of his energy, he was as gentle as a lamb. He borrowed David's thermos cap, and took a drink of warm water (remember, his cap had gotten lost during the scuffle while boarding the train). When he finished he walked over and screwed the cap back onto the thermos. This was unprecedented; normally, when he wanted something, he simply took it, and when he was finished with it he flung it to the ground. If he had done that this time, and David had protested, he might have charged over and stomped it flat out of spite.

The train was about to pull out of the station, and Ma Bo'le's family was orderly and high-spirited. Granted, Joseph had caused a bit of a ruckus, but that did not count, since his opponents had both been from the lower classes, especially the little girl. Sporting a little topknot and wearing a red jacket, she was clearly from the countryside. That little topknot proved it was all right to beat her up.

So Joseph's altercations had no adverse effect on the family's mood. Their spirits were further boosted by the fact that they had all the food they needed and were the only ones in the entire car whose situation could be characterized as favorable.

They sat in facing rows, three children and two adults. They were neat and orderly, dressed for the occasion, and the envy of all who saw them. The children were in short pants, looking spry and alert. This was obviously a well-organized family, destined to emerge victorious from the impending struggle at the Song River Bridge. Anyone in doubt had only to look at little Jacob, who was the picture of vitality, with a bag of food in her right hand, a flashlight in her left, and an eagerness that manifested itself in her constantly wanting to know when they would reach the Song River Bridge.

The train had not yet left the station.

• • •

Boarding the train had brought Ma Bo'le neither happiness nor sorrow—he had calmly done everything he had to do. What remained of their possessions had been placed aboard, and the children were on their best behavior. Admittedly, Joseph acted up a bit now and then, but as long as the boy's mother was there to keep him in check, Bo'le did not have to keep his eye on him.

He felt thoroughly secure. Yes, they were in a third-class coach, which was noisy and chaotic with bawling children and yelling women, and the sounds of people chomping on eggs and slurping water was enough to drive a man to drink. But none of this bothered Ma Bo'le, who sat peacefully, the picture of serenity. He watched the other people and listened to them, but there was no sign that he either saw or heard them. Undisturbed by the racket around him, he was at peace with the world.

It was almost as if the formidable Song River Bridge had lost its power to instill fear. He was not only serene, he was actually comfortable. He had a window seat, and as he took long, deep breaths of fresh air, he enjoyed looking out his window.

All this engendered in him a sense of magnanimity. He even managed to keep his temper when someone shoved something in through the window and bumped his head. His only reaction was a slight curling of his lip as he placed the object on the floor beside him and said to his wife:

"See how much stuff those people are taking? They're going to be in a hell of a fix when they get to the Song River Bridge."

A little later he said to her:

"You see, the train's still sitting here and the crowds are growing."

A little later he commented:

"Just look at all the latecomers. I hope they don't think there are any seats left. They might not even find standing room."

A little later still he pointed something out to her:

"Look over there, just take a look!"

A child was lying flat on her back on the platform with a bloody nose. Bo'le was unmoved by the sight because he could not imagine the same thing happening to his family. Everything was going fine for them. He had entered a private realm of quiet observation.

The train was still in the station nearly a half hour after Ma Bo'le's family had gotten aboard. Normally, this sort of delay would have made him squirm or given rise to outbursts of "Bloody Chinese!" But today he felt that the delay was appropriate, that everything was in harmony.

Once the train finally began to roll forward, he gazed at the horizon to take in the passing scenery. Dusk was falling and the sun was about to sink out of sight. A bright red sunset framed a little bamboo grove behind a village, and water buffaloes moved through rice fields at an unhurried pace. Whenever the train passed through a populated area, small groups of children followed its progress with their eyes. They stood motionless as though transfixed by the monotonous *clickety-clack*. It was impossible to tell by looking at these villages that a war was raging in Shanghai. Night soon fell. It was a moonless, starlit night. The interior of the car was unlighted, the darkness broken only by the burning tip of an occasional cigarette. Bo'le shut his eyes and fell asleep. He slept soundly, as if he were home in bed—he snored, he dreamt, he even talked in his sleep from time to time:

"Bloody Chinese . . ."

His wife heard him, but said nothing.

The train kept rolling along, *clickety-clack, clickety-clack.* His wife kept watch. The children were fast asleep.

Jacob slept in her mother's lap, while David was curled up in a corner, like his father, his head resting on his chest. Joseph, on the other hand, was stretched out, taking up most of the bench on which he was sleeping, as if it were a bed. He was obviously comfortable. From time to time, he kicked his brother in the knee when he tossed and turned. Fearing he might fall to the floor, his mother kept a close eye on him.

By eight or nine o'clock there was a nip in the air. As the children began to shiver and cough, their mother covered them with an overcoat or a sweater. Worried that someone might walk off with their belongings if she fell asleep, she kept her eyes open.

As the night wore on, others on board drifted off as well. The car was soon filled with sounds of deep breathing, snores, grinding teeth, curses, and people talking in their sleep.

Ma Bo'le's wife seemed to be the only person awake. She surveyed the strange looks on the faces of her fellow passengers. Some were chewing their lips, others had wrinkled noses, and all of them gave her an uneasy feeling, since these were sights she had never witnessed before. This was the first time in her life she had ever ridden in a third-class coach. It had been Ma Bo'le's idea; since these were refugee times, frugality was their prime consideration. And that meant traveling third-class.

She grew more frightened by the minute, and was tempted to wake him up to keep her company. But the sight of him sleeping dead to the world stopped her. She forced herself to exercise patience.

All of a sudden, the man sitting directly behind her jumped to his feet with a yell. Nothing mysterious or particularly frightening had happened—a bundle had fallen from the overhead rack onto his head, that's all—but it unnerved Ma Bo'le's wife. She shook her husband out of his deep sleep.

"Paul!" she cried out. "Paul!"

But he was sleeping much too soundly to wake up at her bidding. He knocked her hand off his arm and grumbled:

"What the hell are you doing, what's going on . . ."

"Paul, wake up . . ."

But he didn't hear her. Grinding his teeth noisily, he turned his back to her and went back to sleep.

By the time he finally woke up, the world had undergone a change. The shouts and screams around him were deafening.

He raised his head with a jerk. His wife told him they had arrived at the Song River Bridge. Stretching the kinks out of his neck and rubbing his eyes, he made a single comment:

"Let's go!"

He was evidently less than a hundred percent awake, which was why he grabbed hold of his flashlight but forgot his knapsack and food bags as he dashed down the aisle. He ran back to get them, and when he reached the doorway he saw that there was already a stream of passengers leaving the train.

It was pitch black outside. As he shivered in the cold he thought about his home—they would be asleep in bed now. This made him feel miserable. If it had been possible to get a little more sleep before leaving the train, he certainly would have. Wishful thinking!

So, family in tow, he joined the line of people leaving the train.

The moment they left the car, they were greeted by shouts from all directions. They could not see the bridge, so they joined the crowd as it moved along, heading forward, wherever that led.

They reached it after walking some five hundred yards. During that short time some people ran off like whipped puppies and others were separated from their families. They soon arrived at the bridgehead, Ma Bo'le well ahead of the rest of his family.

Being there was one thing; stopping or waiting there was something else altogether. The people behind him pushed and shoved relentlessly, climbing over their fallen comrades to cross.

Everyone was moving at top speed, shouting as they pressed ever forward. As far as the eye could see there was only darkness. Shouts from far away traveled through the night air as if suspended between heaven and earth. They were distinct sounds, if restrained. They seemed to have been manufactured rather than delivered by human mouths.

Bo'le glanced down at the white water flowing below; it looked like a river of quicksilver, and that sent more shivers down his spine.

Almost immediately he felt his strength ebb. He was burdened by too heavy a load for a skinny fellow like him. After reaching the bridgehead and looking at the water below, he grew lightheaded and, given the weight he was carrying, was in danger of toppling over.

But the people behind gave him no pause; bumping and shoving, they swept him forward until his situation grew desperate. He wondered what was keeping his wife. Just a moment earlier they had maintained verbal contact, but now there wasn't a sound from her. He wondered if her shouts were being drowned out by all the other noise. So he listened carefully and thought he heard her. He listened again, more carefully— no, it wasn't her.

Now what? He could no longer lift his suitcase or carry Jacob, and the food bags were so heavy they seemed to be packed with rocks. The flashlight was more trouble than it was worth—it was bouncing around against his body. But it would take more than an errant flashlight to finish him off. Far more important were his suitcase and Jacob, and it looked like one or the other was going to have to be jettisoned.

But how could that be? His suits were in the suitcase; he could not part with those. His appearance was dependent upon them. A man can get by without inner substance, but not without an outer appearance. You can have all the learning and ability in the world, and no one will care. Your appearance, however, is the first thing people notice.

He was weak from exhaustion, too weak to give any more thought to theories about inner substance and outer appearances. He was feverish, and his heart was beating wildly. He began to see stars and was mumbling incoherently. He might have been calling out to his wife, or to his son David. But his voice was so weak even he couldn't hear it.

He seemed on the verge of collapse—his nerves were shot. He stepped off the rail bed and moved to the side to let the fearful surge of people pass by. It was his bad luck that the tracks had been laid on a steep earthen bank, flanked on both sides by marshland. Water plants, broken and rotting timbers, and coal cinders cluttered the area. He did not know what he'd gotten himself into by moving off to the side. Surrounded by waterlogged plants, he plunged into the water at the base of the rail bed.

He had no idea where he was.

None of the people scrambling across the Song River Bridge were aware that one of their number, Ma Bo'le by name, had fallen off the rail bed. They kept moving ahead. Beams of light crisscrossed the sky above the bridge. The patrolmen on duty were using flashlights to help the refugees maintain an orderly flow. They shouted:

"Don't rush. Take your time."

"Don't push. Be careful."

"Don't shove. Cross one at a time."

They walked among the travelers, lighting their way across the bridge. But there were no more than three or four of them patrolling the entire span, and since their sole responsibility was to shine flashlights, that was about all they did.

Whenever someone was nudged off the bridge and into the river, they paid no attention. Naturally, Ma Bo'le's plunge into the marsh below the rail bed went unnoticed. He was unable to shout and did not know where his suitcase had landed. Poor little Jacob, who had been scared witless by the fall, was standing among water plants, crying pitifully. But the sounds of her crying were drowned out by the even louder cries and wails above him.

The stream of people crossing the bridge moved relentlessly forward. Every trainload left in its wake a number of deaths and injuries. Old folks fell to the ground, never to rise again; children were pushed to their deaths or trampled underfoot; pregnant women gave birth right on the rail bed.

Once the train had departed, out came the patrolmen to search the area with their flashlights. One of them heard the faint cries of a child coming from the vicinity of the bridgehead. When he located the child he asked:

"What's your name?"

Predictably, Jacob had no answer. All that questioning about her name prior to boarding the train had been a waste of time.

The patrolman tried other questions:

"Where's your daddy? Where's your mommy?"

He spoke to her in the Shanghai dialect, which she did not understand, and he shone his flashlight in her face, which so frightened her she cried even harder and screamed, scurrying back and forth in confusion.

The patrolman thought she was putting on quite a show, so he called his buddies over to watch. Before long, three or four beams of light danced across Jacob's body, lighting her up. She bolted, with the frightful shouts of the patrolmen hard on her heels.

"Stop! Stop!"

Fearing that they were trying to catch her, she ran even faster. Since she didn't know where the shallow water was, she headed farther in among the riverbank grasses and suddenly found herself knee-deep.

The three men on the bank, captivated by her actions, tossed dirt clods and small stones in her direction. With remarkable accuracy, these missiles formed a ring around the running Jacob—many nearly hit her. The water that splashed into her face was cold. All the time they were throwing dirt and rocks at her, the men kept shouting:

"Stop! Stop!"

Jacob increased her speed with every shout. She was sure these people were chasing her. Her frantic movements soon led her into water so deep it nearly reached her neck; the shouting men looking down from the rail bed began to worry.

Then she lost her footing and sank.

By the time Jacob had been fished out of the water and carried to the bridgehead station house, Ma Bo'le had also been rescued and brought to the same place.

People at the station house were unaware that he and Jacob were father and daughter, for when the patrolman had discovered Jacob, she'd already run off some distance from where her father lay. They had seen only her; none of them had spotted Bo'le.

He lay on a stretcher; one of the patrolmen held Jacob in his arms. She was crying and struggling to get loose.

Bo'le was in a stupor. His thermos bottle had been smashed; only the empty cover remained slung over his back, until someone removed it. His supply of food was soaked through and his hand-made duffel bag had spilled most of its contents—toothbrushes and soap—owing to the faulty construction of its mouth. It was a shell of its former self. Since it was ruined, it had also been taken off his back.

He was now completely relieved of the hundred-pound load he had started out with. He had no idea where his large suitcase was, or Jacob, for that matter. He couldn't have lost Jacob, not their little darling! And he couldn't have lost his suitcase—all his suits were in it!

He eventually came around. Noticing that the walls of the room were white, he assumed that he was in a hospital or in a hotel room; maybe in one of his former classrooms.

He was thirsty. Recalling that he had a thermos on his back, he reached for it, but for some reason had neither the strength nor the coordination to make the effort. He decided to ask for it instead:

"I want a drink of water."

The sound of his own voice brought him further out of his sleepy state, and it dawned on him that he was not at home or in his Shanghai hotel room. This was someplace he had never been before. He didn't recognize any of the people who were walking around in the room. He felt his nose, which hurt. "Oh-oh! Something's wrong with my nose!"

His nostrils had been stuffed with cotton and a bandage covered the bridge of his nose. He felt it again—he was wounded, no doubt about it. Hadn't he threatened to join the army someday and become a soldier? How had it become a reality? He was filled with remorse. Talk of joining the army had been a ploy to get extra spending money out of other people—his father, his wife—and now here he was, a soldier, after all.

His injured nose did not overly concern him, for he was worried that he might have sustained other, more serious, injuries. He tried lifting his legs and stretching out his arms, only to discover that he couldn't move his left leg. This threw him into a panic; his face was covered with sweat. They've amputated my leg!

He burst into tears, wailing loudly. He'd never wanted to be a soldier, and now he was a cripple! He was inconsolable; regret penetrated to his marrow. Why had he ever become a soldier? It had cost him a leg!

His wife was sitting in a chair nearby, holding Jacob in her lap. The girl was so feverish her face was bright red. Her mother had changed her into dry clothes, but she hadn't been able to find dry socks anywhere, so Jacob sat with her bare feet. Her mother wrapped a towel around her to keep her warm. Drifting in and out of sleep, Jacob held onto her mother's sleeve, as if afraid that someone might try to snatch her away.

Bo'le's wife had heard him ask for water, but since she wanted to avoid waking Jacob by getting up, she told David to pour his father a cup of water. Bo'le refused to touch it; with his eyes shut tightly, he just cried and cried.

It must have been contagious, for Jacob started to cry, too.

Before long, Bo'le detected the sound of someone else crying nearby; he had heard this cry before—it was a child.

He opened his eyes to see who it was. It was Jacob!

Then it all came back: he had been carrying her when he tumbled off the rail bed. He wasn't wounded after all! It had been a bad dream. He called to his wife and asked her to bring him up to date. But he received a cold response. Obviously unhappy with him, she only gave him the barest details of what had happened.

But everything she said filled him with delight.

When she told him how perilously close Jacob had come to drowning, a grin spread across his face. There was a secret happiness in his heart caused by something no one would ever learn about—he wasn't a casualty, after all.

They spent the night at the station house, and then boarded the onward train the following morning. They were exhausted and in sad shape. Not only had their spirits plummeted since boarding the train at Shanghai, but their luggage was a shambles. Of the three canteens they had taken with them, the best they could come up with now was half of one. Joseph's military canteen was more durable than the others', and though slightly dented, it still held water. Ma Bo'le's thermos was beyond salvation and had been thrown away. The only thing remaining of David's thermos was the leather case that had held it; it was still slung over his back.

The food pouches, which had been filled nearly to overflowing, were now empty. Part of their contents had been lost—the remainder had been consumed ravenously in the course of a single day. The butter, the bread—it was all gone.

What about the three children? David was tugging his hair out of sheer boredom. Joseph refrained from getting up and picking a fight, because someone had stepped on his foot during the night, and it was badly swollen. A swollen foot is a lot different than a swollen something else—a nose, for instance, or an eye, either of which is less complicated. A swollen foot makes fighting difficult. So every time Joseph got a notion to pick a fight, he thought better of it.

Jacob was still running a fever. Frightened by nearly everything she saw, she stayed huddled in her mother's lap and held tightly onto her sleeve.

Bo'le's wife had not brushed her hair in a couple of days, and it sorely needed tending to. It would have looked better if it hadn't just been permed. Hairdos like hers were hard to take care of. Her normally large black eyes had lost their luster after two sleepless nights.

Ma Bo'le was the only one among them in high spirits. Whenever anyone asked him why his nose was bandaged, he announced proudly to all:

"I am a casualty of war."

# Chapter Eleven

The train pulled into the Nanjing station, much to everyone's surprise.

"Well, we made it, for better or for worse," Ma Bo'le thought.

As they walked out of the train station, he said:

"Let's get some roast duck. Nanjing ducks are supposed to be the fattest anywhere."

His wife could scarcely believe her ears, and insisted that they find a hotel room first.

It was drizzling when they left the station, so the first order of business was to get settled—children, baggage, the lot—no matter how hungry they were. She won the argument. They went to a hotel.

From the moment they settled in, Ma Bo'le was in an exuberant mood. Even when MPs came by to check on the guests and questioned him, he saw nothing inauspicious in that.

"Where are you from?" the MP asked him.

"I'm from Shandong," he replied.

"There have been more traitors from Shandong than anywhere else."

Ordinarily, if he'd heard a comment like this, even though he'd be afraid to say anything to the MP's face, he would curse silently:

"Bloody Chinese!"

But not this time. He was so euphoric now that the thought never entered his mind. Where had this euphoria come from? He had a broken nose, he had nearly fallen to his death, and he had been unconscious for the longest time—oblivious to all human affairs. His nose was still swollen, as a matter of fact, but all he could think of was that he had not died. If he had . . . but he'd made it to Nanjing, hadn't he? If he hadn't . . .

He experienced an unusual sense of gratitude—he was immensely grateful to the Song River Bridge for not claiming his life.

It was actually a good thing that the bridge had dumped him into the marshland, for it was only through such suffering that he had come to know true joy. Had it not been for the bridge, how could he have known such happiness as he now felt? Ma Bo'le was a contented man; all he needed now was some roast duck.

From his reaction, one might think that he had reached his destination. The air raids over Nanjing were terrifying, day and night, and when Ma Bo'le was in Shanghai, thoughts of what awaited him here had constantly been on his mind, just as the Song River Bridge had obsessed him earlier. But the difficulties of the Song River Bridge were behind him—he had overcome this rite of passage.

Now he was in Nanjing, about to go out and enjoy some roast duck.

Before leaving, he overheard the MPs interrogate the guest in the next room: "Where's your home?"

"Liaoning."

"How old are you?"

"Thirty."

"Where are you coming from?"

"Shanghai."

"Where are you headed?"

"Hankou."

"Occupation?"

"Editor in a publishing house."

"Which one? Got any identification?"

After hearing the man's affirmative response, Ma Bo'le heard sounds of someone rummaging through a trunk.

Following this, the MP asked:

"What did you do before that?"

The man replied that he had been a student at a military academy in Liaoning. He had moved to Shanghai after the September 18th Incident in Manchuria.

"Since you've had military training," the MP responded, "why aren't you at the front? We need men to aid the cause of resistance."

"I changed my calling," the man answered. "I went from the military to the civil."

The MP persisted: "You still ought to be in uniform at the front. You're not supposed to be back here in the rear echelon. The Chinese race has never been in bigger trouble."

Ma Bo'le continued to eavesdrop, but the issue went unresolved and the interrogation apparently ran its course. As he left his room he sneaked a look at the MPs as they were walking out of the room next door. There were three of them; the one in the middle was saying to his comrades:

"He's from Liaoning, a province that's produced lots of traitors."

This time he was merely amused by what the MP said. It was the sort of comment he'd have jotted down for future reference, if only he had some sort of journal. But it was just a passing fancy, as his thoughts quickly returned to food.

"Come on, Jacob, let's go get some roast duck."

He reached out to pick up his daughter, who was sitting on the bed, but he so startled her by coming up from behind that she screamed in wide-eyed terror:

"Mommy!"

Ma Bo'le's roast duck was waiting for them at a riverside restaurant. To get there they had to cross a bridge. The restaurant, some twenty or thirty paces ahead, had been built above the river, which was visible through cracks in the floor. Ducks swam directly below. Joseph got down on all fours and stared through one of the cracks.

"Look at the bright colors," he yelled. "There's a white one . . . one with a green head . . . a big, fat black one . . ." He couldn't take his eyes off them even after everyone else had begun eating.

The roast duck was disappointing, especially the skin, which was tough.

"This restaurant's too small," Bo'le's wife complained. "We shouldn't have had such high expectations for a tiny place like this."

"That's no way to look at things," he retorted. "Roast duck is a Nanjing specialty . . . back home if we took a duck to a big restaurant, do you think they'd know how to roast it?" He capped his pronouncement by picking up a drumstick and biting into it. Blood oozed out.

"Oo, I can't eat this!" he said and spat it out.

He assumed that the wing was his next best bet, which showed his inexperience: it was red and also undercooked. He then picked up the breast, but it looked the same. He could not find a single piece of edible meat with his chopsticks, so he took out his pocketknife and tried cutting off some of the better parts. But even the small pieces without traces of blood were as rank as the rest. All he could do was add a little more soy sauce and vinegar and try to eat it as best he could.

Unable to force himself to eat another bite, he asked for the check, telling the waiter to wrap up what was left on the plate. He was going to take it back to the hotel, cook it some more, and eat it there.

"He's Chinese, so why no curse?" his wife asked him.

"Bloody Chinese!" It had slipped his mind.

Ma Bo'le walked back to the hotel in low spirits. Nanjing duck had let him down. He could have kicked himself for not going to a decent restaurant. No wonder his wife had been critical of the place: just look at the other diners—soldiers, policemen, and people only a step removed from being rickshaw pullers. The food was so bad because the place catered to the lower classes.

A cloud settled over his mood. The ground was wet with rain. Nanjing was certainly different than Shanghai and Qingdao. It was a dreary place, especially after an air raid, when the sense of desolation was increased by the scarcity of people out on the street. The drizzle made it worse.

He lay down on the bed as soon as he was back at the hotel. He was having trouble digesting the duck he'd just eaten—his stomach was churning. He was also depressed about steamship tickets; the hotel attendant had first said that the next ship wouldn't leave for three days, and then it was five. At the moment he was out in the corridor telling Ma Bo'le's wife:

"Tickets are hard to come by. It's raining now, but when the sky clears up tomorrow, the Japanese airplanes will be back."

Bo'le did not want to slip into despair so soon, but by nighttime he could no longer put it off. First, there was the problem of the sky clearing up; then there was the nearly hopeless situation regarding steamship tickets. There was a third problem—the indigestion caused by the duck he'd eaten earlier in the day.

His stomach was sour one moment and burning the next, and he couldn't figure out what was going on. The problem persisted into the night and caused him to sweat freely. By early morning, his energy was sapped almost to the limit; his wife, who had no idea what was bothering him, heard him say:

"Are the stars out?"

He sounded delirious.

"Paul, I think you ought to take an aspirin."

"No. I want you to tell me if the stars are out."

She assumed he must be running a fever. That would explain the delirium.

Actually, he was afraid the sky would clear up and the Japanese airplanes would make a bombing run.

On the following day Ma Bo'le and his family departed Nanjing on a small steamship. The hotel attendant had purchased the tickets for them, for which he'd taken a twenty-percent commission.

But that was only natural. If a man won't shell out a little extra during chaotic times, he probably never will. If he won't part with his money during a national crisis, where will he spend it once the crisis has passed? Life and death situations call for compromises: you pay the going rate. Which is more important, your money or your life? So Ma Bo'le had been willing to write off the attendant's commission.

But not his wife:

"Normally you're eager to curse the Chinese, and you wouldn't be caught dead paying an extra fen for something. But here you are, letting the attendant get away with four or five yuan. Even that would be all right if you hadn't tried to justify it with one of your 'theories.'"

"You always look at things one way! Just think for a minute—what kind of times were those, and what kind of times are these now?"

"So what kind of times are these?"

"Air raid times, that's what."

All this had occurred back at the hotel. Now that they were finally on the steamship, the subject was dropped. As far as his wife was concerned, the sooner they got to Hankou, the better. Besides, the ship had barely gotten underway before the city's air raid sirens had sounded, and getting out of Nanjing quickly was the best move they'd made. The little steamship was unimaginably shabby. Allowing it to travel in broad daylight, thereby contrasting it with the shining waters below, the bright sun above, and the clean air all around, was sheer mockery. It carried the misnomer *Taiping lun*—Ship of Peace—though none of the passengers noted the irony.

Under normal circumstances, the vessel carried something over a hundred passengers. But now, under wartime conditions, she was carrying more than four hundred. The owner insisted that this number was still low, and that if necessary the ship could carry five or six hundred.

There were people everywhere. The poor souls above deck got soaked by the rain and buffeted by the wind. It made sense to load up the decks that way, but they even sold tickets for the galley and the toilet.

If Ma Bo'le hadn't seen it with his own eyes, he wouldn't have believed it. When he went to the toilet, he found someone sleeping there. Then when he went to the galley to rustle up something to eat, there were people lying in front of the stove. He was beyond surprise until some-one explained to him what was going on: the toilet was occupied by a comatose cholera victim, and the galley by sufferers from malaria who, with their special need to keep warm, were huddled up against the stove.

Among the ship's passengers were wounded soldiers and troops who had been relieved. The wounded soldiers were easy to spot, owing to their injuries, which were wrapped and bandaged. Troops returning from the front were a different matter. Although still in uniform, they refused to show their IDs and responded to such demands by pounding the table, stamping their feet, and glaring menacingly.

The ship's owner dared not pursue the matter, even though he knew they had not paid for their passage.

The air was fouled by a stench that normally accompanied a fishing boat, not a passenger ship. In addition to the stench, everything had a clammy feel to it. Whatever they touched was moist and gummy. Ma Bo'le's first action immediately after boarding was to fall asleep. It was the train ride all over again.

He and his family were put up in a cabin next to the owner-captain's quarters. They slept on a steward's bed, a wooden platform covered with a thin straw mat. It was as hard as nails and a breeding ground for bed-bugs, but once they spread out their own bedding, it was quite comfort-able. The bedbugs made an occasional foray, but not often enough to present a real problem. There were far fewer of them here than in the Shanghai hotel room.

It was like being in the lap of luxury. Bo'le slept next to a porthole, which he opened from time to time for fresh air. What he usually got instead was coal smoke and tiny cinders, prompting him to remark:

"The air outside is worse than the air inside."

He shut the porthole.

The ship steamed on, taking the slumbering Ma Bo'le along with it. It moved lethargically through the water, a sluggish, lackadaisical pas-sage. When the river grew choppy, rather than smooth out the ride by heading into the waves like other ships, it placed itself at the mercy of the heavy swells, listing sharply with each surge of water that rolled beneath it, the decks groaning and creaking in a sorrowful chorus from stem to stern.

It was an innocent ship, and eminently practical, incapable of struggling against superior forces. If dictated by necessity, it would think nothing of rolling over and dumping its human cargo into the river. Fortunately, the winds on this trip were not *that* strong, so the ship was merely buffeted slightly, and then allowed to proceed as it plied a course on the Yangzi between Nanjing and Hankou, carrying passengers in both directions.

Each time it made one of its trips, the ship lost rivets and screws, and on each trip from Nanjing to Hankou, one of the deck railings would be newly broken or part of the deck newly caved in. The caved-in portions were covered with boards; broken railings were replaced with ropes. Nothing was ever repaired. Someone asked the owner:

"Why don't you make some repairs?"

"Why should I? They cost money." No clarification was forthcoming

For Joseph, who had an abundance of energy, the ship was a playground. He toured it from one end to the other, curious about the engine spaces below-decks, a noisy place that he found especially intriguing. He was eager to go down, but when he first looked through the hatch and saw the ladder leading down into what was nothing more than a black hole, his courage waned. One of the passengers seated near the engine called out to this neatly dressed little boy:

"Hey son, come on down. We'll light the way for you," the man said, and struck a match.

So down Joseph went, where he was met by the powerful odor of lubricating oil and a blast of hot air. He did not like it down there, so he turned to climb back out. But then the man who had lit the match thrust a little round object into his hand. It was a warm rivet. Joseph liked his little hexagonal toy at once and immediately stole two more off the bulkhead.

The chief engineer, his face black with oily smudges, walked up just then, frightening Joseph. He looked down at the boy's hand and asked him:

"What've you got there?"

Joseph opened his hand. The man laughed when he saw the rivets, then mussed Joseph's hair.

"I've never seen anyone as clean as this kid . . . go on, kid, you can play with them."

Joseph returned to the deck with four rivets; he gave two to Jacob and kept two. David got none. He wanted to see what they were, but Joseph slapped him.

"I'll stick one in your eye, and you see if you can get it out!"

David was on the verge of tears, but his mother dragged him away. She asked Joseph where he had gotten the things he was playing with.

He told her.

"You're a force to reckon with," she said. "No place is off limits to you, not even a dangerous place like the engine room."

That was all she said, so Jacob and Joseph went back to their game.

After a while, the ship's owner approached them. Mrs. Ma was afraid he'd be angry when he saw that his ship was being dismantled right under his eyes, so she pretended she had just this moment discovered what was going on.

"Joseph, what a naughty little boy . . . where did you get those things? Put them back, and be quick about it!"

"Let them play, it's all right. Do they have enough? If not, there's more in the engine room. The place is loaded with them."

She was impressed by the man's easy-going nature.

"Go ahead and play, but be nice," she said. "And don't squabble."

There were so many passengers aboard the ship that at night the snores were as loud as thunder. It sounded like the ship was carrying a cargo of croaking frogs. During the day, the sole activity seemed to be eating. They had to eat in shifts, given the limited space in the galley and the shortage of bowls and chopsticks, and so there was a constant stream of people in and out of the galley, where they took turns preparing meals. There were flies everywhere, attracted by the overpowering stench of food that had been spilled onto the decks and trampled into a gooey mess.

There were no bathing facilities, the decks were never hosed down, and the toilet was too small to be of much use. When nature called, as often as not the passengers simply relieved themselves in the vicinity of the facility, thus creating a provisional toilet that kept expanding.

Hankou's silhouette came into view when as the sun came out. Situated on the bank of the Yangzi, the city was enshrouded in a bluish haze. The passengers began gathering up their things, as if the slightest delay might keep them from disembarking at all. Old folks out on the decks were always left behind. Once again, it was survival of the fittest.

Nearly everyone had finished packing and getting their belongings together by midday. All they had to do was wait to dock at Hankou to leave the ship.

But it seemed to take forever. Noon came and went, and port was still off in the distance.

The ship steamed on, but did not seem to be going anywhere, as if it were mired in quicksand; each wave, each whitecap, seemed to stick to the keel and hold it fast. Hankou was right there, but it was just beyond reach.

Some of the passengers had been to Hankou before; others were first-time visitors. The old hands acted like members of the city's Chamber of Commerce, with talk of its landmark, the clock tower at Jianghan Pass, visible from a great distance. Once it was in sight, you could say hello to Hankou.

First-time visitors squinted into the distance, but no matter how hard they tried, they could not see Hankou's famed landmark. Even after lunchtime, it still had not come into view. By three or four o'clock in the afternoon, nothing had changed—the clock tower remained elusive.

By dinnertime it had yet to make an appearance.

The people were flabbergasted that any ship could travel so slowly.

"Are we going to have to unpack our bedding and spend another night here?"

There was no doubt that another night aboard ship was virtually assured. But hope springs eternal, so the passengers stayed on deck to watch and wait, silently nursing their frustrations.

"Well, we won't make it today," said one of the sailors, shattering the passengers' hopes once and for all. They had been saying that the ship would dock today all along, but never with much conviction. They had used words like "possibly," "maybe," and "hopefully."

In their impatience, however, the passengers had interpreted these comments as meaning they would "dock without fail" today.

By early the next morning, the river was alive with junks and other small boats. The passengers' passivity had given way to displeasure; their ears were assailed by all sorts of river noises—shouts, the scraping of oars, and the singing of tow ropes—but they were too busy once more tying up their bedding and grumbling to watch the scenes that accompanied these sounds. There were complaints of sore backs, sore legs, aching stomachs, and runny eyes caused by cold winds. The prevailing opinion was that had they docked the night before, none of these symptoms would have appeared.

Word was then passed that the ship would dock within the hour. But even that thought did not lighten the passengers' mood, and their mutterings continued.

"A ship like this should not be allowed to carry passengers."

"Remember, this is China. In any other country, a ship like this would have been scrapped long ago."

"This rust bucket is worse than an old water buffalo . . . and still they make you buy a ticket . . ."

The owner listened to these exclamations of discontent from his cabin, until they became unreasonable. At this point, he stuck his head out of the hatch, listening closely at first, and then reacting to what they were saying:

"You're not taking China's situation into account when you talk like that. Naturally, a rust bucket like this wouldn't have any place in an industrialized nation. But what kind of nation do we have? We used to be a nation of wooden ships. Now we've got steamships, and even if they're not much, they're still steamships! They may be slow, but they're better than wood! Nitpicking is the vice of traitors. Now, when the nation is united in resistance against the enemy, we must tighten our belts and give what's asked of us, whether it's money or the sweat of our brow. That is the true spirit of a son of Han, the legacy of the Yellow Emperor."

His lecture finished, he pulled his head back in through the hatch and headed below-decks, just as Ma Bo'le woke up.

Bo'le had been sleeping so soundly that he was aware only that someone was speaking somewhere above him. Ever since the Song River Bridge, he wanted to do nothing but sleep, and it was getting increasingly difficult to get out of bed, his body ached so.

The ship's owner had reached the bottom of the ladder.

His eyes bloodshot, Ma Bo'le asked him:

"What's going on?"

The man shrugged with a smile.

"I've got this two-thousand-yuan rust bucket insured for eight thousand. If it capsizes, I collect the insurance money, while as long as it stays afloat, I make two or three hundred on each passage. Now you tell me if it's worth it, friend . . ."

He gave Ma Bo'le a couple of slaps on the shoulder.

Ma Bo'le was ready to curse the man—Bloody Chinese!—but the slaps on the shoulder, which proved that the fellow held him in high regard, changed his mind.

"Which insurance company?" Ma Bo'le asked. "Who would insure a ship like this?"

Ma Bo'le's father had once been in the insurance business, and Bo'le had spent time hanging around the office. He knew a thing or two about insurance.

The ship-owner winked.

"The rules were bent a little, but that's how things are done in China." He was in such high spirits that he slapped Ma Bo'le on the shoulder again.

"I tell you, friend," he said with merry confidence, "in China, anything's possible as long as you're willing to bend the rules!"

Just then, Ma Bo'le's wife descended noisily down the ladder, carrying Jacob in her arms and dragging Joseph by the hand. As she reached the bottom she overheard them talking about the ship.

Being a cautious woman who was always afraid of trains derailing, any talk of capsized ships was normally taboo to her. But not now. After hearing the man out, her reaction was one of indifference, as if she had no regard for her own life. She turned to her husband.

"Paul, see how someone can quickly turn an investment of two thousand yuan into ten times that . . . why couldn't you buy a cheap ship like this and get it insured? Then even if it didn't capsize, you could make two or three hundred on each trip. If it did, you could collect the insurance money."

"It's not as easy as you think," he said. "You can't insure a ship that's falling apart. Who's going to insure a ship today that will probably capsize tomorrow?"

"Bend the rules!" suggested the ship-owner.

"Excuse me?" Ma Bo'le's wife asked.

"Go out and bend the rules!"

Meanwhile, the people on deck were still grumbling.

The ship-owner climbed back up the ladder to give them a piece of his mind. A few of the wounded soldiers gathered round, and one of them said:

"Let's hear what the captain has to say!"

A solemn silence settled over the crowd.

"Why am I doing this?" he asked, then answered his own question: "You people have become refugees in order to flee to safety. And me, why do I ply the route between Nanjing and Hankou? For you, that's why. In other words, I am doing this for China and her people. If not, why would I feel obligated to be in this line of work? Take this ship, for instance; what's to stop me from using it to carry cargo? During a national crisis, everyone has to contribute his share. If a man is armed, he should be up at the front; if not, he should be working in the rear echelon. When you're living the life of a refugee, you must be patient and ride out the hard times. Prattling on and on without helping the situation and sowing seeds of dissension are the attributes of a traitor."

By the time he finished, the lesser issues of the ship's decrepit condition and slow progress had been discarded. The passengers were too intent on contemplating China's glorious future. They were so moved they broke into song with no regard for class standing—workers, merchants, peasants, students, soldiers. They all sang "March of the Volunteers!"

". . . Arise. Stand up and cast off the shackles of slavery.

"Create a new national heart out of your flesh and blood.

"The Chinese race faces its greatest danger;

"We must unite in sprit,

"Brave the enemy's cannonade,

"March forward,

"Forward, forward, forward . . ."

As they sang, whitecaps crashed into the ship's bow, spraying froth into the air.

The placid water off the stern gave no evidence of the waves that were crashing against the bow. The ship was surrounded by a lonely white mist that covered the river and both banks, seemingly lying in wait for a "refugee ship" to swallow it up.

When the clock tower at Jianghan Pass finally came into view, the passengers all had the same thought:

"We made it, we actually made it to Hankou!"

They could not have been happier. They considered themselves children of fortune, a sort of chosen people.

Before long, the ship stopped in the middle of the river opposite the clock tower. They weren't about to dock after all; instead they had to undergo an inspection by the quarantine inspectors, who motored out in a small white launch that looked like a shiny silverfish. The inspectors wore white smocks and caps, and white gauze masks over their mouths.

Their launch zipped across the water, leaving a trail of white caps in its wake. It stopped about thirty feet from the heart of the river, where the chief inspector called out:

"Any sick people aboard?"

"No," answered the ship-owner from the deck.

Satisfied, the inspector waved them on.

"You can go!"

With that the ship carrying Ma Bo'le, as well as two or three victims of dysentery and a man with cholera among the passengers, steamed up to the pier.

These, the chosen people, came alive, so elated they could barely control themselves. They were like someone who has bought the winning lottery ticket. They were so happy they seemed to have taken leave of their senses; they yelled, they shouted, they scampered off the ship and onto the pier, where they scattered to the four winds. None of them—not a single one—paused to take a final look behind. What dangers lay in store for the little ship from this day forward? No one gave it a passing thought.

# Chapter Twelve

Ma Bo'le had reached Hankou, but he did not stay there long. After spending two nights in a hotel, he and his family moved across the river to Hankou's twin city, Wuchang, where his father's friend lived. Back in Qingdao this man had been a Christian, but whether that was still true was anybody's guess. There may have been a hint in the bronze Buddha statue that stood in his living room.

Ma Bo'le had paid a courtesy call on Mr. Wang his first day in Hankou.

"You folks move over to Wuchang," old Mr. Wang had said. "It's a nice, quiet place. We've lived here for nearly ten years. Moved right after we came from Qingdao. Been here ever since . . . we . . . I have a vacant house you can . . ."

Surprisingly, Mr. Wang hadn't lost his Shandong accent after all these years. It was music to Bo'le's ears.

Presently, two plates of snacks were brought into the sitting room, one for Ma Bo'le and one for old Mr. Wang. They were homemade spring rolls filled with bamboo shoots, bean noodles, and bean sprouts, and they looked delicious. Just seeing them was enough to convince Ma Bo'le that life was indeed worth living.

At first he was too polite to eat, but the rolls proved to be irresistible. The appetizing shells, made from egg-enriched flour, were so neat and appealing, and so yellow, they dazzled his eyes.

He daintily broke a tip off of one, put it into his mouth, and savored it. He told himself not to eat too much, to avoid making a fool of himself.

But as he was chatting with old Mr. Wang, he unconsciously broke off another small piece and put it into his mouth.

Their conversation was long and covered a great many topics. Mr. Wang wanted to know if Ma Bo'le's father's insurance company had any shares for sale.

"No, they've been taken off the market."

Bo'le stuffed another huge piece of spring roll into his mouth.

Mr. Wang's next question came before Ma Bo'le could swallow.

"I hear that he donated a parcel of land for a new chapel. Is that true?"

"Not yet."

Into Bo'le's mouth went a whole spring roll.

This time his mouth proved inadequate to the task. It was a little like the train filled with refugees or the little ship and its teeming passengers. There did not seem to be any space left in his mouth. The spring roll was stuck.

Ma Bo'le panicked. He couldn't force it down whole, and he couldn't move it with his tongue. He was in a real jam. Eventually he managed to get it down somehow, although the strain showed in his reddened, tear-filled eyes.

He did not take another bite for a full half hour.

The men chatted on and on, until Ma Bo'le's gaze landed once again on the spring rolls, and he was tempted to pick one up and pop it into his mouth. The maidservant walked in with another plateful of rolls that she'd just taken out of the pan. She held it out to him, but he declined the offer:

"No, thank you, I've had enough."

She put it down beside him anyway.

"Don't eat any," Ma Bo'le reminded himself. "Do not eat any!"

He looked away from them, forcing himself to concentrate instead on his answers to old Mr. Wang's questions. Letting his gaze wander was risky business, so he fixed his eyes on the movements of old Mr. Wang's mouth. Then, while he was amusing himself by observing the man's yellowed mustache, the old fellow opened his mouth and inserted a spring roll right below the bushy line.

As if on cue, Ma Bo'le followed his lead.

He ate one after another, this time without letting any of them get stuck. Down the hatch! Old Mr. Wang was too busy eating to ask any questions. This saved Bo'le the trouble of supplying answers and made it possible for him to finish off the plateful with a clear conscience. When he had eaten the last one, a glistening ring of oil girded his lips.

Having also eaten his fill, old Mr. Wang said:

"Well, are you going to move to Wuchang?"

"We sure are."

What went unsaid was:

"I'd be crazy not to move as long as there are delicious spring rolls like these around."

"What's their Wuchang house like?" his wife asked when he returned to the hotel.

To which he replied:

"Wuchang spring rolls are unbeatable!"

This put his wife in a foul mood during their move from Hankou to Wuchang. She scowled as she boarded the ferryboat and, even when strong winds mussed her hair until her head looked like a mushroom, she refused to touch it. Anger bulged like a balloon. She did not say a word throughout the crossing.

"Mommy, look!" Jacob called out. "That pigeon landed in the river! It's in the water!"

Her mother stood there morosely. Jacob tugged on her sleeve and persisted:

"Do you think it's the same white pigeon that used to fly around our house?"

David laughed at his sister.

"That's a water bird, not a pigeon."

"We don't need you to tell us that," Joseph said. "I know a water bird when I see one."

"How would you know?"

"How would *you* know?"

"I saw a picture of one in a book."

"Me, too."

David did not think much of Joseph's knowledge; Joseph did not think much of David's strength.

Ma Bo'le saw a fight brewing between the boys, so he separated them, commenting to his wife as he did so:

"Can't you see what's going on? Don't you care that people will laugh at us?"

She blithely ignored him.

This ferryboat was remarkably similar to the steamship that had carried them from Nanjing to Hankou. Buffeted by the winds, it creaked and groaned on the trip, which took all of thirty minutes.

The famous Yellow Crane Tower loomed up ahead.

Everything had turned out to Ma Bo'le's satisfaction: he had a place to stay, his refugee days had come to an end, good food awaited, and his wife was with him. His financial problems had ended the day she joined him. As far as he was concerned, life was good and getting better. He was so happy he began to chant the famous "Ode to the Yellow Crane." It went:

"The yellow crane is gone, never to return / Leaving behind only Yellow Crane Tower . . ." From there he drew a blank.

His wife stood nearby, still silent, for she was in a determined mood. Neither water birds nor Yellow Crane Tower interested her enough to warrant a passing glance. She was far too concerned with what their house in Wuchang would be like. She'd been told nothing about it, and her imagination did not come to her aid. Which direction did the windows face? How about the doors?

"I wonder how many bedrooms it has. One? Two?"

The fact that she even had to ask the question displeased her before the words were out, so she kept them to herself. Her anger mounted. Turning to him, she glowered.

But he remained blissfully ignorant as he stood there with his hands buried in his pockets.

"The yellow crane is gone, never to return / Leaving behind only Yellow Crane Tower."

He got so carried away he was virtually shouting, and all eyes were on him.

"Bloody Chinese!" he thought. "Can't you appreciate art?"

The ferryboat nestled up to the pier and disgorged its passengers, who up to that moment had all stood quietly on the decks, but as soon as the ferryboat docked, they came to life. Some leaped over the rails before the gangplank had been lowered; then, once it was down, the remaining passengers swarmed across, the hale and hearty surging into the lead, leaving the very old and the very young cursing and screaming in their wake.

Ma Bo'le picked up Jacob, the motion taking him back to the Song River Bridge.

He was sweating as he walked ashore. His nose, which had not yet healed from the fall, was still bandaged. But there was nothing to worry about. He had a house to live in, and he was set financially.

His wife spotted the bronze Buddha as soon as she entered Mr. Wang's living room. "Well," she said to herself, "it looks like our Mr. Wang is no longer Mr. Wang the Christian." She and the children sat on the sofa, all but Joseph, who jumped up and down on it until the blue slipcover was a mass of muddy footprints.

His mother stared daggers in him, but he ignored her, and her face turned from red to white. She glared at Bo'le, who was continuing his conversation with Mr. Wang from the previous day. Wondering if he'd spilled tea on himself, he looked down at his lapels. Nothing wrong there. *Yackety-yak*—he and old Mr. Wang chatted on.

They kept it up until the spring rolls were served, just like the day before. This time Bo'le limited himself to two.

The snacking finished, they said good-bye to their host and set out with their belongings to the new house, wherever that was.

A servant led them to a small compound at the intersection of Mount Mopan Road, where two large stones flanked the gate, and a loquat tree stood inside. This was to be their new home, at least for a while. Bo'le went up first to have a look—he banged his head on the ceiling at the bottom of the stairs and then stepped on a dead rat when he reached the top. The second floor was being used as a playground by hordes of the furry, squeaking animals.

The house was deserted, but the air inside was not as bad as they'd expected. The only problem was the overabundance of rats, but they could live with that, since rats are afraid of people. They stopped scurrying as soon as Bo'le walked into the room and cowered in the doorway, staring at him with their tiny, shiny rodent eyes. There were at least five of them there, all staring intently at Bo'le.

It was a two-bedroom house.

Ma Bo'le was happy with the place precisely because it was rundown and because it had rats. It fit perfectly into his philosophy of refugee life: frugality came first and foremost.

His wife followed him upstairs, and we can assume that she did not share his opinion of the place.

Once they had settled in, their days took on a sense of normalcy. Immediately after rising each morning, Ma Bo'le stared at the loquat tree beyond his window, soon developing an affection for it. On rainy days its leaves shed their water, drop by drop, and in the still of night the raindrops beat a steady tattoo on the ground.

As he sat at the window gazing silently at the tree, sometimes with a book in his hand, he considered himself to be a lucky man, with food and drink whenever he wanted it and a loquat tree right outside.

He looked ahead to the coming days and weeks with an upbeat mindset. Particularly gratifying was the existence in the neighborhood of a shop called Anyone's Guess, where they sold steamed, stuffed buns called *baozi*. Within days he became a regular customer.

Whenever he and his wife had words, he went out for *baozi*, and after eating five or six of them was able to return home shorn of the anger he'd left with. He put this method to the test time and again, and it never failed.

Anyone's Guess was located only a couple of blocks from where they lived. Above the shop's front door hung a very old white signboard with black lettering, which had the elegant airs of an ancient scroll that had mistakenly wound up above a common storefront. The shop did not advertise and gave no indication, by symbols or anything else, of the nature of the business inside. No one would have known from the words "Anyone's Guess" on the signboard that *baozi* were made and sold inside. The shop relied on word-of-mouth advertising for its flourishing business. No self-respecting man from Hankou would think of visiting Wuchang without making a stop at Anyone's Guess to pick up some *baozi* to take home. Even if he had just finished a meal, he would eat one or two of the buns inside the shop while they were hot, praising their quality with each bite, then walking off after wiping his greasy mouth with equally greasy hands.

There were no seats in the shop. Locals ate hot *baozi* at the counter—standing—and were never given preferential treatment. The shopkeeper charged and treated everyone the same.

No one was ever greeted at the door.

Ma Bo'le ate *baozi* twice a day, as a morning snack and again at four or five in the afternoon. Not content to merely buy and take them home, he usually hung around inside the shop to see how they were made, in preparation for the day he left Wuchang. Lacking an Anyone's Guess to frequent, he could make them himself once he mastered the art.

Like *baozi* everywhere, these were made of flour rolled into cups, filled, and crimped at the top. In this shop, however, a pinch of sugar was added to the flour, giving the buns a slightly honeyed taste. But it was the meat filling in which the greatest difference lay.

Instead of chopping up the raw pork, the owner threw large chunks of meat into the pot, and then chopped it up fine after it was cooked. Even then it had to be braised along with bean paste before it was ready to be made into filling. Nothing else was added, not onions or ginger, and that was the secret recipe for the *baozi* from Anyone's Guess.

Bo'le passed the results of his investigation on to old Mr. Wang, who was one of Anyone's Guess' most loyal customers. In fact, it was he who had introduced Bo'le to the delights of the buns from Anyone's Guess.

Miss Wang, the demure eldest daughter of the Wang family, put Bo'le's praise into perspective:

"Anyone can appreciate flowers, but few can embroider them. If everyone could make buns like that, why would anyone ever open a shop?"

Miss Wang, known for her refined nature, had been one of Bo'le's childhood playmates. It had been ten years since they'd last seen one another. The change was most obvious in her; she had left Qingdao as a teenager and was now a grown woman of twenty-three.

She had been a student at Wuhan University, which was located on Mt. Luojia. Since graduating the year before, she seldom went back, but whenever she thought about the sparkling green water of the university's East Lake, she felt an intense longing to see it again. One of her favorite pastimes had been to go rowing on East Lake, which she could see from the window of her dormitory room. She had taken this pastime pretty much for granted then, but thoughts of the lake now reminded her of the swift passage of time—those few years were like a dream.

During her school years Miss Wang had had a sweetheart. In reality, he was probably just a close friend, but her schoolmates preferred to think of him as her sweetheart. She'd heard that her friend had recently gotten engaged to be married, but she did not know if there was any truth to the rumor. She'd nearly asked him about it the day before, when he came calling, but somehow never got around to it.

She sat for a long trying to compose herself, but it was no use. Her eyes filled with tears as she was overcome by sorrow that seemed to appear out of thin air; as people in the living room laughed and talked, in her room the tears flowed.

For some strange reason, Miss Wang always grew lonely when others were carefree and happy. Not unlike Ma Bo'le.

One day she decided to take in a movie during a light rainfall, so she put on her raincoat, picked up an umbrella, and walked out the door with a determined air. Her mother's objections fell on deaf ears. Once she reached the street, she refused to hire a rickshaw, preferring to walk the whole way. "What right," she thought, "does anyone have to be transported by the sweat of others?" It was shameful.

She walked to the pier at Hanyang Gate, where she boarded a crowded ferryboat, found a seat, and then stood up almost at once for a countrywoman with a child in her arms. As she turned around, she came face to face with Bo'le. This unexpected sight gave her a start.

She and Bo'le had said their good-byes in Qingdao the year before his marriage, so their accidental meeting on the ferryboat had all the elements of their playmate days. At first they did not exchange a word, as they experienced a brief, uncomfortable sense of unfamiliarity, and merely nodded to one another. After a few seconds, he broke the ice with what must have sounded appropriate to the occasion:

"Crossing the river, I see."

That was it—one simple comment.

They did not see one another again for the rest of the crossing, and once the ferryboat docked, she left in a hurry, almost a trot. The uneven pavement was a minefield of puddles, so by the time her frantic dash had taken her to the theater, her shoes and stockings were soaked through.

The chance meeting left Bo'le with a measure of unease, for, after the boat docked, he could not find her anywhere—she had disappeared.

He put the matter out of his mind and strolled over to visit a friend who had just arrived from Shanghai, to see if there was any news worth listening to. There were rumors of fierce battles, and he wanted to know if the Chinese soldiers were holding on or retreating.

He was thinking as he strolled slowly along the bank and looked up just in time to spot Miss Wang running ahead of him, holding an umbrella. He checked his first impulse to call out to her, since he had nothing to say, and he merely watched her widen the distance between them. After seeing her turn a corner, he continued on to his original destination. He was surprised to bump into his Shanghai bookkeeper and one-time garret mate, Chen. After remarking on the coincidence of seeing one another in this new place, they decided to travel together to see the friend, after which Chen informed Bo'le that he was planning to go to Hong Kong, where a job in publishing awaited him. He wrote down a contact address.

The following morning, Bo'le walked to Anyone's Guess to buy some *baozi,* as usual. Since he wasn't really hungry, he nearly stayed home, but the children begged him to take them, and so he did. When they got the buns home, he declined to eat any. Instead he brushed off his suit and went out.

When he returned, little Jacob greeted him with two of the buns held in outstretched hands: "Here, Papa, these are for you."

He went out again in the afternoon. His wife assumed that he was on his way to Serpent Mountain for a cup of tea, so she asked him to take little Jacob along to get her out from under foot. He walked off without his daughter and, surprising even himself, went straight to the Wang house. Miss Wang was apparently not home. Unwilling to admit to himself that he had gone there to see her, he sat in the living room and chatted with her mother before getting up and taking his leave.

That evening he came again. This time he was told that Mr. and Mrs. Wang had gone to Hankou to take in the opera.

"Is Miss Wang in?" he asked the maidservant.

Asking specifically for her surprised the maidservant, who paused before she said: "I'll go see." In the hallway, she asked one of the bondmaids: "Mistress said she was going to accompany her parents to the opera. Did she?"

Before the girl could open her mouth to reply, Miss Wang parted the heavy, claret-colored curtains to her room and stepped into the hallway. She was on her way to fetch water, teacup in hand. It was obvious she had been lying down, for her hair was slightly mussed, her collar button was undone, and she was wearing slippers.

"What's all the commotion about? The moment my mother is out the door, the rebellion begins."

"No, ma'am," was the response. "Mr. Ma is asking for you."

She wondered which Mr. Ma it was.

"On the phone?"

"He's in the living room."

She set her teacup down on the table beside the door and peeked into the living room. As she parted the curtains, she saw Bo'le sitting there. "Paul!" She was so startled she uttered his name without meaning to. It was too late to return to her room to touch up her hairdo and put on some shoes, so she buttoned her collar and walked into the living room.

They sat and almost immediately began talking about Wuhan University. She told him a little joke about one of the professors, over which they had quite a laugh.

After a while, the maidservant served tea, while they sat there as if they were either both guests or both hosts, chatting on and on until nine o'clock, when he finally left. Old Mr. and Mrs. Wang had not yet returned from the opera.

Miss Wang went to her room and started a couple of letters. She was so tired she lay down, but sleep would not come. She heard her mother return home and listened with interest to her talk about the antics and funny makeup of the clown in the opera as she passed through the living room on her way to her own room.

Since Miss Wang had put out the lamp, the room was now lit only by faint moonlight. She enjoyed lying awake at night, for there were so many interesting sounds to be heard. The bells on rickshaws moving down Mount Mopan Road, which were impossible to hear in the daytime, came through clearly. The world seemed to grow smaller at night. She rolled over and, presently, fell asleep.

# Chapter Thirteen

From that night on, Ma Bo'le was a frequent visitor to the Wang house, especially when the children, who were cooped up inside most of the time, were misbehaving. Miss Wang made it a point to be home as often as possible. If she planned to take in a movie or go somewhere else, the reminder that Paul might drop by was enough to make her change her plans.

The Wang's living room often looked like the site of a soiree. Mrs. Wang felt the need to chaperone, and if Mr. Wang had nothing better to do, he joined them. Mrs. Wang often commented to her daughter about how Paul had done this or that in his youth, almost as if it were yesterday. She sometimes spoke with such tenderness she might have been talking about her own son. A friendship that had seemingly ended or had simply ceased to exist after the passage of so many years got a new lease on life. It could not have come at a better time, since the once freewheeling Bo'le had begun to feel constrained by his role as husband and father. Thoughts of "wild-oat sowing" days crept into his consciousness and quickly merged with recollections of the enjoyable times he and his childhood playmate had shared.

One evening, when Bo'le was invited to join the family at dinner (he had told his wife it was Mr. Wang who had extended the invitation),

Miss Wang was called away for a phone call. She went to answer the telephone at the end of the hall and did not return.

Sounds of crying emerged from the rear of the house.

Her mother went to her room and asked why she was crying, but got no response. So she turned on her heel and left, letting the curtain fall closed behind her and leaving the impression that her daughter's sudden tearful outburst was nothing to be concerned about. She came back into the living room, where Mr. Wang had not paused in his discussion about wounded soldiers at the front to ask his wife what was wrong.

Bo'le offered his opinion that since the war involved the entire nation, everyone should do his part. He spoke of his determination to don a uniform and fight the Japanese.

"I even wrote to my father to ask his blessings in my decision to join the army."

"There's no denying that it's the responsibility of all patriotic young men to take up arms," Mr. Wang offered his opinion, "but it's enough for the rich to contribute money and the able to contribute labor. There's no need for the rich to contribute labor too."

Seeing that his talk of joining the army had not struck the responsive chord he had anticipated, Bo'le backed off.

"The army doesn't want intellectuals like me anyway. What I meant by joining the army was to be a medic at the front."

"I don't think that's called for either," Mr. Wang advised. "Who said you have to go to the front to serve the national cause? Our chief commissioner says that the rear echelons are more important than the front lines. We need people here, too. Why, take me, for example: I'm a member of the Price Stabilization Commission. The people's livelihood is of utmost importance, and what is 'livelihood' if not food on the table? There's no justification for raising food prices during our War of Resistance! We're lucky to have a government with the foresight to create a Price Stabilization Commission. We're responsible for overseeing the work of the major commodity organs."

When he finished, he asked Ma Bo'le:

"Are you interested in finding work?"

This took Ma Bo'le so completely by surprise he didn't know what to say. But after a thoughtful pause, he replied:

"Sure."

"Then I can find you a position with the Price Stabilization Commission."

Just then the telephone at the end of the hall rang again. It rang for a long time before Mr. Wang finally rose to answer it.

"I don't know what those girls are doing, but the time will probably come when no one will answer the phone."

It was a business call. After giving two or three short responses, old Mr. Wang hung up and returned to the room

"I stocked up some charcoal," he said to Ma Bo'le, "and now the price has gone up, so I'm going to sell . . . it slipped my mind while we were talking . . . that's what the phone call was about."

With that, he put on a black wool cap and took up his cane, then walked out with the sedate airs of a man upon whom the welfare of the nation depended.

With Mr. Wang gone, Bo'le felt that he should be going, too, since it did not seem right to have Mrs. Wang keep him company by herself. But he could not translate his feelings into action, owing to his concern over the absence of sounds coming from Miss Wang's room. She had probably stopped crying by now, so why hadn't she come out? Bo'le was hoping that Mrs. Wang would find out what was going on, but she had apparently forgotten all about her daughter's tearful outburst. He dropped a hint to remind her:

"The scenery at Wuhan University, where Miss Wang was a student, is quite beautiful, I hear. Have you ever been there?"

"Yes, I have. Guiying took me there in the summer . . . the water is as green as emeralds and there is a lovely mountain behind it . . ."

Taking Mrs. Wang's lead, he began referring to Miss Wang as Guiying.

"Has Guiying tried finding a job?"

"Not yet. That daughter of mine doesn't have the patience she had as a child. The older she gets, the worse her disposition becomes."

Bo'le could think of nothing else to say. He knew it was time to go, but he preferred to stay a while longer. Several more minutes passed, and though he had no reason to stay, he still could not bring himself to leave. He covered his hesitation by leafing through the newspaper. He eventually took leave of his hosts and walked out of the compound through the flower garden.

As he walked past a trellis, he carelessly brushed up against a rosebush and pricked his cheek on a thorn. He felt it to see if the skin was broken—it wasn't—then let his finger wander up to his nose, where he felt the still noticeable scar caused by his fall at the Song River Bridge. The night was clear, the moon overhead full and radiant as Bo'le walked out of the compound.

When he emerged from the lane onto the street, he spotted the nearby military hospital, which housed some six or seven hundred wounded soldiers. Knowing that there wasn't much worth seeing there, he turned back and went straight home.

His wife, who had not yet gone to bed, was doing needlework. The sight made him angry—all she ever did was sew.

"It's late, why are you just now getting home?"

He went over and lay down on his canvas cot.

"Why just now? If I were a soldier, I wouldn't be coming home at all!"

Assuming that something unpleasant must have happened, she ignored him. After a few minutes, she reached over and turned out the light.

• • •

One day Bo'le and Miss Wang arranged to meet at a teahouse, where they talked about the institution of marriage. By then he had felt stirrings, wondering if somehow a budding romance had taken hold.

"Doesn't it make sense for everyone to get married?" she asked.

"Marriage is diabolical."

"If both parties are willing, that's another matter, isn't it?"

"No, it's always diabolical."

The enthusiasm with which he responded earned her sympathy, so she told him the story of her life over the past few years.

That friend of hers who was reported to have become engaged had not only not become engaged after all, but had even proposed marriage to Miss Wang.

She brought the subject out into the open to enlist Bo'le's aid in analyzing the situation from a theoretical perspective. But it sounded to him as if she were using it as a personal rebuke. He withheld his opinion, for he thought it unlikely that the similarity between her story and his situation could be a mere coincidence.

He stood up and recommended that they leave the teahouse and go home. She implored him to stay a while longer, to which he replied tersely, "No," and then walked to the door. She had already found someone else.

Miss Wang returned home, broke out a bottle of her father's brandy, and got so drunk that night that she couldn't eat a bite of food the next day, and instead spent the entire time crying.

Her mother had never broached the subject of her marriage, not once since she had grown into a woman. But it was time to break her silence now.

"If you have your heart set on someone, all you have to do is tell me. If he's a man of sufficient means and good background, we'll be happy to go along." Seeing that no revelation was forthcoming, she tried to coax it out of her: "I've always let you have your way, so if something is weighing on your mind, just tell me." But the harder she tried, the louder her daughter cried, until all she could say was: "Don't cry. Be a good girl and stop crying. You'll make yourself sick."

Miss Wang forced herself to get out of bed the next day. As she and her parents were chatting in the living room, Bo'le dropped by, stopping in the garden to pass the time of day with the gardener. Miss Wang ran to her room as soon as she heard his voice.

Ma Bo'le wondered if Miss Wang's parents thought there was something going on between him and their daughter, since Mrs. Wang seemed somehow distant, limiting her comments to commonplace matters, as if Bo'le were just another visitor. When the maidservant came in to pour tea, he was sure she gave him a funny look. In the hallway a few moments earlier, the young bondmaid had shied away from him as if he were a total stranger. It was a drastic change from his usual reception, for she normally smiled at him gaily, as if he were a member of the family.

Even Mr. Wang did not have much to say to him today, and, after a couple of brief pleasantries, he picked up the newspaper and went inside.

Bo'le wanted to leave, but had worked himself into such a state of anxiety that he couldn't move. Beads of nervous perspiration beaded his forehead. He began to fear that if his blood got any hotter, he might melt on the spot. He was bedazzled and totally disoriented.

The sound of Mr. Wang coughing in his bedroom made Bo'le shiver. A house cat brushed against his shoe, and he thought it was a snake.

"Why haven't we seen Mrs. Ma lately?" Mrs. Wang asked him.

"Why is she asking about her?" he wondered. "Is she trying to tell me something?"

He did not think it likely. What was there to know? He and Miss Wang had seen each other only a few times, and all they'd done was talk. No improprieties. And yet he knew it was time to leave, having gaining an awareness that a fantasy he had created was crumbling. The burden of family, exacerbated by unstable living conditions on the road and fears for the immediate future, had stoked the fires of romantic liaisons, a throwback to his carefree days in Shanghai with a lover and no children to look after. Reality and conscience made for a potent awakening and, for the first time, he asked himself what he was doing and whether or not his wife was aware of what was going on. If so, how could she have remained so nonchalant, so trusting? Bo'le's "midlife crisis" had come early and left quickly.

Soon afterwards, Miss Wang became engaged, and her wedding date was not far off. Two days prior to the wedding, Ma Bo'le received a wedding invitation in the names of her parents. He could scarcely believe that her wedding plans had jelled so quickly. Getting married was one thing—that he could accept—but the urgency?

Then there was the unfamiliar name of the prospective groom. It was such a common name: Li Changchun.

Bo'le ripped up the invitation before he'd even taken careful note of the date. His wife, who planned to attend, picked up the scraps to piece them together, at least enough to get the necessary information. But to her surprise, he knocked them out of her hand before she had a chance.

"What sort of 'noble' family would give their son a name like 'Everlasting Spring'?" he growled. "As far as I'm concerned, they should have called him 'Life's End.'" With this, Bo'le's days as a jilted suitor ended, and *baozi* from Anyone's Guess made its reappearance on his table.

"Long time no see, little *baozi*."

There were tears in his eyes as he picked up his first bun after so long. It was a touching moment.

"How could I have given these up for her?"

After polishing off eight of the *baozi*, he felt that he had more or less paid off his emotional debt and could once again face his beloved steamed buns. So he stopped, went over to his bed, and lay down to sleep.

It was one of the most refreshing sleeps in recent memory. He awakened with a heart brimming over with resolve to fight the Japanese, no doubt caused by the rousing War of Resistance songs on the lips of soldiers who were just then marching down the street.

He ran outside to take a look.

"With all this excitement, who could resist the urge to fight the enemy?"

• • •

Thousands of troops marched by Jianghan Pass singing songs of the Resistance; they marched by night and they marched at the crack of dawn. Troops from Guangxi, from Guangdong, from Hunan, Hubei, and everywhere else came and went in the area between Yellow Crane Tower and Jianghan Pass. Every one of them—old and young, fat and thin—had a rifle slung over his shoulder. Eyes straight ahead, they were the defenders of the Fatherland. A solemn silence fell over the crowds of onlookers, who believed that nothing could destroy the great Chinese nation.

There were a few, however, who lacked vision and whose attention was focused on troops from Guangxi wearing unlined trousers in the middle of winter and shivering in the cold.

"Look at those men in their unlined trousers! We're wearing quilted pants and we're still freezing our asses off!"

Usually it was women who said things like that. Ma Bo'le looked around to see who had said it this time; it was a white-haired peddler in his sixties who was carrying a little basket of fried dough sticks for sale.

Ma Bo'le seethed with anger.

"That's women's talk! I never thought I'd hear it from someone claiming to be a man!" He snatched the old man's basket out of his hand, scattering dough sticks all over the street. A crowd of curious bystanders immediately surrounded them. He had intended to let the miscreant off the hook after frightening him, for though he was infuriated that a useless old man like that could be a son of the Republic of China, his basic sense of humanity dictated that he spare him because of his age. But that was not to be. He had not taken into account the curiosity seekers who gathered round.

"He's undermining the soldiers' morale!"

He wished he hadn't said that, but words sometimes have a mind of their own and actions have consequences. His unwarranted accusation, which would cost him some sleep for days afterward, incited a rickshaw puller to kick the man to the ground. An M. P. walked by and added fuel to the fire:

"Beat him," he called. "Beat the old traitor!"

The ground around them was soon littered with the remaining dough sticks from the basket. The old man, ignored if not forgotten by all, lay on the ground, cowering with fear.

Gone was Bo'le's desire to become a soldier. The more he watched the ragtag column of troops, the more amused he became; and the greater his amusement, the keener his disinclination to join them. Eventually, he concluded that being a soldier was nothing to get excited about. It was the same whether he was one or not, for with all the time he spent watching these soldiers, he could almost be considered one of them. And since he was already living a regimented life, it didn't make much sense to go out and actually join the army.

It did not take long for Ma Bo'le's sadness to return. Miss Wang may have been on his mind again, or perhaps he was growing concerned about his uncertain future. On his latest stroll along the riverbank he was surprised to see that the soldiers had changed, just like him, and that now they went around hanging their heads in dejection. As luck would have it, he spied a group of recently arrived wounded soldiers; they had been sent over from a distant battlefield, and since none was seriously wounded, they carried their bedrolls on their backs as they walked down the street. Naturally, neither they nor their uniforms looked to be in very good shape, and Bo'le was disgusted by what he saw.

"They're a bunch of beggars, nothing but beggars! The defenders of the nation have changed from warriors to beggars."

This sight alone was enough to shift his sorrow into high gear. He returned home, lay down on his bed, and brooded over the fact that national affairs were in the same sad shape as those of his family.

From that day forward, Ma Bo'le's light-hearted mood lessened daily, and even the Anyone's Guess *baozi* did not seem as tasty as they once had. That realization planted a seed. Maybe the purchased *baozi* actually *weren't* as good as before. Then why not make "better" ones at home? In typical Ma Bo'le mercurial adjustment, the very thought swept away the clouds of despair.

"How about you and me going out and selling our own *baozi*," he proposed to his son, David, one day. "Tomorrow I'll make a little box for you to carry on your back. If our food at home ever runs out, you and I can sell *baozi*. I'll make them and you can hawk them on the street."

This turned into a regular routine.

"We'll specialize in selling to the proletariat," he'd say to David. "People like rickshaw men. We'll keep the price low and make our money on volume. Two fen apiece, the same price that sesame cakes sell for. Who could possibly prefer sesame seed cakes to our *baozi*? If I were a rickshaw man who could choose between the two at the same price, I'd pick *baozi* over sesame cakes every time. You can tell they're delicious just by looking at them. Besides, they'll have meat filling."

Bo'le sometimes gave this spiel to his friends and sometimes to his wife. At other times he rehearsed it alone, and when he visualized the buns being snatched up by hungry rickshaw men, he shouted dramatically, as though he were in front of a movie camera: "I'm going to drive the competition out of business!"

On occasion he called David over to run through the sales pitch. His son would strap a little stool onto his back with the legs sticking up and hawk his imaginary wares. "Hot *baozi*! Very tasty—take them into battle and please be hasty! Hot *baozi*! What a fine taste—go grind the invaders into paste! Ding-dong, ding-ding-dong." Bo'le was impressed by how quickly David caught on. The creative pitch gave him a glimpse of his eldest son's verbal talent. Now it was time to teach him a sales pitch aimed exclusively at rickshaw men.

"Rickshaw men, come on over! Have *baozi* to eat, then hit the street! Rickshaw men, come on over! Try my *baozi*—a special treat! Ding-dong, ding-ding-dong."

When Joseph saw how much fun his brother was having running around pretending he was selling food, he tried to wrench the stool off his back, saying he wanted to do it too. But David was having too much fun with his sales pitch to quit, so Joseph kicked him in the shin and punched him in the stomach. David yielded tearfully to his brother, who ran downstairs to sell his imaginary *baozi*, and before long, hit a playmate in the eye and drew blood.

His mother looked out the window and saw her son wielding his little wooden stool like a weapon.

"How dare you refuse to buy my *baozi*!" he was screaming. "Now let's see if you want some . . . now let's see if you want to buy some . . ."

Swinging his weapon with each verbal assault, Joseph looked like a whirlwind as he demonstrated his martial skills.

"He's started a fight," his mother said angrily.

His father reacted happily to what was going on.

"As long as we can sell *baozi*, we'll never starve."

Only a few days later, Bo'le decided to take up sandal repair, which he considered preferable to selling *baozi*. First of all, there was no need to go out and drum up business. Secondly, he didn't have to worry about capital—all he needed was an awl and a length of hemp.

"If someone wants his sandals resoled, what will you use?" his wife asked him.

"I won't resole them. I'll just patch them up."

A few days later, he decided to become a tailor. After that it was a taxi driver, then a paperboy, and finally a performer in a Chinese-opera troupe. But all his plans went a-glimmering, and he soon reverted back to his old habit of sitting at home and brooding.

"Life makes no sense.

"The world is full of crafty merchants and hooligans.

"These endless nights, when will I break out of this tangled web?

"All the people in the world are shackled in economic fetters."

Days of sadness were once again upon him.

He did not take shelter when air-raid warnings sounded, for death would be the easy way out—the horrors of life outstripped the fear of death.

His friend Chen had taken a job in Hankou in the film industry before leaving for Hong Kong. The producer of a movie about the War of Resistance was looking for someone to fill a comic role, and Chen came looking for Bo'le to audition for the part.

Why not? It beats staying at home. But when he discovered that they wanted to make him up like a clown, he turned his friend down. "I wouldn't be recognizable as a human being!"

Ma Bo'le was saddened by everything he saw, particularly true at night, as he watched water dripping off the leaves of the loquat tree outside his window. He ate and slept like everyone else, differing only in his ubiquitous tendency to sigh. Although he was forever burdened with anxieties, he was in decent health, his appetite was good, he slept well, and he took daily strolls. But he anticipated a gloomy future.

This time the gloom persisted for six or seven months. But every cloud has its silver lining. For Ma Bo'le it was the general retreat from Wuhan, as the enemy forged its way into China's interior.

"It's back to being a refugee," he announced.

This breathed life into him. He was like a soldier on the eve of a long march, or a racehorse before a big race. He was bursting with unharnessed energy; no one had better stand in his way.

He jumped out of bed and said:

"Quick, let's buy boat tickets."

"Where to?" his wife asked him.

"Where everybody else is going."

Everyone in Hankou had dreams of fleeing to Chongqing.

# Chapter Fourteen

For the second time in less than two years, the Ma family was on the Yangzi River heading west. It was September 1938, only days after Hankou fell to the Japanese. But this time they traveled in style, to Ma Bo'le's delight and Mrs. Ma's credit. She had gone to Mr. Wang with a request to help get tickets for the family on a ferry still in possession of all its rivets for a trip upriver to the new center of government, Chongqing. The relative comfort in their second-class cabin for the five-day trip through the three gorges, up the dangerous rapids, and past the mountain wall that guards the province of Sichuan was made perilous by occasional strafing by Japanese fighter planes. They sailed mainly at night, stopping in cities like Yichang in Hubei province for provisions and safe harbor. The shipping lanes were busy.

This time there were no port inspections or delays when nestling up against the pier, which put Ma Bo'le in a celebratory mood as he fought his way through the disembarking crowd onto the pier at Chaotianmen Port, where the Jialing River flows down from Gansu to meet the Yangzi. With Jacob in his arms, he scurried past the transportation queue, where boatloads of refugees were waiting with increasing impatience to get a ride into town. Chaos reigned, with battered old buses, rickshaws, sedan chairs, even some pony carts drawn by tiny Sichuan horses competing for fares. His wife followed at a distance, her sons in tow—Joseph already mocking the pier-side coolies for the funny way they talked and David, still green around the gills from five days of seasickness—grumbling as she tried to get the porter with their luggage to move faster.

Probably out of gratitude for the loss of Ma Bo'le as a prospective son-in-law and in response to Mrs. Ma's pleas to his Christian conscience, Mr. Wang had telegraphed a friend in Chongqing, a Mr. Gao, to have transportation available to take the Ma family to a rented house in the Beipei district, in the far north of the city, on the west bank of the Jialing River. They were stunned by the uncontrolled crowds and the devastation from a Japanese bombing campaign that had begun only weeks before.

"Is this what I'd hoped would bring my wife and her money to Shanghai from Qingdao?" Bo'le asked himself, What was I thinking? He wondered how he was going to cope in a place like this with four other mouths to feed. "Maybe she should have just sent the money and stayed home. Now what am I going to do?"

"Bloody Japanese," he muttered. It would take him a few minutes to realize what he'd just said. But, always having his wits about him, he made a quick adjustment: "They're worse than the bloody Chinese!"

"What are you mumbling about, Paul? And what's the matter with Jacob?"

Bo'le looked down at his daughter. He was holding her so tightly she was crying. "Bloody Chinese!" This time he got it right, even though the target of his complaint was his own family. "Maybe she has a stomach-ache," he shouted back at his wife. "I know I do." Turning to the little girl in his arms, he teased, "Want me to let go of you again, like back at the bridge, you little crybaby? You don't see anybody else crying, do you? That's because we're at war, and nobody cries during a war!"

"I told you not to eat those clams on the ship," his wife said. "They didn't smell right. But you wouldn't listen to me, you and your spoiled daughter. You're worse than the boys. At least they said they weren't hungry. David, especially. He's still sick. Look, there's a car, it's probably ours. Go ask the driver. And help me with this luggage."

Ma Bo'le knocked people out of his way as he ran to a black car idling in front of a pier-side warehouse, the driver leaning against it, smoking a cigarette and grinning at the chaos around him.

"Hey, you, I'm Ma Bo'le," he shouted to the man before he even reached the car. "Did Mr. Gao send you to pick us up?"

The man flipped away his cigarette, said something Ma Bo'le didn't understand, and pointed to a rough-looking motorized pushcart a hundred yards or so down the pier.

"No, Mr. Gao. The friend of Mr. Wang in Wuchang, the businessman, my rich father's friend. Understand?"

More grinning, more smoking, and, after lighting another cigarette, more pointing.

By now Jacob was crying harder than ever as she tried to get out of her father's death grip.

"What are you waiting for, Paul? Open the door so we can get away from this mob. David just threw up and Joseph knocked a little girl down. I'm at my wit's end and all you can do is stand there and stare. Snap out of it!"

"It's not our car," he said in a choked voice. "This moron, who doesn't even speak real Chinese, keeps pointing to that thing." Now it was his turn to point.

"That's for us?" his wife exclaimed. "How are five of us and our luggage supposed to ride in that?"

But that is what they did, once the man sitting up front assured him that Mr. Gao had sent him for Mr. Wang's friends. It took several repeats for Ma and his wife to understand the man's singsong accent. He showed no sign of helping them with their luggage, but he did wait till everyone was seated before chugging off, releasing a noxious cloud of burning vegetable oil. Happily for all—anxious Paul, his fuming wife, sickly David, uncontrollable Joseph, and terrified Jacob—the Beipei district, where they were headed, was not far from the docks. Days later, once they had settled in, they would talk about the seemingly endless ride that had made their teeth chatter and their joints ache; faulty memories are a boon to wartime survivors.

It was early May, when clear skies had appeared after the winter fogs exposed the city to waves of Mitsubishi bombers of the Imperial Japanese Navy, flying wingtip to wingtip as they released their bombs over the helpless city. The bombing campaign would continue through July, with thousands killed and hundreds of buildings destroyed. At first the Chinese had no answer to the attacks; the city's residents simply lived in a constant state of panic, until an alert system was finally worked out. Ma Bo'le knew nothing of that, of course, but his imagination filled his head with terrible images of death and destruction. He kept looking around. "There must be a way out of this," he thought aloud. "Why did I urge those runty Japanese to hurry up? I thought they'd never come, and now they might never leave? What *was* I thinking?" In his head he had already begun the hunt for an exit, near or far.

Chongqing, China's newest melting pot, swollen with hordes of downriver refugees who were bringing new customs, new demands, new dialects, and new problems to the city, was adapting slowly and poorly to its new status as the temporary seat of government. It was not a comfortable or pleasant place to begin with, and was now made nearly intolerable by Japanese air raids. Bombed out buildings were replaced with flimsy, temporary structures constructed of mud and bamboo in which people were forced to live and work. It was noisy and dirty and smelly. Its climate, one of the country's worst, was an ideal choice for the national government headquarters, for in such an atrocious climate there were few weeks in a year in which Japanese bombers could visit the city. But for people from Shanghai, Wuhan, and points east and north, it was a terrible place, unworthy of the horrors they had endured during their flight from approaching war.

Food was expensive and in limited quantities and varieties. Once the enemy had blockaded China's coastal cities, imported goods reached the hinterland only in small amounts trickling in from Hong Kong and over the Burma Road. That often led to profiteering and hoarding. Mrs. Ma, who had recently enjoyed the luxury of a private kitchen and well supplied markets, adapted to the new environment better than the other members of her family. There was still enough money to take them through the hard times, as long as those times did not last long, and her ability to cook whatever the local peddlers could provide kept her family well, if not happily, fed.

Bo'le and his eldest son held on to their dream of preparing home-made stuffed buns to sell to neighbors or, if that was asking too much, to coolies who supplied the neighborhood with labor—from delivering water to repairing collapsed bamboo structures and transporting them in their rickshaws and pushcarts, motorized and human-powered. Memories of the *baozi* from Hankou's Anyone's Guess, as well as the oily spring rolls in Mr. Wang's home, would sometimes sustain and sometimes torment Bo'le in the coming weeks and months of relative deprivation. That, as much as the prospect of earning a bit of money selling the buns, was a driving force to become a food peddler. If he ate only one out of every ten they made, his craving would be satisfied at little cost to the family.

"Where do you expect to get meat for the filling?" his wife said after David told her what he and his father had in mind. "Have you forgotten that you entertained the same idea back in Hankou? Tell me, how did that turn out? Besides, what will our neighbors think if they see you two peddling *baozi* for two fen apiece? We may not be living like we did back home—which is where I'd rather be right now—but let's not take pride in living like refugees."

That incensed Ma Bo'le. Being a refugee was a mark of honor to him, however unpleasant it got to be. If you weren't a refugee, you were either a member of the despised (to him, at least) upper class, who lived a life of luxury in big houses and cars that ran on gasoline, or you were, worse, a traitor. He would not let his pampered wife turn his children into traitors. Like him, they were refugees, and if they felt like eating fried rice once in a while (who didn't?), chose to sleep in comfortable beds, and enjoyed street food, which helped a poor man support *his* family, he preferred not to consider them as traitors. Peddling inexpensive food was what refugees did, with pride.

There were, however, more practical matters to be dealt with.

The Beipei district had so far been spared the devastation dealt to other parts of the city, despite the proximity of a makeshift and heavily guarded armory. Before the war, residents had lived in houses passed down by their ancestors in relative comfort, if not opulence. In recent years maintenance had fallen off for obvious reasons. The house Bo'le and his family were living in needed attention in enough areas to keep him busily occupied, mainly doing things for which he was spectacularly unqualified. Not one to ask for help with unfamiliar jobs, he rose to the occasion, often under his wife's tutelage, achieving nearly as many successes as failures. The house was in no danger of falling down any time soon.

As in Shanghai, Bo'le seldom strayed far from the neighborhood where he lived. A mixture of local residents, long-term visitors, and recent refugees occupied the squat houses, many partitioned to accommodate multiple families, a few cheap hotels, and some odd shelters. Noisy and chaotic, they were the source of a fog of cooking smells, outdoor toilet facilities, and smoke from coal briquettes. Rats, of course, kept the humans company. Many of the structures were occupied by students at universities that had relocated to Chongqing from besieged coastal cities like Shanghai.

Not long before sunset one evening, Ma Bo'le left the house in the midst of a squabble involving his wife and two of three children, unmindful of the shouts for him to stay inside. He walked down Benyue Road in the provisional university area, scouting possible routes for peddling *baozi*, once he and Joseph figured out how to make them. He stopped abruptly when he spotted a ramshackle building with a cross over the door. "Well, I'll be, a Christian church. Wonder who goes there." He walked up for a closer look just as a cluster of people emerged in animated conversation.

"Everyone made it out alive, praise the Lord," he heard someone say. What caught his attention was not the sentiment, and certainly not the reference to the Lord, but the accent—it was someone from home. He rushed back to tell his wife that there were people from Qingdao in the neighborhood, and not just anyone, but Christians. She could hardly believe her ears, and demanded to know more. Relishing his far-too-seldom role as deliverer of worthwhile information, Bo'le gave her what amounted to a step-by-step account of his excursion that morning, including an expanded, and totally fabricated, version of the conversation among the parishioners. For one of the rare occasions in their married life, she was happy to let him ramble on without interruption. Mrs. Ma, who had lived uncomfortably among southerners ever since leaving their home in Qingdao, wanted to know every detail. After he finished with a flourish, she responded with determination:

"That's where we're going next week, all of us. It's time to get reacquainted with Jesus." With a look that invited no objections, she turned to the messenger of the welcome news and said, "He is our weapon against China's godless invaders and a guarantee that your father will be proud."

No objections were forthcoming.

Bo'le, who had more or less forsaken his Christian roots, had hoped for something more in the area of congratulating him for finding a prospective clientele for local food specialties, like nicely filled stuffed buns. But at least she hadn't reacted negatively to his discovery, and joining a church could satisfy both desires.

On the following Sunday morning, Ma Bo'le, his wife, and their three children, dressed in the best they could manage, took their first outing as a family beyond the immediate neighborhood, following his imagined peddler's route to what turned out to be the Beipei Christian Missionary Church on Yutang Wan, off quiet Benyue Road. They walked proudly through the front door, where a mixed congregation of mainly older people sat in makeshift pews as a middle-aged man—the pastor, they assumed—spoke to the twenty or more citizens in front of him.

"Praise the Lord!" Mrs. Ma uttered, creating an immediate silence as heads turned to see the newcomers. Welcoming smiles told her that it had been a wise move. "Praise Jesus!" she announced louder, just in case.

The pastor interrupted his sermon to welcome this family of believers, inviting them to find seats in the cramped room. Four members of the Ma family did just that, all but member number four—Joseph—who struck out for a table by the window, where a modest arrangement of snacks awaited the conclusion of the service. He dug in. This unmannerly, but not uncharacteristic act forced member number two—Mrs. Ma—to glare at member number one—Ma Bo'le—who took member number five—Jacob—off his lap, climbed over member number three—David—and dragged the errant member back to the herd.

To the relief of all, the service ended within a quarter of an hour, when the pastor invited everyone to enjoy the light snacks and a cup of tea before reemerging into the chaos of the secular world outside. Mrs. Ma seemed transported to an Elysian field, not by the words of religious conviction, but by the sound of the pastor's voice—she could almost tell where in Qingdao the man was from, and she stopped short of running up and throwing her arms around him (such impulsive acts were the province of her husband).

As the worshippers, all of whom were Christians, but not all from the north of China, stood around eating and talking, introductions were made. One elderly couple nearly cried out loud when they learned the identity of Bo'le's father, for the husband was the man who had polished the transparent stones in a pair of eyeglasses that had found their way onto the nose of old Mr. Ma. He was also the one who had nearly cost himself his attendance at the Ma home by foretelling grand futures for *both* of the old man's grandsons, David and Joseph. Since he and his family lived nearby, they invited the Mas to come to their temporary home to get acquainted. As they made their way, forced to walk single file down a rubble-strewn lane, Bo'le made mental notes of the few potential sites for sales. The residents he saw were poor, but possibly not too poor to buy his inexpensive *baozi*.

After hosts and guests walked in the door, Mrs. Ma began asking questions almost before everyone was seated:

"Do you have news of Paul's parents?"

"Are they all right?

"Has the house suffered under the Japanese occupation?

"What about Paul's younger brother and sister-in-law?

"Is Mama Geng still there? How about the little slave girl.

"Are their possessions safe?

"What's happening to the city?"

She took a breath.

"Is the church still standing?"

She'd almost forgotten that one.

Generally satisfactory answers were forthcoming, although the unknowns were troubling, especially the question about family possessions. While the last telegram received from home indicated that the foreign occupation did not seem as oppressive or cruel as it was in southern cities like Nanjing and Shanghai, some houses had been taken over by Japanese forces, and only by paying out large sums of money had the Ma family been able to stay put. Mama Geng and the other servants had been sent back to the Shandong countryside; upkeep was the responsibility of Bo'le's brother, a young man of decent character and modest talents, and his wife, now ensconced as the sole live-in daughter-in-law.

By the end of the friendly inquisition, Mrs. Ma was in tears, as were David and Jacob. Bo'le and Joseph remained stoic and unmoved. Joseph was, generally unmovable in any situation. Bo'le still fumed over his father's parsimony during his days of suffering in Shanghai, while willing to pay out large sums of money just so he could continue to live in luxury. He appeared not to give a damn about his elder son. Now that China was in danger of being overrun by a foreign power, the term "bloody Chinese" hardly seemed appropriate, although if anyone qualified for that distinction, it was his father.

By afternoon, Mrs. Ma, emotionally spent, gathered her brood around her to say good-bye to Mr. and Mrs. Li, as they turned out to be, and returned home for dinner and a rehash of the morning and afternoon's events. Thankful to her husband for the discovery, she went into the kitchen to make fried rice, minus the hard-to-get eggs, for the whole family. He looked forward to that night, after the children were in bed.

Refugees in the provisional capital from the northern provinces were relatively rare, owing both to the distance and to the restraints imposed by the Japanese occupiers. The pleasure in meeting people from home lasted only as long as nostalgic impulses were satisfied, since there was virtually nothing new acquaintances from back home could do to make living in the harsh climate and constant dangers of Chongqing any easier or more pleasant. As a high tide floats all boats, air raids and deprivation dispensed suffering to all.

One of the first things Ma Bo'le's wife did in the wake of the conversation with the couple at church was to locate the local telephone and telegraph office, where she sent a telegram to her father-in-law in Qingdao, telling him where they were and assuring him that they were getting by as well as could be expected. She reported that they had just returned from a makeshift church, where the pastor was from Shandong, and had met an old friend of his (she passed on his name). She asked about conditions back home, and told them she would write to give more details. She did not tell her husband about the telegram, knowing that he would want her to exaggerate their already precarious situation in Chongqing and ask his father to wire more money. After she and the children had arrived in Shanghai, she'd reluctantly shown Paul a bankbook with funds that would allow them to subsist at least until the war ended, which they hoped would be soon, and they could return home. She did not, however, reveal to him that she had come with not one, but two bankbooks, the second worth more than the first, as a hedge against a longer war, unexpected expenses, and her knowledge of what that news would mean to her husband. She was not about to ask her father-in-law to send more, although, like Bo'le, she was concerned that he was depleting the family fortune and her inheritance by bribing Japanese officials who had set up a pseudo government in Qingdao. Requests such as those

Bo'le wanted to make inevitably spawned Biblical exhortations that she had long since grown tired of hearing. Better to appease the old man, and if he wanted to send more money—an unlikely scenario—she would not be unhappy.

Ma Bo'le suffered more than most people, not only because he was forced to rely on his wife for everything he wanted and answer to her for everything he did, but because the war seemed to be following him. Each escape—from home, from Shanghai, and from Wuhan—had led to new dangers. His sad eyes and hunched back promised a tale of despair, which he was eager to tell anyone who would listen. His wife was not one of those people, and the children were either having too much fun (Joseph), too sick to care (David), or too young to understand (Jacob, his pet).

Now that he had traveled as far west as possible, there was nowhere to run to if things got worse. His mantra of "Then what'll I do?" had become unanswerable, whatever the "then" might have been in his apocalyptic vision of the future. The "bloody Japanese" had taken away all his sites of refuge, provided no discernible exits, and turned him into a hopeless refugee; the sadness that regularly descended on him increased the distance between him and his family. Since they were doing fine (all but David), why wasn't he? Because he was Ma Bo'le, and they weren't.

Ever since learning that bookkeeper Chen, whose health had begun to improve when he'd found work at the film studio in Wuhan, had flown to the British colony of Hong Kong, Bo'le considered the possibility of joining him one day, since the Japanese would surely never attack the white foreigners. Or would they? Chen did not think so, but Bo'le, who had spent all that time in the foreign concession areas of Shanghai, wasn't so sure. His natural pessimism assured him that bad as his situation was at the moment, it was only bound to get worse, wherever he was. And, let's face it, Chen had never impressed him as particularly loyal or competent. No, he'd have to stay put, for now at least, and hope that the Japanese would go home as soon as they got whatever they'd come for.

Ma Bo'le had never been a fan of popular sayings—he preferred to create his own comments on life. But now that he was as far from his family home as he would ever be, forced to dress and eat and be entertained in ways he'd never imagined, he found the saying "when going to a new place, adopt local customs" or, as Pastor Ma back in Qingdao was fond of saying, "When in Rome do as the Romans do," suddenly useful. Now that his suits rested in a suitcase somewhere under the Song River Bridge, along with all the ties he'd brought south from Qingdao, he began dressing like the locals, wearing whatever he could throw together, a combination of Western attire and more traditional Chinese wear sold by local shopkeepers, including cloth shoes and sandals. Since they had arrived in the spring, only weeks ahead of the furnace-like summer, he and the children wore as little as possible, and even that did little to stem the flow of sweat and the appearance of a variety of skin problems like heat rash. Naturally, that affected David the most, but even Joseph sometimes had to be stopped from scratching himself bloody. When she itched, Jacob just cried.

Getting around was another challenge, especially owing to Bo'le's long held beliefs about the rich, whom he spurned, and the poor, whom he pitied. To get into town, the choices were few. He could try to squeeze onto one of the few buses and risk injury to life and limb. Always crowded to near bursting, the aged vehicles, which ran on whatever fuel was available, were long past retirement age, but could not be replaced. The cost in terms of money was low, but in terms of comfort, ease of travel, and temperament, it was far too high for him. The only viable alternative were the rickshaws, vehicles he had refused to ride in back home, owing to his professed distaste for having one man pull another, and by the way his father had used and abused the family puller, all, of course, in support of the Christian adage that hard work is good for the soul. Even worse for Bo'le's tastes were the bamboo sedan chairs, used to carry passengers, mostly bound-footed women, up and down Chongqing's long flights of stone steps to the rivers and over the many hills, the sedan-carriers' blood pumping proudly as they shuffled along, seemingly holding their breath in order to hear the sound of their own straw sandals against the stony ground.

Children carrying shoes on shoulder poles or crates of vegetables on their backs, old men and their oxen, woman herding the increasingly rare pigs to market, and idle strollers like Ma Bo'le all gave way to these coolies, who sped along like a fast-moving, unstoppable stream.

Ma Bo'le felt a degree of pity for the hard-working sedan carriers, but could not deny the floating customer base they provided for his entrepreneurial activity of selling homemade stuffed buns. For the first time in memory, he was beginning to consider making the best of a bad situation, rather than complain about the unfairness of life, at least where he was concerned. Also, in uncharacteristic fashion, he convinced himself that the war would end one day—a day he needed to begin planning for.

# Chapter Fifteen

One morning, during one of Mo Bo'le's aimless walks around the neighborhood, a man and woman speaking Japanese came down the street toward him. "What's going on?" he nearly blurted in complete shock. "Who are those people and what are they doing here? This spells trouble." When they reached him, they smiled and said "Good morning" in Chinese before entering a walled compound at the end of the street. He ran home, where his wife was preparing broth for sickly David and trying to keep Joseph from storming after rats with a broom.

"We're in big trouble," he said breathlessly. "We have to get out of here, it's not safe, there are spies among us!" He collapsed onto the bed and buried his face in his hands, knowing there was no place they could go from here. All they could do was wait to be buried in rubble as the agents of death flew back to report to their emperor that the Chinese people were all dead or dying, that the nation was lost, and that five thousand years of recorded history had come to an end.

His wife stopped what she was doing and looked at him as if he had finally lost his mind. David burst into tears, Joseph, the future high-ranking military officer, whooped his delight, and Jacob slept on.

"Stop that, Paul! You're scaring the children. What did you see?"

"A couple of Japanese walking in our neighborhood without a care in the world."

"Where did you see them?"

"Right outside, on the street, proud and arrogant as can be. They were speaking Japanese until they saw me, and then switched to Chinese, so I wouldn't know who or what they were. But oh, I knew. Don't forget, before we left Qingdao, I had lots of experience with the Japanese. I watched how their sailors went around raping and killing and stealing . . ."

"Nonsense!" she said. "All those sailors did was come in their ships, walk around town, visit Japanese residents, and sail back home."

"That shows how much you know. They've got spies everywhere, and one day we'll wake up to see a flag with a big red dot in the middle flying over the city."

"Where exactly did you see these terrible people?"

"Not two blocks from here. They went into a building behind a high wall."

"The one with a blue door?"

"That's the one."

"You can forget your secret-agent theories. They're Japanese dissidents. I met them at the market a few days ago and had a chance to talk to them. Her name is Chitian Xingzi—I forget how she pronounces it in Japanese—and he is Mr. Ludi Heng. They live with another woman, who teaches an international language they call Esperanto, or something like that, to local university students. We see them in the market every day. He's a journalist and she was a famous ballroom dancer in Japan. They're wanted by the Japanese authorities for antiwar activities. He's written stories exposing the cruel behavior of the Imperial Army and Navy. They both speak Chinese and are very friendly. Tell me, how many Chinese actually greet you out on the street?"

"Esper—what? What kind of language is that? Japanese secret code, I'll bet. Don't be fooled. Remember what their sailors did in Qingdao only a few years ago. That blue door is probably a sign to the pilots not to drop bombs on them."

"Paul, you're a fool."

"Better a live fool than a dead sage. I'm telling you, keep your distance from people like that."

Whenever he was out of the house, Bo'le was surrounded by a glut of incomprehensible dialects, thanks to the influx of refugees from all over the country. Not understanding what people were saying had not bothered him much in Shanghai, since his demeaned, impoverished circumstances had kept him indoors most of the time. Never a particularly gregarious northerner, he shunned "locals" whenever he could. That included not only Shanghai, but Hankou as well, his visits to Anyone's Guess the one major exception. In Chongqing he had needed to get away from his squabbling children from time to time to keep his sanity, which put him in contact with all sorts of people, who, fortunately, had no more desire than he to converse with strangers.

One Monday afternoon, as he was out walking after a weekend of air raids, he went up to a noodle stand and asked for a bowl of spicy rice noodles. The man at the counter did not understand Ma's accent. Ma gesticulated, fanning his mouth with his hand and shaking his head, so it wouldn't be too spicy, but did not do well enough to get his point across. As his frustration mounted, a man stepped up and asked if he could help. His accent was pure Shandong—music to Ma Bo'le's ears! He introduced himself, told the stranger he was from Qingdao, and said he was hoping to get a bowl of spicy rice noodles. Five minutes later, he and his new friend, who spoke to the proprietor in the local dialect, were both enjoying a bowl of the Sichuan treat. The man was from Qufu, the Shandong birthplace of Confucius, and, like his forebear, his name was Kong. Within minutes they were chatting as if they'd known one another for years, Ma Bo'le characteristically painting the saddest picture of life in Chongqing he could manage, whether he actually believed it or not.

Following an hour or so of pleasant talk, they arranged to meet again and then went their separate ways.

"What are you smiling about?" Bo'le's wife asked when he walked in the door, suffering a minor shock at seeing her usually downcast husband with a wide grin on his face. "If you knew how to whistle," she said, "I think that's what you'd be doing next. What's going on?"

"I just had a bowl of noodles with Lao Kong."

"Who's that?"

"Lao Kong. He's from Qufu. A really smart guy. He can already speak the local dialect. He says he can speak half a dozen dialects, and he knows a lot more English than anyone in our family. 'Beer. Boy. Good-ah ma-ning. Hah! The old man had us fooled."

"How did he learn all those dialects?" his wife asked.

"He says he absorbed them as he passed through regions along the way from Shandong to Chongqing. He came here because he wants to help the government stand up to the Japs. He says they're turning North China into a sort of prison. After all this misery from the damned Japs, I've finally found someone I can talk to. He lives on Hot Spring Road, near a local orphanage. I'm going to meet him again on Friday."

"I'm supposed to go to that orphanage to help out Friday. I thought you'd stay home with the children."

"When did you start working at an orphanage?"

"I didn't, but Mrs. Huang, who goes there twice a week to teach the children handicrafts, asked if I'd like to go along one day. We met at the market yesterday, and since you're home most of the time, I told her I'd go with her on Friday. Maybe I can find something outside the house besides cooking, cleaning, washing, and trying to keep the children entertained. So you can arrange to meet your Lao Kong some other day. I'm going to the orphanage."

"Why not get one of the neighbor women to watch the children that afternoon. That way we can go together, and I'll meet Lao Kong there."

"Where were you planning to meet him? And what time?"

"I'm going over to his house tomorrow to arrange all that, it if you can watch the children."

"I can't believe what I'm hearing. Don't tell me you're a changed man, all because of one of Confucius' descendants."

"Maybe I am," Ma Bo'le said, not quite sure if that was true. "All this bombing is starting to get to me."

Over the days that followed, he spotted the couple, plus another woman, walking around and greeting local residents, all of whom did not seem to have the same concern he continued to harbor; he stopped trying to convince his wife after the third time she laughed and called him an idiot over his belief that the foreigners were in reality undercover agents for the Japanese invaders.

He did not mind confinement, so long as he was the sole inhabitant. Add a wife and three children to the mix, and he did not do so well. While the family was fortunate to have space to move around in a city whose populace was swollen with refugees and government hangers-on, Ma Bo'le needed space to suffer properly. One sunny day, as he stood amid the rubble behind their row of buildings, he heard a scraping sound he could not identify. He walked around front and spotted an out-of-breath youngster pounding the ground with a broom.

"What's going on here?"

Though Bo'le knew about the orphanage in the area, he'd never seen one of the children, especially one wielding a broom, if that's where this boy came from. It gave him a good feeling, partly because neither of his sons would be caught dead doing anything that resembled work (like father, like sons), and partly because he knew what it was to feel abandoned, which is how he characterized his stay in Shanghai. Before he could ask the boy what he was doing, he reflected on the fact that even though he heard them raise the flag every morning at the orphanage and sometimes could tell that they were flying kites, they seemed to live a world away from him.

So he stood there watching the boy sweep and pound the ground with the broom, which that was as tall as he was; it looked more like play than work. He seemed to mumble or hum something as he moved the dirt from one side of the walkway to the other until he was red in the face.

"Lin Two," a man shouted good-naturedly as he crested the hillside and walked over to the boy. "What are you up to now?"

"Is that his name?" Bo'le asked the man, who wore a nametag.

"Yes, he's one of our favorites. Officials who visit the orphanage all ask to see him. He arrived from Hankou, where he begged on the streets for years. Then he came to us and quickly outshone the other children in making friends and mediating childish disputes."

"What's the broom for?" he asked.

Lin Two just shook his head and walked up to him.

"How old are you?" Ma Bo'le asked.

Again Lin Two just shook his head. The man said he was eleven. He had no memory of his parents, did not even know his name when he arrived.

"He thought it might be Lin, and since there was another orphan named Lin, an older boy, we began calling him Lin Two. He seemed to like it. He's become a leader of sorts," the man said, "after gaining the trust of the other children and us adults with his winning attitude. He has the uncanny ability of knowing what to do in just about any situation. He's taught us all to make the best of a bad situation." It had taken Ma Bo'le a lot longer than Lin Two to achieve that worldview.

Bo'le smiled. Thanks to Lin Two, it seemed there might be hope for the country after all. He turned and walked inside, where Jacob was bawling, Joseph had pinned his brother to the floor and was pulling his ears, and Mrs. Ma was clearly looking for help or a fight, one or the other, or both.

"Bloody Chinese!" Mo Bo'le sputtered as his hopes were once again dashed. He slammed the door on his way out, but an air-raid warning stopped him in his tracks. The door opened and out rushed Mrs. Ma and the children, heading to the local shelter. Ma Bo'le joined them.

The raid on this day targeted a distant district, where muffled explosions still made the ground shudder. Once inside the shelter, Bo'le looked around to see who else had made it there. The three "spies" were huddled in a corner, looking not afraid, but pensive. Once the squadron of airplanes had dropped their loads and flown back to their base in Hankou, where Chinese spotters notified Chongqing authorities whenever the bombers were on their way, Mrs. Ma dragged her husband over to where the Japanese stood and made the introductions. He was guarded, but not hostile; they were friendly, but not exuberant. Their spoken Chinese was accented, but comprehensible—no worse than some of the Chinese who wound up in Chongqing from God knows where. Mrs. Ma invited them over when they were free. Surprisingly, her husband raised no objections.

The couple and the second woman took her up on her offer a few days later. Bo'le was especially taken by the language teacher—whose name was Midorigawa Eiko—not because she was beautiful, since she wasn't, but because she smiled and complimented him on his outspoken patriotism. He had told them about all his "acts of resistance" against their countrymen back in Qingdao and later in Shanghai. During what turned out to be an unexpectedly pleasant conversation, she invited him to sit in on one of the study sessions with students who wanted to learn Esperanto, which she described as the only true international language. But only if he had nothing else to do, of course.

Ma Bo'le had plenty to do, but nothing that counted as a productive enterprise, though he would not have admitted that. One day he showed up at the blue-doored compound after seeing a clutch of students walk through the gate. She was happy to see him, and introduced him to the class. The youngsters in turn introduced themselves as patriotic university students, most but not all of them local.

Ma Bo'le was no stranger to a foreign language. He knew how to say important phrases such as "Hello, how do you do," in English and felt more comfortable saying "sorry" than "*duibuqi*" when a foreigner stepped on the back of his shoe. It was a start. Compared to the instructors he had observed during his "auditing" days in Shanghai, Miss Midorigawa was not only an effective teacher, but one who instilled in her students the unnatural (for Chinese youth) willingness to be called on and to ask questions. Bo'le found the sessions much to his liking, though it took a while for him to become an active participant.

Over the weeks and then months that followed, he attended just about every study session Miss Midorigawa taught and was, in fact, her most conscientious student. He spent nearly every waking hour not devoted to the few odd jobs his wife would allow him to help with studying the basics of a language he was told was developed in the name of world peace, an elusive goal, to be sure. For him, learning the strange language made him feel as if he could hold his head high around his new multi-lingual friend and it might even help him order food in the future. He was a frequent visitor to the blue-door building, armed with questions only the "*instruistro*," as she asked to be called, could answer.

Contrary to what one might assume, Bo'le's frequent absences and his uncommunicative presence at home were a blessing to his wife. Truth be told, she was puzzled by her husband's interest in studying the foreign language. She did not mind taking care of the children and managing household affairs now that he had stopped complaining about a great many things and appeared, mistakenly as she would learn, to have abandoned his harebrained schemes to bring in a bit of income. The pampered daughter-in-law of a wealthy family with servants was finding this more self-sustaining lifestyle to her liking. She was getting quite good at life on the run, and had hopes that her husband would find himself in the same frame of mind one day.

• • •

Joseph was lost.

One morning, after breakfast, Ma Bo'le went down the street to ask his *instruisto* some questions about the Esperanto dialogue in a book she had lent him entitled *Eta Peter*. She wasn't in. Back home his wife sat their sons down to continue a lesson in a Chinese character book she'd brought from home. Jacob, with a scratched face and a bruised arm, was sitting in the corner, sniffling over being yelled at by her mother for fighting with playmates at the orphanage. The first time Mrs. Ma tried teaching the boys how to write characters, she realized that she should have brought two books or worked with the boys separately. The problem, as always, was Joseph, not just because he was a terror much of the time, but because he bedeviled his older brother as a matter of pride. And now she had Jacob to deal with.

"That's not how you write that, stupid!"

"It is so."

"Is not!"

"Stop that. You're both right. David is writing it in cursive, Joseph. You're making it the simple way."

"Granddad liked the way I write. He said my writing is bold. David writes like a girl."

"I do not!"

"Yes, you do, Miss David."

"Mother!" Nothing brought tears to David's eyes quicker than being called a sissy. This was one of those times.

"That's enough, both of you. Joseph, keep your hands to yourself, and stop being a brat."

Bo'le walked in with his copy of *Eta Peter*, saw what was happening, and immediately turned to walk back outside.

"Stop right there! Where do you think you're going? Wherever it is, take Joseph with you. I don't have a minute's peace when he's around. Look, your other son is about to cry, and when that happens, Jacob joins in. I've got things to do. Joseph, put on a jacket and go with your father. Besides, I'm supposed to spend a few hours at the orphanage. I can take David and Jacob with me." All three children perked up at the news, Joseph because he was getting out of the house with his usually inattentive father, which opened all sorts of possibilities; David, who was quiet and timid at home, tended to come out of his shell when there were playmates with similar temperaments; while Jacob simply rejoiced in the prospect of not being bullied by Joseph for a whole afternoon and looked forward to the lunch all the children were served at the orphanage.

Bo'le had not planned to go anywhere. He thought he'd practice a bit of Esperanto dialogue at home, since Instruisto Midorigawa was not home to answer his questions, and then work on the only pair of leather shoes he'd brought from Hankou. Cleaning the mud from the soles and around the edges with a stick was a legacy from his down-and-out days in Shanghai. The difference now was that he cleaned the tops with a rag and added a bit of color with coal dust and water, though that did not last long. But when he saw what was happening in the house, he instinctively turned to run without even taking off his jacket. The last person he wanted to spend the morning with was his younger son; the last person that son wanted to be with was his mother. Joseph won.

It was a cold, cheerless day, with a customary layer of fog drastically lowering the visibility. That, of course, wasn't always a bad thing, since bombed-out buildings and pitted streets did not offer anything worth looking at, and the fog kept the enemy planes in their Hankou hangers. Father and son were barely out the door when Joseph picked up some rocks and started flinging them at anything that moved.

"Stop that! You might hit somebody."

"I don't care."

"Well, I do, and your mother certainly would."

"She won't care. All she cares about is that sissy David."

"She doesn't play favorites."

"She does too, and so do you—all you care about is that crybaby Jacob."

"That's nonsense."

"No it's not. You both hate me. Grandpa's the only one who lets me do what I want."

It was at times like this that Joseph's father wondered if anything in the world could tame his own father's spoiled grandson. Not normally given to thinking much about anyone, let alone his incorrigible middle child, thoughts of Lin Two, the little ex-beggar who was such a hit at the local orphanage, raised an inescapable conclusion: Joseph was one step from becoming a little monster. He could imagine the boy one day getting into serious trouble or turning his back on his own parents, almost, it seemed, a family trait. What in the world could he, a man who had played virtually no role in the upbringing of his son, do to rectify the situation? Nothing came to mind.

As they walked along aimlessly, both grumbling, but for different reasons, some people out for a stroll in the safety of the dense fog emerged up ahead. It was Ma Bo'le's *instruisto*, Midorigawa, and the Japanese couple. He greeted his teacher in Esperanto:

"*Bonan matenon.*"

Miss Midorigawa smiled. "*Saluton.*"

"I have some questions about *Eta Peter*," Bo'le said. "Funny meeting you here."

"Do you have the book with you?"

"Right here."

"Let's go to our place and get out of the cold. We can talk there."

The four of them walked the short distance to the building with the blue door, Ma Bo'le trying out some of his Esperanto on the way:

"*Kiel vi fartas?*"

"*Mi fartas bone, drank on.*"

"*Ne dankinde.*"

Midorigawa's hosts, who were ignorant of Bo'le's earlier suspicion that they were spying on the neighborhood for their fellow Japanese, were impressed by his diligence. He appeared to be doing well with the difficult language. While Bo'le had no trouble entertaining racial prejudices, he appeared to be in the process of moderating, at least temporarily and selectively, his abhorrence of the squat invaders who had chased him from city to city, thanks to the reception he'd been given at the residence of the three Japanese intellectuals.

"Where's your son?" Mr. Kaji asked suddenly as soon as they walked in the door.

"What?" Ma Bo'le had forgotten all about Joseph, who was nowhere in sight. He ran outside.

"Joseph!" he shouted.

No answer.

He tried again. "Joseph, stop hiding and get over here."

Still nothing.

For the next several hours, after saying good-bye to the Japanese, a panicky Ma Bo'le searched for his son, shouting his name until he was hoarse. There was no answer. He startled the few people he encountered as he walked aimlessly, calling out for the boy.

Joseph was truly missing.

It had been a long time since Bo'le had gone on one of his poetic rants, but the current situation certainly called for it.

"Now what? I can't go home without Joseph. What am I going to do? That damned kid, just like the bloody Chinese."

"When a child goes missing, his parents worry.

"When his parents worry, people feel sorry for them.

"When people feel sorry for them, they feel guilty.

"When they feel guilty, life loses its meaning.

"When life has lost its meaning, you lose your own son.

"When the child is found, everyone is happy.

"When my wife learns that I lost our son, she'll kill me.

"When she kills me, she'll be alone with the children, except for Joseph. I'll be dead."

Ma Bo'le thought himself into a frantic, cold sweat. The fog took its time lifting and darkness could not be many hours off; his son, maybe dead by now, could be nearby, and he wouldn't know it. He had to keep shouting his name and hope that he'd hear him. Throughout a lifetime of misadventures, some comical, others life threatening, Ma Bo'le had never actually lost one of his children. His heart skipped a beat and he choked up—he was crying.

"Joseph," he sobbed, "where are you? Answer me. He's dead. I just know he's dead. I can never go home again. I'll have to kill myself, save my wife the trouble."

In total despair, he walked in circles, oblivious that the fog had finally begun to lift. He asked every person he encountered if they had seen a boy alone. No one had and no one would have taken note if they had, since children out alone were a common and heartbreaking occurrence. Bo'le was at his wit's end, now convinced that Joseph was dead or had been kidnapped, and that he would never see him again. After what seemed like forever, he turned to head home, feeling that his world was coming to an end. Tales of children torn to pieces by packs of wild, rapacious dogs (not true), rumors of children being caught and severely punished by citizens for stealing food and other rare commodities (partly true), and stories of youngsters being hurt or killed by falling rubble from damaged buildings (commonplace) affected him more than any of the horrible events he'd witnesses or imagined during his days in Shanghai.

As he was rehearsing a litany of horrible outcomes, possibly to ease the impact when one of them turned out to be true, he looked up and saw that he was on Benyue Street, not far from the church. His father had said so often that the church was a refuge granted by God that Bo'le was willing to believe—or hope, at least—that it was true. Exhausted and foot-sore, he nonetheless started running and did not stop until he was at the door. He opened it and there, in the arms of a matronly woman, was his terrified son, his face dirty and tear-streaked, his clothes torn.

"Joseph, where have you been?" Ma Bo'le nearly fainted from relief.

"I found him in a bomb crater some distance from here," the woman said. "I didn't know what to do with him, and he was too scared to talk, so I took him by the hand and started walking, hoping he could show me where he lived or meet someone who knew him. When I spotted this building, he ran to it. Now I'm not a Christian, but I've heard people call this little church a kind of sanctuary, so here we are. There's no one else around, so you must be his father."

Joseph ran to his father, wrapped his arms around his legs, and bawled. For possibly the first time in his life, Ma Bo'le shed tears, not of anguish or self-pity, but of joy. The woman walked quietly off with a smile at the reunion she had brought about.

A half hour later, father and son, their tears dried, were on their way home, Joseph hanging onto Ma Bo'le's sleeve, not saying a word. He acted like a different boy, while his father walked like a changed man—for the moment, anyway. Neither of them was about to tell the truth of what happened to Mrs. Ma.

Despite the settling darkness, the rest of the family had not yet returned from the orphanage. Maybe, Bo'le was thinking, they expected us to find something to eat outside; he was not the least bit hungry and relieved that he might actually have time to calm his son down and clean him up a bit. A brief prayer to that end might have occurred to him, but time was not on his side, for the door opened before he could even wipe his son's tear-streaked face.

Once inside, Mrs. Ma herded David and Jacob upstairs so she could throw together a simple dinner. When she saw the panicked look on her husband's face and then the scrapes and torn clothing on Joseph, she gasped. Her first reaction was: "Paul, what have you . . ." but she quickly relented and turned her attention to her son, who was trembling and crying, refusing to let go of his father's sleeve.

"What happened to you?" she asked.

"I fell into a hole."

"You did more than that. Just look at you. And why is he shaking like that?"

"We took a long walk in the fog," Bo'le replied, "having a great time trying to guess where we were, when he fell into a bomb crater. First, he was scared, and then I was. But he's fine, just bruised and dirty. See how happy he is to be home?"

"Are you sure that's all? He doesn't look happy to me."

"What else could there be? Ask him, he'll tell you. He fell into a bomb crater."

Just then there was a knock at the door. Bo'le opened it saw that it was Instruito Midorigawa. What was she doing here at this hour?

"Oh, good," she said, spotting Joseph behind him. "I see you found your son. Where was he?"

Bo'le looked over his shoulder to see if his wife had heard. But she was too busy cleaning the dirt and tears from Joseph's face to pay attention to him and their visitor, or to have heard anything said. The boy was still crying, David was asking a bunch of questions, and Jacob was complaining that she was hungry.

"Everything's fine," he said hurriedly as he took the relieved woman's arm and walked her outside.

"She doesn't know he was lost, just that he fell. She'd kill me if she knew."

"*Mi komprenas,*" Midorigawa said. "I understand. Come by tomorrow and we'll go over your questions on *Eta Peter. Adiau.*"

Bo'le went back inside and was surprised by the scene that met his eyes: Joseph was sitting quietly in a chair, listening to David tell him what he and their mother had been doing at the orphanage: he and some playmates had played numbers games while Jacob napped, and now they were laughing over some of the silly answers. Joseph nodded and tried to smile, but then stood up and ran to his father. There was not a sour comment or a tempestuous act; the word that came to his father's mind, for the first time in Joseph's life, was "docile." The boy had already forgotten that the man he was clinging to had abandoned him, left him alone for hours, cold, sore, and scared silly. He recalled only that a kind woman had found him and brought him to the church, where his father had appeared in the doorway when he thought he'd never see his family again. He had been saved in a church, praise the Lord!

# Chapter Sixteen

Once the winter months arrived, the Chongqing populace could breathe a sigh of relief. The bombing stopped and the city was a beehive of activity, with teams of residents digging more shelters into the surrounding mountains and building them where people lived and worked. Funerals for the air-raid victims were no longer held and burials had been supplanted by cremation. Rubble was cleared, food stocks were replenished, and some forms of social activity and entertainment were once again a part of daily life. Even young men and women met to talk and flirt and try to forget the other realities of their existence.

For Ma Bo'le, winter, one of two horrible seasons in Chongqing, could not have been more welcomed., Since the Beipei district and its sites, including the church in which his wife and children continued to worship, and where he and his younger son had found a form of "salvation," if not redemption, were so familiar, he explored parts of the city that were new to him. One day he strayed into a compound that turned out to be a damaged Buddhist temple of some sort. The domestic religion held as little interest for him as did the foreign Christianity, but the building, which had so far escaped total destruction, and the cassocked monks seemed to beckon to him. His sleep had been interrupted in recent weeks by nightmares of terrible things happening to one or more of his children, usually the already once-lost Joseph: kidnapped and sold to Japanese soldiers for bayonet practice; crushed by a falling building; dismembered; and other images so ghastly he woke up in a cold sweat. Nothing, it seemed, had ever truly frightened Ma Bo'le before, not even the attacks in Shanghai, and not the demeaned existence he found himself in before the arrival of his wife. He even celebrated bad times, as if they were somehow ennobling. But the day Joseph went missing changed that. The fright of losing his son, the feared reality of not having the boy around ever again, and the terror of facing his wife changed him—not completely, but significantly.

And so, the ancient wooden building, a sanctuary to many people, summoned him in through its gate, over which an undamaged signboard announced: Chang'an Monastery. He did not know what he might be seeking there, maybe only a temporary diversion, but he experienced a sense of peace and serenity the moment he entered the main hall, where silence reigned and all the idols wore looks of melancholy: the Long Brows Immortal, the Crouching Tiger Immortal, The Red-Legged Immortal, the Dharma Immortal, and many he could not name from his religion schoolbook, each on its own pedestal, filling the hall on both sides. Only the big-bellied Maitreya Buddha was smiling. Ma Bo'le took that as a sign that Fate had smiled down on him when he found his missing son in a church, and he turned to leave, relieved that, he hoped, the nightmares would stop. He made his way through the muted crowd of worshippers, cloaked in the smoke of a thousand sticks of incense, and serenaded by the ritualistic clacking of wooden fish shapes, emerging into the rear compound, where peddlers were selling snacks to hungry pilgrims. He went over to see what they had.

A pair of small boxes hanging from one peddler's carrying pole held a cornucopia of sweets. There was peanut brittle, sweet puffed rice, and caramelized walnuts. Another man sold seeds and nuts from a long bamboo basket, with white seeds at one end and dark blue peanuts at the other. One coin bought a handful, poured from either one end or the other, to go with a cup of tea or a bowl of vegetarian noodles, all available for anyone willing to stand to drink or eat. The monastery was a favorite stop for locals and refugees—some, but only some—for religious purposes. In earlier days, Bo'le would have cursed—silently—people who were only interested in stuffing their faces and enjoying life. "Don't you stupid people know what's coming?" he would have fumed. "How can you buy snacks when the country is facing annihilation!" Now he envied them. The business of annihilation was on hold, so of course they enjoyed what they could while they could. He walked up to a man who had some still-warm *baozi* in a covered basket.

"How much?" he asked.

"Three fen each, two for five fen," the man said.

Ma Bo'le walked away.

• • •

Six months passed, peppered by the occasional bombing, taking refuge in the neighborhood shelters, repairs, and, for Bo'le, more studying. But still no job, as his wife reminded him often. He did not know how to go about finding work, and the prospect did not appeal to him. What was he good at? What skills did he possess? This was neither the time nor the place to open another publishing house, and he was not fit for physical labor. Grudgingly admitting that they could not rely indefinitely on the money she had brought from home, he took stock of his prospects. By a process of elimination, he arrived at the one thing both he and his sons had dreamed of doing and something they loved to eat, not to mention a popular item among monastery visitors: peddling stuffed buns with a vegetarian filling. Meat was not allowed on the monastery grounds. He figured that without seriously interrupting his studies of Esperanto, he could go out on the street like the peddlers at the monastery and bring in some badly needed revenue.

The first order of business, after nagging his wife until she reluctantly agreed to do the cooking, was to find some bamboo steamers and baskets to carry the buns out onto the street. Then he went back to the monastery and bought two buns, thus saving two fen in the process. He and Joseph ate them once they'd cut them open to analyze the ingredients. He then went to a neighborhood provisional open-air market early the next morning, bought what was available for his purposes, had his wife cook up a batch, and calculated the cost of the ingredients, coming up with a figure of four fen apiece. *Baozi* that looked and tasted better than those in his first batch sold at the Buddhist monastery for one for three fen or two for five. His and David's attempts to peddle *baozi* to the coolie class at what the peddler had charged for two barely made it a single day.

"We'll eat these ourselves," he said to his sons. "A bunch of poor peasants in unsightly rags have a monopoly in this business. We'll have to think of something else." But nothing else came to mind, and he remained jobless. He knew that his wife, mellowed by the highly welcomed weight of responsibilities thrust upon her, would run out of patience one day if he did little but study Esperanto, take walks, and read to the newly obedient Joseph. Even his neighborhood sojourns lost some of their appeal with the knowledge that he was on the outside looking in where family life was concerned.

Despite the realities of refugee life, an aura of normalcy existed in neighborhoods like Beipei. Virtually all available living quarters were occupied—commonly over-occupied—so new neighbors were a rarity. But one day a second, newly arrived Japanese couple moved in with their compatriots, fellow resisters of Tokyo's militarism. They spoke little Chinese, but were happy to share their experiences with their friends' friends. Eager to hear news on the progress of the war and wary of propaganda broadcasts on the radio, Bo'le and his wife called on the blue-doored house one afternoon and, over tea, listened to what the newcomers had to say, interpreted by Kaji and Ikeda. The war, they said, was going badly, especially in places like Nanjing, where stories of atrocities saddened and depressed their listeners. Chinese troops, they were told, were fighting rear guard actions most of the time, and outside assistance from the West was minimal. Bombings were taking a terrible toll, on land and over water. Not long before they arrived, as they were traveling on the Yangzi, they learned that a slow-moving steamer carrying hundreds of passengers had taken a direct hit by a Japanese bomb and, because it was so un-seaworthy, it rolled over and sank, with mass casualties.

"Do you happen to know the ship's name?" Mrs. Ma asked anxiously.

"It was the *Taihei maru*," was the answer.

Kaji interpreted: "In Chinese it would be something like *Taiping lun*."

"That was ours, the Ship of Peace," Ma Bo'le announced unnecessarily.

Wide-eyed, Joseph's mother gave him a searing look, the image of plucked rivets in his hand all she could see. Then she shuddered with the realization that they could easily have been among the victims, but for the providence of time. For some reason, the intervention of a celestial being did not occur to her. She'd seen and heard too much to go down that road.

The latest arrivals left soon thereafter, on their way to Yunnan and, they hoped, Burma, where they had a better chance of eluding the Kempetai Secret Police, who were hot on their trail. Bo'le never did get their names, only that they represented a militant faction of dissidents. Their friends, Kaji and Ikeda, went with them, now that Midorigawa's husband, a Chinese linguist named Liu, had sent word that he was on his way after leaving the Communist stronghold of Yanan. Now her husband and a writer she'd met in the home of another writer, Lu Xun, in Shanghai a few years before had moved down from the mountain district of Geleshan and were staying with her until they could leave for Hong Kong, where people had arranged quarters for them.

Several days later, Ma Bo'le and his wife made the twenty-minute walk to the orphanage, where she had been an eager volunteer since becoming acquainted with Lin Two, who had returned with his broom nearly every day since the first time. She'd introduced him to the children, who had quickly learned many things from their older "brother." He had grown up in Wuhan. After his mother died, his father had put him in the care of a cousin and left for Yanan. Badly treated by the cousin, he ran away and spent several years on the street, along with a legion of orphaned and abandoned children. A friendly missionary had seen him and talked him into coming to Chongqing, where he entered the orphanage. The director and a couple of the other neighborhood helpers wanted to put Mrs. Ma to work full-time to take advantage of her motherly instincts.

After dropping his wife off at the orphanage, Ma Bo'le went to meet his new friend for what he hoped would become a regular walk around town. It did not stay regular for long, as air raid sirens caught them by surprise while they were strolling through a park. Men, women, and children who had been on the street were now thrown into chaos and began to run. Dust swirled in the air as pounding feet sought shelter. Panicky shopkeepers lowered steel grates over storefronts, sneaking terrified looks into the clear sky before taking refuge inside.

In less than fifteen minutes, the sirens stopped and the streets were deserted, as residents hunkered down in air-raid shelters or found refuge where they could. Ma Bo'le and his new friend, assuming that the danger had passed, went outside to make sure. They hadn't gotten far when they spotted an old man who had taken cover under the statue of a lion and was signaling them to come over. They had no sooner reached him than the sirens started up again, and this time they heard the sound of aircraft overhead.

"Can you see them?" the old man asked.

"I count six," Bo'le said.

"Only six? Are they heading our way?"

"It doesn't look like it."

The words were barely out of his mouth when an entire squadron of Japanese airplanes—dozens of them—filled the sky and began dropping bombs somewhere in the Beipei area. The ground shook.

"Look at us, we're good people, we've never done evil things, we're not going to die . . ." The old man sounded more defiant than afraid. And on this day he was right, as no bombs fell on the park. But flames and black smoke were not far away. Bo'le and Lao Kong got up, dusted themselves off, said good-bye to the old man, and hurried to the Beipei district. They emerged onto a road where sedan bearers were carrying the injured down a hill to safety. Bo'le, who had held people who rode in rickshaws and sedan chairs in contempt ever since his days at home in Qingdao, had never considered the possible virtues of that mode of travel. Now he did. Lao Kong led him over to a makeshift tea stand, where some sedan bearers were resting from their backbreaking labors.

There they struck up a conversation with a couple of the spindly, leathery, obviously undernourished men, who seemed ageless.

One of them had a bowl filled with some powder, which he was stuffing into bamboo tubes.

"Is that for firecrackers?" Ma asked him with Kong's help.

"No," he replied without looking up. This is gunpowder."

"What are you making?" Ma said skeptically.

"Bombs to use against the Jap invaders."

"Where'd you learn how to do that? Were you a soldier?"

"I fought against the communists in Hunan."

"The communists have formed an Eighth Route Army," Lao Kong explained, "and they're fighting the Japanese."

"We didn't know that," one of the other bearers said. "We Chinese have to stick together. Maybe we should join them. That's the only way to send those bastards back where they came from!"

They turned as shouts from up the hill alerted them that there were more victims. They unhesitatingly hoisted their poles onto their shoulders, and fell into a syncopated rhythm as they walked up with their chairs.

"I never expected to see so many patriots among a bunch of coolies," Bo'le commented to Lao Kong. "To them it doesn't matter if you're here with the government or in Yanan with the Communists, since we're fighting a common enemy. Maybe I've been complaining a little too much."

"Could be," Lao Kong said. "I thought the coolies and what they were doing was something you might want to see."

On the way back to the orphanage, Ma Bo'le experienced a range of mixed emotions and a nascent sense of shame over his lack of patriotism. Though that would migrate away from his consciousness as personal events claimed his attention, the seeds of national pride and survival may have been planted thanks to some unschooled laborers.

•  •  •

Mr. Li and his wife called on them one day. Bo'le was out with Joseph, but Mrs. Ma was home with the other children. They told her they had bad news. A friend in Qingdao had written to say that the Japanese authorities had commandeered many large compounds, including the one belonging to the Ma family, and that old Mr. Ma had suffered a fatal heart attack when they came to evict him. They had little news about Bo'le's mother or the rest of the family, but they believed that she had left with a few possessions; luckily, that included some valuable pieces of jewelry and gold, which she could sell on the black market to cover living expenses. The Qingdao friend had asked Mr. Li to tell Ma Bo'le and the family not to return to Qingdao, where they had fallen on terrible times. They were rounding up suspects for all sorts of things, and someone had mentioned that Ma Bo'le had been spotted looking in the windows of a Japanese home years before. He was suspected of being a spy, though his actual offense was mere voyeurism.

Realizing the inadvisability of telling Paul, at least for the moment, his wife decided to wait until the next time he brought up the subject of returning to Qingdao. After all those years of marriage, she still found it difficult to predict how he might react to bad news; she did know, however, that he did not handle setbacks well.

Bo'le was still spending several hours each day studying the Esperanto books his Japanese tutor had lent him. He had come a long way since learning that all nouns ended in "o," that every adjective ended in "a," and that the emphasis was always placed on the second syllable. And he was hardly ever alone. The one-time incorrigible Joseph refused to leave his side, sitting obediently while Bo'le studied with his Esperanto tutor, entertaining himself by repeating new foreign words, whether he understood them or not. He went wherever his father went, even began talking like him. If his rice bowl was empty, he'd say "Now what?" or launch into a Bo'le-like monologue:

"When I finish my rice, my bowl is empty.
"When my bowl's empty, so is my stomach.
"When my stomach's empty, I'm hungry."

Bo'le would smile and say to his wife, "Like father, like son."

Then the day finally came for Mrs. Ma to reveal the bad news from Qingdao. There was no way to sugarcoat what had happened to the family back home

"What are you telling me?" a staggered Ma Bo'le uttered. "How could Father be dead? And is Mother really gone? And what about Pastor Ma and his wife? It's gone, everything, it's all gone. We can't ever go back! This is terrible!"

"Now what?" Joseph supplied the key sentiment.

"I know how shocked you must be, and how sad you will be as this sinks in," his wife commiserated, "but now we have to plan for the future. There will be no more money coming from home, and what I brought with me can only go so far. I know how much you enjoy studying, but it's really time for you to be thinking about how to bring in some income. I know I've said this before, but I'm talking about something you've never had to consider before, and that is getting a paying job."

The Qingdao news had barely begun sunk in, and now this. "Bloody . . ."

But more bad news was on its way, news of the sort Bo'le had never anticipated, though he probably should have, since the country was at war, after all. He learned from someone at the church that a letter was waiting for him at the post office. "Who could be writing me here?" he asked his wife.

"We already got the terrible news from home," she said. "Who even knows you're here?"

"Nobody but Chen."

"Well, go get it, then we'll know."

Bo'le returned from the post office two hours later, visibly shaken

"What's wrong? Who's it from?"

"From Lao Chen in Hong Kong. Lao Zhang is dead."

"Who?"

"Big-eared Zhang, I never told you about him. Someone I knew in Shanghai, a friend of Lao Chen's, a good guy who went with him to Wuhan. I didn't have a chance to see him there."

"What happened?"

"He was always saying he wanted to go to Yanan to join the communists and fight the Japanese. I never thought he'd do it, but Chen thought he would. He didn't make it. He was visiting an uncle who taught at the university in Linfen, when a Japanese bomb hit it, and he was assumed to have died along with some students and bystanders. Those goddamned Japs! Why don't they go home and leave us alone?"

Like all refugees who arrived in Chongqing in 1938 and 1939, Ma Bo'le expected to be there for only a year or two. But he and his family stayed on—where else could they go? Throughout the city, broken families were commonplace, with wives and children remaining in Shanghai or other coastal cities, while the men, especially those who came west with the Chiang Kai-shek government, made the best of a lonely life in the wartime capital. Children went without schools, babies went without milk once they were weaned from their mothers, women went without presentable attire, and men went without women. Ma Bo'le and his family were luckier than most, thanks to the arrangement by Mr. Wang back in Hankou. They lived in two small but adequate rooms, plus a makeshift kitchen, with a public toilet nearby. While not as "luxurious" as their accommodations in Hankou, the rooms were a stark improvement over his windowless room in Shanghai. For that he had his wife to thank. She quickly became part of a wives' community, women helping each other get through days of deprivation and danger. She was now working full-time at the orphanage, where her motherly instincts were so strong it surprised even her. The children were drawn to her, even though some of them could not understand her dialect. She acquainted herself with Lin Two and met his friends, all of whom needed more than a temporary mother; it was a start. As one of a handful of Christian families in the neighborhood—however suspect their devotion might be—they went to church on Sundays, clear skies—good weather, no airplanes—permitting. Mrs. Ma would take David and Jacob over to Yutang Wan Street in the morning, where they would sit through the service, followed by a fellowship hour or two, where news and advice were exchanged. Paul and his little acolyte showed no interest in praising Jesus. Praise him for what, for Christ's sake?

A degree of normalcy settled in for Ma and his family during the early winter months. He continued his study of Esperanto and often went for tea or a stroll with Lao Kong, until the man revealed that he was being sent to the interior, though he wasn't permitted to say where or why. Now that she was a regular at the orphanage, Mrs. Ma left Bo'le to deal with their children and basic household affairs. David had started attending a provisional neighborhood school, and loved it. Joseph did not join him, fearful of becoming lost again. He accompanied his father when he went to see Instruito Midorigawa, though he steadfastly refused to leave his father's side or learn any of the strange language. Jacob, being Jacob, hardly made a noise, preferring her own company over all others. The still frequent bombings had beaten the rambunctious nature out of all three children. They obediently followed their father, or mother, when she was home, to the shelter at the first sign of enemy aircraft.

Late one afternoon in November, the air raid warning sent them to safety, and as soon as they were inside, the shelter shook with the force of explosions that seemed closer than usual. It was not unexpected, given the nearby armory. By design or accident, the bombers appeared to have more or less found it that day, despite its camouflage.

When they emerged at the all-clear, a pall of smoke and rubble greeted them. The armory had been badly damaged, but the homes had escaped the devastation. Mrs. Ma, who had stayed home that day with Jacob, who was running a fever, confirmed that the neighbors who hadn't made it into the shelter were safe, and then she rushed to the orphanage, which had not been so lucky. A stray bomb had hit the schoolroom before all the children had gotten out. Three had been killed, along with their teacher. Lin Two was among the victims. This time her prayers were heartfelt, albeit too late to do much good. She did not have the heart to tell the children.

Nothing—not news of his father's death in Qingdao or the loss of the compound, not even the death of Big-eared Zhang—hit Ma Bo'le with the force of the death of the boy who had swept their yard, befriended his children, and so completely won over his wife. It was slow going, but Ma Bo'le was changing, thanks to a smiling, energetic eleven-year-old boy who didn't even have a proper name.

• • •

Early one December morning in 1940, Mrs. Ma walked spiritedly in through the door, told David and Jacob to change their clothes and find something to do, and called Ma Bo'le outside. When Joseph came with him, she sent him back inside. She had something important to discuss with her husband.

"One of the Qingdao women at church this morning told me that her husband wants her to leave Chongqing and go to the British colony of Hong Kong, where he has taken up a position at the local YMCA. She had told him about the Ma family from Qingdao, and he had said there was a need for a Christian man who speaks a non-Cantonese dialect and has some knowledge of English to perform a number of odd jobs. He said that even Esperanto might be a welcome addition, since people from so many places lived in or visited the YMCA hostel. There would be modest wages, plus room and board in the hostel." She wanted Paul to go to church with her the next week and talk to the woman, who would soon be leaving on one of the daily national airline flights to Hong Kong. This was a chance for him to become a wage earner for the first time in his life and lessen the financial burden on her while she remained in Chongqing.

Bo'le, who had made friends only with Lao Kong, the Japanese couple, his tutor, and, briefly, the young woman from Manchuria and her husband, who were staying with her, saw Hong Kong as a welcome alternative to life in the bombed-out capital. Never one to shrink from an adventure or a change of scenery, he nonetheless did not want his wife to think he could hardly wait to be off on his own again. So he refrained from showing too much emotion.

"What about the children?"

"If Mrs. Gao finds you to be a good fit for the job—if you'd come to church with us once in a while, she'd already know you—you'll have a seat on the flight. Her husband sent her a pair of tickets. Take Joseph with you, he can sit on your lap. He hasn't let you out of his sight since that day he hurt himself. Though I'd never have expected it, among the children, he's having the most trouble dealing with the disruptions and the daily fear. He's even having trouble sleeping, so getting away from Chongqing would be good for him. I have enough money for the three of us here for the foreseeable future. We'll join you in Hong Kong after you're settled. Now that your father is gone, you're the head of the Ma family, like it or not. It's time for you to act like it."

At that moment, Ma Bo'le could barely keep from hugging his wife. He turned his back to her to wipe his eyes.

"Are you sad again?"

"No, I'm happy."

She reached out and gave him a brief, unprecedented hug.

# Chapter Seventeen

On January 17, 1940, Ma Bo'le and his younger son joined Mrs. Gao and boarded a twin-engine Douglas DC-2 to make the five-hour, perilous flight from Chongqing to Hong Kong. The passengers were too sick on their first ever airplane ride to carry on a conversation, which the noise of the airplane would have made virtually impossible anyway. Ma Bo'le and his son were green around the gills by the time the plane had landed.

Kai Tak Airport, in the center of Kowloon, a British colony that was on war footing but had so far been spared the trauma of hostilities, was eerily deserted when the CNAC flight carrying Ma Bo'le, his son, Mrs. Gao, and a dozen or so other airsick passengers arrived from Chongqing. The muggy air in the city added to their discomfort. Bo'le and his son set out for the YMCA hotel on Salisbury Road in a car that had been sent for Mrs. Gao; it was a vast improvement over the vehicle that had delivered them to their quarters from the pier in Chongqing. The short ride from the airport to the Tsim Sha Tsui district was a disorienting experience, as they traveled on the left side of streets, which seemed more crowded than even those in Shanghai. Gaudy storefront signs and billboards, some in Chinese and English, presented a stark contrast to Chongqing, where rubble was the predominant sight.

"Do you speak Chinese?" Ma Bo'le asked the baffled driver, who found the northern dialect as incomprehensible as his Cantonese was to his passengers. Throughout the ride, Joseph's face was glued to the window; he was used to seeing bombed-out buildings and littered streets, something the British government would not allow, and was dazzled by all the activity and vehicles.

When they passed the luxurious Peninsula Hotel with its white-clad, gloved doormen (boys, actually) guarding the entrance, Bo'le could hardly believe his eyes. He knew he had entered a different world, one far from the war, a true land of opportunity. His sense of adventure, however, was muted by the foreignness, the opulence, and the hustle and bustle of the place, a far cry from the Teutonic stuffiness of the German concession back home in Qingdao. He could not compare it with Shanghai, since he hadn't explored the city very much at all.

"Hey, look at that, Dad!" Joseph pointed to the harbor, where ferries were shuttling to and from the island across the water.

"Oh, no!" Ma Bo'le blurted out at his own first glimpse of Victoria Harbor, where warships were berthed or at anchor. Images of the Japanese naval "breakwater" in Qingdao years before made him shudder. Then he saw a different flag than the Japanese rising sun and breathed a sigh of relief.

Nathan Road was clogged with buses and cars and rickshaws; pedestrians crowded the sidewalks, on which a dizzying array of shops and street vendors conducted business in a fashion more orderly than Bo'le had seen in any of the cities he'd lived in. He'd heard that the British government ruled with an iron fist. He first witnessed the white man's rule in front of the Peninsula Hotel, where a British official was watching two Chinese policemen beat a man whose load of goods had fallen onto the hood of a green Rolls Royce. His father, who revered foreigners, would have viewed the scene with pride. But not Ma Bo'le.

"Bloody foreigners," he fulminated, "I hope the Japs drive you into the sea!" Pan-Asian cooperation, the Japanese militarists' catchphrase, appeared to have found a bit of relevance in Ma Bo'le.

A couple of blocks later, after dropping Mrs. Gao off at nearby St. Andrew's Church on Nathan Road, the car pulled up to the twenty-year-old building that housed the hotel and a variety of facilities the Association used to promote wartime services and organized worship, plus, as he would learn, a Refugee Relief Section, a War Service Team, and a program called the "Bowl of Rice Movement," serving the poor.

"This is better than I thought," Ma Bo'le said to Joseph, who was clearly overwhelmed by the sights and sounds of Kowloon. "It's the kind of place real Christians come to, not that fallen-down so-called church in Chongqing. Let's go inside and look around."

"Wow!" was the boy's reaction. The place was massive, yet peaceful, serene even, filled with objects and an aura he had never imagined. He was no stranger to religious symbols and rituals, thanks to his grandfather, a true but hypocritical Christian, and his mother, who saw the practical value in acting like a believer. But this was not a church, it was a colossus, a place where he thought he could spend the rest of his life. Such revelations seldom come to a boy not yet into his teens.

"May I help you?" The voice was not loud, but it seemed to echo off the walls.

"What?"

"Do you speak English?" It was a tall, redheaded, rosy cheeked, collared man wearing a beatific smile.

"What?"

"Do you speak Cantonese?" the man asked in heavily accented Mandarin.

"N—n—no."

"Any Chinese at all?"

"Yes."

"So, may I help you?"

"My name is Ma Bo'le, I came from Chongqing. I'm supposed to work here. This is my son, Joseph." He turned. Where was Joseph?

"Are you looking for Mr. Gao?"

"Joseph! Where are you? Pardon?"

"I asked if you are looking for Mr. Gao?"

"Yes."

"Follow me."

"Joseph!"

He waited for Joseph to come running up so they could follow their host into the administrative offices to meet the man who had offered him the job. But there was still no sign of his son.

He was led into a spacious, if sparsely furnished anteroom, and from there into a small office. A middle-aged Chinese man wearing a pair of glasses with thick lenses stood up from behind a rather messy desk, and thrust out his hand.

"Hello, Mr. Ma. I'm James Gao. Welcome to Hong Kong and the YMCA. You have already met our director, Mr. Smythe. I hope you had a stress-free trip. My wife, whom you met in Chongqing, and I would like to invite you and your son to tea one day after you've settled in. As soon as I wrap up a bit of business here, I'll show you to your quarters. I'll only be a moment." Bo'le looked behind him—no Joseph. He got up and went back into the lobby, where he found his son waiting anxiously for him to come fetch him.

"Joseph, come with me. We're going to see where we'll be living in this new city." Not yet completely comfortable with his younger son's changing nature, he assumed that getting the boy to keep his hands to himself and his mouth shut would be a struggle, and was worried that the boy could make their first day here their last if he acted up as before. His fears were not realized; Joseph simply took his father's hand and smiled.

James Gao led father and son to a modest second-story suite with a kitchenette and a private bath. Bo'le was speechless.

The first thing James Gao did in the rooms where the newcomers would stay was explain Bo'le's duties, which were, initially, janitorial, helping the staff when needed, and dealing with Chinese refugees who spoke no Cantonese. Ma Bo'le could hardly believe his good luck. The second thing James Gao did was ask father and son to kneel and pray with him. As we have seen, they were old hands at this, if a bit rusty, and Bo'le knew he would have to become a lot more "Christian" than he'd been up to then if he was to hold on to this "heavenly" job.

A flood of refugees from Guangzhou and points west had filled the hotel on Salisbury Road and would keep Ma Bo'le, who had informed James and others that at home his parents and his wife had called him Paul, busy from his earliest days in the hotel.

"I never knew there were so many Christians in China!" he said to James Gao.

"They don't have to be Christian to find refuge here, Paul" James said. "We just wish we had room for everyone who came to us. Once they're here, we treat them with Christian charity, which will be easy for you. Do your best. I'll keep you in my prayers."

"God bless you," Ma Bo'le was quick to reply, which brought a smile to James' face.

"Once you have a chance to rest and have a look around, we'll need to get young Joseph into an English class. His other schooling will, I'm afraid, have to wait."

"God bless you again," Ma Bo'le said, hoping he wasn't going overboard.

Traffic on Salisbury Road—like all foreign enclaves in China, street names were given in two languages, the less important one usually Chinese—pedestrian and vehicular, civil and military, was heavy, but in Bo'le's eyes, remarkably orderly. This was not so with the commercial entities along the way, where Cantonese merchants and customers interacted with passion and volume. Beggars of all ages were everywhere, especially places frequented by Westerners. All this would take some getting used to.

Joseph would go outside only in company with his father or, on rare occasions, one of the female staff members, with whom the only shared language was gestures. He would master Cantonese in time. He preferred to stay indoors, either in their rooms or in the chapel.

Among the generally light tasks assigned to Ma Bo'le was an occasional trip across the harbor to deliver or pick up items on Hong Kong Island, a short fifteen-minute ride on normally smooth water. The round trips on the Star Ferry, which left the pier only blocks away, still made him jittery, having recalled the perils of water travel on the Yangzi. Blessedly, the trips, to places like Central, Wan Chai, and as far as Repulse Bay, entailed no missed meals and minimal absences from his son. Among the most disorienting experiences was an early summer trip with Mr. Smythe to the racetrack at Happy Valley on Hong Kong Island, where well-heeled Chinese and Western fans of horse racing acted as if Hong Kong would be spared from war. Smythe assured Bo'le that the Hong Kong Volunteer Defence Corps, which was exclusively British, was up to the defense of the island. He would be proved wrong.

Bo'le was also sometimes sent to pick up books at Swindon Book Company, the British-owned English-language bookstore on Lock Road, near St. Stephen's Church. Never much of a serious reader, he was intimidated by the sanctity of the place. The buyers and browsers, a mix of Chinese and westerners, paid him no attention, to his enormous relief. He had no interest in looking at titles, even those in Chinese. Every time he opened a book in such a place, he recalled his father's Biblical proscription and shrank back. Some youthful experiences never lose their impact, especially for Ma Bo'le. On the first day of August he spotted a bulletin board notice of a memorial service on the fourth anniversary of the death of the writer Lu Xun. Like most Chinese youth, Ma Bo'le had read Lu Xun's famous story "The True Story of Ah-Q," but his attention was caught by the name of the northeastern writer he'd met briefly at the home of Instruito Midorigawa in Chongqing. Since he had never been to the Confucian Temple on Caroline Hill, he decided to go to the free memorial.

Two days later, he told James Gao he had something he'd like to do that afternoon. Joseph, who had an English class, raised no complaint when his father said he was going out for a few hours. That pleased Bo'le, not because he was tiring of his son's excessive attentiveness, but because he seemed to be regaining some of his former independence, without the concomitant antisocial strain. Bo'le took a bus to Caroline Hill, then walked to the Confucian Temple, where the memorial was just getting underway. He was happy to see his fellow northerner up at the podium, speaking about her friend and mentor, Lu Xun. When she limited her presentation to brief remarks about the revered writer's life and works, he thought, "Everybody knows that," but immediately regretted such an ungenerous thought. She seemed gaunt and drawn, as if unwell. She did, however, look confident and stylish in a dark cheongsam. He planned to go up and ask her if she had any news about his Japanese friends, especially Instruito Midorigawa, but after all the speeches were over, two songs to Lu Xun were sung by the audience, followed by a pair of short plays adapted from his work. The memorial ended with a premier performance of a silent play on Lu Xun's life, which the northeastern woman had written while in Hong Kong. It took longer than he had hoped, and since he needed to get back to Tsim Sha Tsui for evening fellowship, he left, vowing to look her up some other day.

Fighting in China made communications difficult, but Ma Bo'le, whose letters to his wife never seemed to get mailed, was able to telegraph her in Chongqing that he and Joseph were doing fine. He did not forget to ask how she and the other children were getting by.

Over the months that followed, as the level of anxiety rose in the population, given the news of what was happening in China's interior, Ma Bo'le was encountering grumpier temporary residents. The number of refugees from the attacks on Canton in 1938 had dwindled, while those from the interior increased. Recalling his father's disdain for the Chinese, he could not help but compare the ragtag refugees who landed on his doorstep with the British rulers of the colony, including the men who ran the YMCA. Often, when the refugees made life difficult for him, he silently cursed: Bloody Chinese! Somehow, that made him feel better. It also made him feel superior. He urged Joseph to work hard at his English lessons (which he shared with his father, who fooled himself into thinking he spoke it well) so he could stay above the people who filled the hotel rooms.

Finding his old friend Chen proved to be harder than he'd expected. The address he'd been given in Wuhan turned out to be the office of a small publisher in Kowloon. But when he went there, he was told that his friend had moved, with no forwarding address. So he placed an ad in a Hong Kong newspaper, asking Chen to look him up at the YMCA. Three days later, as he was sweeping the area around the neglected flower garden, Chen called to him from the other side of a flagstone walkway. He and his one-time fellow down-and-outer had not seen one another since their brief meeting in Wuhan. The reported death of Zhang muted the reunion. Chen told him that he had written some anti-Japanese articles for a local newspaper and was afraid he might be in trouble. Bo'le offered to help by hiding him in the YMCA cellar without telling anyone. Since he had the run of the place, he could bring him food and news, and did so for several days. Then one day Chen disappeared, but he left a short note so Ma Bo'le wouldn't worry that he'd been found. He thanked him, of course, for the risk he had taken. Bo'le wondered if his association with the Japanese trio in Chongqing might also be discovered. He must be careful.

Finally, at the end of 1941, nearly five years after Ma Bo'le had watched Japanese warships line the harbor in Qingdao and disgorge their complement of sailors intent on intimidating the local population with their "war games," the war he had been predicting, the war he had been fleeing from, the war he had once hoped would hurry up and begin, reached him in all its fury. On December 6th Japanese aircraft attacked the city, killing Chinese and British alike. Ground troops of General Sakai's 23rd Army advanced on Kowloon a week later, and the battle was over almost as soon as it began. Hong Kong Island fell soon thereafter, and the Japanese occupation of the colony was complete. An Instrument of Surrender was signed on Christmas night at the Peninsula Hotel, which served as the Japanese Command Post in Hong Kong. Members of the YMCA staff waited stoically, prepared for the worst, when they learned that British and other foreign citizens were being rounded up and sent to Stanley, an internment camp for non-combatants, on the southern tip of Hong Kong Island. Mr. Smythe passed his authority to James Gao and prepared to leave, but not before sending Bo'le with the orphan children, Joseph included, to nearby St. Andrew's Church, which would be their home as long as the streets were unsafe. Bo'le stayed with James to help keep the YMCA open. Over the days that followed, he checked on the children regularly and brought them books and other things they would need. He also gave Association money to the church for food and other necessities. One day, on his way to St. Andrew's, he was nearly bowled over by scores of rickshaws and people careening down Nathan Road, fleeing to the already chaotic Star Ferry, which was in the hands of the Japanese military. The sound of gunfire and the rumble of tanks had the populace in full-blown panic.

He returned immediately to the YMCA, knowing that the war, which had chased him from city to city, was now on his doorstep, the final exit on his escape route from Qingdao. Uncharacteristically, some might say, his thoughts were of his son, not himself. James Gao told him that one of their colleagues was moving his family to a hilltop Buddhist monastery in the New Territories, not far from the Chinese border, where his cousin was a resident monk, and that his wife and children were leaving with him. Joseph was welcome to go along if Bo'le wanted. Two days later, after seeing his frightened son off to what he hoped would be a protected sanctuary, Bo'le prepared to face the enemy that had threatened him and his family for so long.

For a while, the YMCA was left alone by occupying troops. Many of the people who had taken refuge there had moved out once they found less conspicuous places to live. But that ended when the war turned sour for Japan, and increasingly atrocious behavior by the occupiers threw the populace into further panic. One day, after returning from St. Andrew's Church to see how the remaining children were doing, Ma Bo'le walked in the door at the YMCA, and was confronted by a squad of Japanese marines, led by a Chinese-speaking officer. They took him into a room and began questioning him about his dealings with Japanese dissidents. Shown a photograph of Kaji and Ikeda, he denied knowing them. The beatings commenced almost at once, and continued until the interrogators were satisfied that he was telling the truth. Where had he learned Esperanto, they wanted to know. From books, he said, refusing to tell them about his studies with Instruito Midorigawa, since they appeared not to know about her.

After an hour and a half, the squad emerged from the room with Ma Bo'le, who was bloodied and hogtied. The few remaining staff members of the YMCA stayed out of sight, but watched from an upstairs window as Ma was hoisted onto the bed of a military truck, along with some other prisoners.

It was the last they would see of him, and the war continued.

January 1985.

David Ma has been sitting at his radio station desk, nursing a pot of tea, for a couple of hours, deep in thought as he reflects on what he has finished reading, now for the second time. The rare, likely unique experience of reading a novel by an unknown writer about his family during the war years has rocked his emotions. While not all of the contents square with the facts as he knows them, there can be no doubt that he has been reading about his family, about himself.

That's us, he says to himself, and yet it isn't.

His initial anger over the characterization of his father as a coward has expanded to include what must be seen as an invasion, a tabloid-like exposé of the details of his family's life, cloaked in the guise of fiction.

In the four decades since the war ended, David has thought little about what those years have been like, for him and for his family, at least until now. They were a sorry lot when he, his mother, and his sister arrived in Hong Kong and found his father in terrible health, the victim of a long and brutal incarceration. Joseph had returned from the monastery where his father had sent him to escape the violence in the city, and the family was reunited for the first time in five years.

Post-occupation living conditions in Hong Kong were poor, but the family was safe from outside violence for the first time in years. And yet surviving day-to-day would not be easy. By conserving the money she'd brought with her to Shanghai, David's mother had enough for them to live on, if they economized. She found a modest flat in the New Territories, more commodious than the cramped space in the YMCA, and a real improvement over their living conditions in Chongqing. Thoughts of those days, which David has largely avoided, have come rushing back in fearful clarity. He dreaded the horrific bombings and hated the dank, stifling shelters that kept them safe as explosions sounded overhead. He shudders at the recollection of the always present smell of fear. While he and his family were spared the worst effects of wartime as they traveled from Shanghai west to Chongqing, images of those terrible times have been unleashed by the fictionalized history of his family. He could not hold back the tears as he learned of the death of young Lin Two in a bombing of the one place that been a sort of sanctuary; his mother had never told them. To his surprise, his own memories of his father during those days are scarce and unformed. He has been forced to rely on an outsider's narrative to gain a picture of his father during the war, especially in Hong Kong, when he and the rest of the family stayed behind in Chongqing. It had always been an article of faith to him that Ma Bo'le was a caring father, often a victim of outside forces, though a survivor. But if what the novel reveals is reflective not only of the events of his childhood, but also complicated family dynamics he had never before considered, he concludes that his father was not a bad man, just self-centered and often thoughtless. Though David was the eldest child, the prized first son, Joseph, the apple of his grandfather's eye, was his father's favorite. He was a source of both pride and consternation.

His father had not been around much during the trying days in Wuhan and Chongqing, David reflects, leaving the care of his children and the running of the house to David's mother. That changed after Joseph was lost, but only until his brother and father left for Hong Kong. In essence, David admits to himself, to him his father was an absentee parent. And then, after everyone was safely together again, Ma Bo'le, frail to begin with, became a semi-invalid. David takes several deep breaths to overcome the image and the latent smell of the sick room at home. As the eldest son, he was responsible for his father's care while their mother was busy at home. He sat with his father when he could, even reading the news to him once in a while, and sometimes helped him downstairs to sit in a chair outside, where Ma Bo'le had a chance to breathe fresh air and escape the confining space of a room he had grown to despise. Not long before Ma Bo'le died, a broken man, Joseph surprised everyone by coming home one day with two *baozi* wrapped in newspaper. Their father had wept when he saw them. The others nearly did as well. It was a wonderful gesture. He slowly ate what he could of one of the still-warm and greasy treats, and when he finished, he smiled, something they had not seen in a very long time. David sighs as he contemplates how central he was in the story and the family's history, especially after the war, and thoughts that had lain on the periphery of his memory begin to form; he conjures up images of his brother and sister, trying to understand things he had always accepted uncritically.

An intense sadness grips David as he probes more deeply into memories he has, consciously or not, suppressed for years. How, he had often asked himself, had Jacob, the cheerful little girl of their child-hood years, become so rebellious after arriving in Hong Kong? He had avoided answering the question until he realized that the anonymous novelist had revealed aspects of his sister's behavior that hinted at what she would become later, and that he had forgotten. The telltale scar over her eye, the result of her mischief-making at home, had found company in the scrapes and bruises she'd brought home from the orphanage, after fighting over toys with playmates there. He had forgotten that. Had she missed the attentions of her doting father? Was she burdened with fears that he might put her in danger again? Something was hidden in the mind of a sister he thought he'd known well.

After the war, Jacob had dealt poorly with the abrupt change in sur-roundings and attitudes, and had had a terrible time adapting to life in Hong Kong. She seemed distant from her father almost from the instant of the family's reunion and refused to go into his sickroom. She was smaller than her classmates, owing to poor nutrition in Chongqing, and less well prepared for the lessons, especially in English. David recalls sadly the day she came home crying, her pants wet. When their mother asked what had happened, she said she hadn't known how to tell the English teacher she had to pee, and she'd wet herself. How humiliating that must have been, and it might have stuck with her, especially after she was mocked by kids in school who called her "crybaby." Then in high school she'd made friends with the sons and daughters of working class parents, and from that evolved feelings of contempt for what she termed the "colonial overlords." In 1967, she was arrested for participating in violent anti-British demonstrations. Upon her release, she returned home, where her mother tried to talk to her about what she was doing. Sullen and defiant, she was not moved by her mother's reminders of what they had all gone through to stay together and thrive in the new environment. A few days later she left home and returned to the flat she shared with like-minded firebrands. David hardly saw her after that. She had no desire to maintain contact with him or with their mother, whom she viewed as lackeys of the colonial government. Then, without warning, one day in 1972, Jacob, who had rejected that name and now called herself Ma Hong—Red Horse—sneaked across the Chinese border from Hong Kong and joined comrades in Guangzhou. She left a brief, unsentimental note for her mother. They had not heard from her since.

Joseph's journey had gone in a different direction. Oh, how he'd hated Joseph! David recalls. As far back as their days at home in Qingdao, his younger brother had made his life a living hell. That changed when he had gotten lost in Chongqing, the full details about which, if the manuscript was to be believed, he had not known at the time. And then the brat had gotten to go to Hong Kong instead of him. Joseph had had it so easy, David has long believed. Or had he? David had envisaged his brother living the good life all those years, eating fried rice every day, safely out of harm's way. But now he knows that Joseph could not have been happy on a remote hilltop where he'd had to learn Cantonese to communicate and was introduced to Buddhist teachings, all the while deprived of contact with his family.

After returning to the family circle, Joseph did well enough in school, but did not make friends easily. His personality, formed by his thuggish behavior back home in Qingdao, the timidity that followed his accident in Chongqing, and his life with the monks in the hillside monastery, often put him at odds with his fellow students. He had tried hard to fit in with his peers and, partly for that reason, was detached at home, a situation that grew worse after graduation, when he was in a relationship with a girl whose parents disapproved of his background and status. He was devastated by the breakup, and David still recalls the day Joseph told his mother that he was quitting his job and returning to the monastery to drown his sorrows in Buddhist texts. Her pleas for him not to go were futile. So David accompanied her to the monastery to talk his brother into coming home. He refused to see them. They returned days later, and this time he emerged, his head shaved and wearing a novice's robe, fingering a Buddhist rosary. He told them he had taken the religious name Hengguan and was renouncing all ties to the mundane world. He no longer had a family. They did not see him again, but one day learned that he had traveled to Taiwan, where he'd been initiated into monkhood. He'd said he'd found his true calling, but David knew that his brother had simply lost faith in the real world.

As a storyteller, David knows that the character who holds a tale together is often not the most prominent one. In the Ma family, that person was his mother. He has few cheerful memories of Chongqing, but trips to the orphanage with his mother are among them. The other children were fond of her, and being her son made him popular among them. After bringing David and Jacob to Hong Kong, the first few months had been especially difficult as she tried to make a home for them in a new, and at first, not particularly welcoming, environment, trying to manage with no knowledge of the two languages spoken in the colony. Taking care of her husband, getting all three children into schools, and putting food on the table wore her down.

David's most vivid memory of his mother during the early days in Hong Kong is of her putting on the one dress that had accompanied her throughout her travels, pulling her hair into a tight bun, and forgoing sandals for real shoes every time she went to the market. He'd asked her why she went to so much trouble just to buy food, and can still recall what she'd said, almost word for word: "We are no longer refugees. This is our home, and I don't want women to look down on us. Call it pride, call it face, I don't care, but the Ma family will not be laughingstocks here, that's why." He'd thought she was being overly dramatic, when now he knows he should have been proud of her.

Their mother managed to keep the family together for years, despite the obstacles, including the eventual loss of her husband, but in the end not even she could keep outside forces from turning two of her children in directions she never quite understood. The departure of Joseph and Jacob within the space of a couple of years was a terrible blow, but the months and years that followed were even worse. In the end, it all combined to destroy her will to live and, heartbroken, she simply slipped away.

Though what he has just read is a sort of family history, it has been filtered through the consciousness an outsider, and both disturbs and perplexes him, especially what he characterizes as the nonsense about his father's so-called infatuation with Miss Wang. Though he admits that his father may have strayed from his marriage vows at home in Qingdao, this particular episode in the manuscript reads like a second-rate romance novel. Carrying on with the daughter of a family friend while living at home with his family seems ludicrous. Yet he knows that pointing out what he considers a flaw in the narrative will sound defensive, which he wants to avoid. He reminds himself that nothing he says will change what was written and that it is what strangers will read. He is not sure how he feels about that and even asks himself if it might have been better, less stressful, if it had been published without his knowledge. But no, he is grateful to the Society for giving him the chance to read it before it winds up in the hands of people he doesn't know and who will make judgments independent of him.

The disintegration of the Ma family will always haunt David, essentially its sole survivor, and he is in no mood to talk to the young woman from the Historical Society about what he has read, or to reveal his thoughts to her. But he made a promise, and is expecting her at any minute.

His brooding is interrupted by a knock at the door.

Ms. Lam takes a seat across from him, searching his face to intuit what is on his mind. She detects a look of melancholy, but David's years as a public figure come to his rescue, as he easily, if somewhat mechanically, greets her with an apologetic smile. She can see in his eyes that the manuscript has had an impact on him. He looks older, somehow.

She looks down at the manuscript, obviously eager to hear what he has to say. Although David tries to prepare himself to deal with specifics in the work, after being bombarded with memories, he is not sure where to begin. He cannot bring himself to disclose recollections that have only moments before begun to surface for him. He is not thrilled with the picture it paints of him as a child, but must admit to himself that it seems accurate. Everyone else is pretty much the way he remembers them, although the line between reality and fantasy is hard to pin down.

So as to avoid opening the conversation by seeking his reaction to how the manuscript portrays David's father, Ms. Lam tries to take his mind off of the war years and concentrate instead on what happened to the family after they settled in Hong Kong, the part of the manuscript that was left unexplored.

David has lived most of his life in Hong Kong, and yet at this moment he feels like an interloper, a "mainlander" whose moorings were cut loose by the war. In the main, there are more questions than answers raised by what he has read. What *did* happen to the Japanese couple and the Esperanto teacher his parents were so fond of? How had his mother managed to get him and his sister to Hong Kong, which had been sealed off by the Japanese? Are the answers to these and other questions important to him now? Will they become important later? He cannot hazard a guess. He also knows that he is not done with the question that began this sequence of events: Was Ma Bo'le a coward? Not during his days in Hong Kong, if the second author has dealt honestly with the material. But before that. David will likely give a great deal of thought to it in the days to come.

For now, though he has a family of his own, he cannot drive out the feeling that he is still somehow alone, a middle-aged man who has just read someone else's narrative of a life he had all but forgotten. Reintroduced to parents and siblings who shared his experience, he laments that they have all left him, and wonders how his brother and sister are coping, away from the only settled home they had after leaving Qingdao. He would give anything to see them again, and struggles to keep from breaking down in front of his guest.

"Now that you've read the manuscript, do you have any idea who could have written it?" Ms. Lam breaks the silence as David is caught up in his thoughts.

"I've thought about that for days, but I haven't found an answer. I'm not sure I even want to know."

She smiles. "Before we publish, we would be pleased to add something from you to increase the appeal to readers and give you a chance to let them know how you feel."

David has expected this, and though he has mixed feelings, he knows what he needs to say. While it is clear to her and her colleagues that he is the David Ma in the novel, it is really just a name in a piece of fiction, and he sees no reason for his true identity to be revealed. It would complicate his life and do nothing to affect the reception of the book. People can read it as a novel, he assures himself, as history, as a promotion of Hong Kong values, or as something else. He notes the surprised look on her face as he tells her, "I'd rather it not be known as 'my story.'"

But he has thought of at least one thing he can contribute.

"As a courtesy to me and to my family, and especially to a man of whom I am proud, my father," he says, "I ask only that you include the following statement at the beginning of the book:

THIS IS A WORK OF FICTION, NOT THE TRUE ACCOUNT OF A REAL FAMILY.

# *Author/Translator/Author*

In 1940, Xiao Hong, a writer from Northeast China (Manchuria), wrote a novel entitled *Ma Bo'le*. It was published in Chongqing the next year, when she then wrote and published serially a sequel she called "Book Two." The final installment appeared in a Hong Kong magazine in November, with the note, "End of Chapter Nine. More to come." That did not happen. Two months later, shortly after the Japanese invasion of Hong Kong, she died of a combination of a throat infection, a botched operation, and a fragile constitution, at the age of 31. She was buried in Repulse Bay. For decades after, no one in China or elsewhere had heard her name; her books sat undisturbed on library shelves. Now, more than half a century later, she is celebrated as one of China's foremost writers of the Republican era; her childhood home, a stop on the Northeast China tour circuit, has been refurbished and shares space with a museum devoted to her and her work.

   In the early 1980s, after a decade of writing and talking about Xiao Hong (Zhang Naiying) and translating much of her work, including two other novels and a multi-chaptered quasi autobiography, I began a translation of *Ma Bo'le*, taking it slow, since I did not think a Western publisher would be keenly interested in the translation of an unfinished novel by an obscure Chinese writer. I cannot recall when it happened, but at some point I decided that I would complete, in English, what most people agreed had been planned as a trilogy. It has taken me more than twenty years to get up the nerve to fulfill that promise.

After completing and editing a rough translation of the first two "books," I picked up the thread of the original story, which ends as the protagonist contemplates leaving Wuhan with his family and traveling to Chongqing, the wartime capital of the Chiang Kai-shek Nationalist government. As I wrote, I located the narrative in places where Xiao Hong had visited or lived—Qingdao, Shanghai's French Concession, the Beipei district in Chongqing, Lock Road in Kowloon, Hong Kong—wherever possible, and included actual events and situations, such as her friendship with three Japanese intellectuals, the only true-to-life characters in the novel. For a speech Xiao Hong gave in Hong Kong to commemorate her mentor and friend, Lu Xun, who had died four years earlier, I cited actual reports. I even had them—author and protagonist—meet on at least one occasion. I then translated and included snippets from essays, stories, and occasional pieces Xiao Hong wrote during that period to include her "footprint" in the final third of the work. Beyond that, I had to follow my instincts in pulling everything together, since she left no indication of how she planned to end the work.

The novel is unique, not just to Xiao Hong's oeuvre, but in the modern history of Chinese fiction, through the twentieth century and up to the present day. It has been reissued several times in Chinese and has been written about extensively. In it the eponymous character travels from Qingdao south to strike out on his own in the days prior to full-blown war with Japan. Once Shanghai is attacked, Ma Bo'le, whose wife and children have joined him, follows the route his author took from one besieged city to the next, ending, as she did, in Hong Kong.

History plays a significant role in the novel. Many of the national events are factual; the remainder complement and expand the recorded history, with an eye to enriching the narrative. In those cases, it isn't what happened, but what could have happened.

Ma Bo'le (pronounced Ma Bwo-Luh), a picaresque character in the mold of self-preservationist Yossarian in *Catch-22* or the slothful Ignatius J. Reilly in *A Confederacy of Dunces*, has few peers in the modern Chinese-language tradition. Nobelist Mo Yan's bumbling "investigator" in *The Republic of Wine* and Taiwanese pedant Dong Siwen in Wang Chen-ho's *Rose, Rose, I Love You* come close. Ma Bo'le anticipates them all by decades.

When first published, the novel, marked by humor, cynicism, and a number of solipsistic fictional characters, was not well received by many, who thought that only patriotic, incendiary anti-Japanese literature ought to be made available to a public experiencing the terror and displacement of war. That Xiao Hong defied such sentiments is remarkable in itself; that she did so on the run, as it were, when her relationships with the men in her life were rapidly deteriorating, and when she was in failing health, is extraordinary. And, we mustn't forget, the second half was written against a monthly publishing deadline.

The first book was published without chapter divisions; the second was divided into nine chapters. I have retained the three parts, but unified them into seventeen chapters, bookended by reflections on the story and two parts of a fictional dialogue between a representative of a fabricated Hong Kong historical society and the grown son of the novel's protagonist following the discovery of a long-lost, anonymous manuscript—the "work."

No part of Xiao Hong's novel has ever been published in English translation, until now. I toyed with the idea of trying to replicate Xiao Hong's writing style, but found it more reasonable to allow for a second "author" to complete the unfinished work; had that actually been done before I weighed in decades later, a second sequel would probably have been written by the novelist Duanmu Hongliang, with whom she had been living for nearly four years. He has written about their lives in Hong Kong and elsewhere, but offers no insight into where the novel was headed.

Some of the language in the original work, while offensive, is historically correct and reflective of the Chinese original. To set the scenes as accurately as possible, I have called upon a number of biographies of Xiao Hong in Chinese, my own among them, and have drawn upon a variety of contemporary reports on China and Hong Kong, including Theodore H. White's *Thunder Out of China* (1946); *China: After Seven Years of War* (1945, Hollington K. Tong, ed.); Philip Snow's *The Fall of Hong Kong* (2003), John M. Carroll's *A Concise History of Hong Kong* (2007), and Anna Louise Strong's *One-Fifth of Mankind: China Fights for Freedom* (1938). Many of the named establishments and locations in Shanghai, Wuhan, Chongqing, and Hong Kong actually exist, or did at the time.

I have spent more than four decades in the wonderful company—figuratively, intellectually, literarily, and emotionally—of Xiao Hong. I can only hope that she would have approved of our collaboration.

Xiao Hong (1911-1942) was one of the most important Chinese novelists of the twentieth century. With a literary output covering less than ten years, her impact is still felt today with such novels as *The Field of Life and Death*, *Memories of Mr. Lu Xun*, and *Tales of Hulan River*. She is the subject of the 2014 biopic, *The Golden Era*.

Over the course of his career, Howard Goldblatt has translated more than sixty works of Chinese literature—including the works of Nobel Prize-winner Mo Yan and Chu T'ien-wen—has won the National Translation Award, and received a Guggenheim Fellowship.

**OPEN
LETTER**

**OPEN
LETTER**

**WWW.OPENLETTERBOOKS.ORG**